P9-BZR-910

D0015356

1 9 9 0

OTHER BOOKS

BY ABBY FRUCHT

Snap (Novel, 1988)

Fruit of the Month (Stories, 1988)

LICORICE

A NOVEL BY

Abby Frucht

GRAYWOLF PRESS

Copyright © 1990 by Abby Frucht

A portion of this novel first appeared in the *Kenyon Review* (New Series, Summer 1990, Vol. XII, No. 3. Copyright © by Kenyon College) under the title "Steps Out."

Michael Zimmerman's company, humor, and understanding were wonderful as always. For their insightful readings of the manuscript-in-progress, the author thanks Michael Zimmerman, Tom Hart, Carolyn Frucht, Yopie Prins, Katrina Kenison, Gary Engle, and especially Scott Walker. And many special thanks to Howard Frucht for his inspirational remarks about the medicinal properties of licorice.

Publication of this book is made possible in part by grants from the National Endowment for the Arts and the Minnesota State Arts Board. Graywolf Press is the recipient of a McKnight Foundation Award administered by the Minnesota State Arts Board, and receives generous donations from other foundations, corporations, and individuals.

Published by GRAYWOLF PRESS
2402 University Avenue, Suite 203
Saint Paul, Minnesota 55114
All rights reserved.

ISBN 1-55597-137-7

Library of Congress Cataloging-in-Publication Data
Frucht, Abby.
Licorice : a novel / by Abby Frucht.
p. cm.
$18.95
I. Title
PS3556.R767L53 1990 90-3652
813'.54-dc20

First printing, 1990
9 8 7 6 5 4 3 2

F O R   M I C H A E L

who has good taste

CONTENTS

L I C O R I C E

PART ONE

The Day the Supermarket Closed

NO NOISE. Just a shadow. In a fraction of a second, I'm scared. But it is only a flock of geese. White-bellied with black-bordered wings, they fly close to the tops of the quiet trees like a single, giant kite. Ordinarily, snow geese don't come here—they fly north to the marshes surrounding the power plant, now defunct, or east to the flats where they vanish among tall reeds. Here, the bodies of water are simply too small, the fish miniscule. The geese swoop low above the reservoir, then soar over the woods out of sight. Gone, they might have been a gust of wind, leaving ripples on the water. There are the same people fishing; some boys and their father who fish every day. Squint-eyed as men, the brothers sight the lengths of their homemade poles as if aiming into the murk to shoot. They're not fishing for sport, but hunger. The skinny father watches from a distance, perched on concrete blocks, not scowling, not impatient, not anything, really, but fatherly, like someone overseeing homework from the other side of a tv set. He watches turtles basking on a log and slipping off. Every so often he rises, throws a cigarette butt to the gravel, walks around the water's edge and stares down into the bucket near the boys' tackle box. It's a toy bucket just deep enough to hold these tiny fish they're catching. Bluegills, no bigger than cocktail crackers. No one would eat these fish unless they had to, every night, dipped in flour and fried. You hold a fish by its tail, slide it into your mouth, pull it out between clenched teeth to skim off the flesh, like eating artichoke leaves. I wonder if they dip them in butter and lemon. Our town is so small that the geese are now several towns over, but this family lives on the other side of it, in another world, where the houses are built from my neighbors' cast-offs; extra doors, discarded windows, some shingles, cinder blocks and the boards from some old bookcases. Sometimes a sink, a carpet remnant, a length of fencing or a set of porch steps. Because the doors do not properly close, the front yards of these improvised houses are as cozy as parlors, like the tv rooms under the awnings in trailer parks.

"Hi," the older of the two boys says as I pass, and I watch him throw a fish back into the water, too small to nibble, the size of a quarter. In the bucket are crowded fifteen or so of the bigger ones, tails barely undulating.

"Catching anything?" I ask stupidly, and the boy points into the bucket with his elbow while hooking a fresh worm. Nearby, a submerged bullfrog grunts in its city of algae until a second frog replies. Why don't these boys eat frog legs, too, I wonder, but can't bring myself to ask. We're eating dinner tonight at our friends', Ben and Leah's. Leah's a potter, and each meal is a feast of platters and bowls. Last time, around a tray of steaming corn tortillas sat platters of beef, chicken, and beans, bowls of peppers, hot sauces, sour cream, chopped olives, tomatoes, onions, and a dish of guacamole. Also, some margaritas in Leah's squat mugs salted and chilled.

I say goodbye to the back of the younger boy's head just as his line starts to wobble, then follow the trail to the fork. There, it slopes down into woods near the creek, the fallen logs cushioned with fungi and moss. But somebody is already sitting on my log

–it's Joe with the piercing eyes. This evening, Joe keeps his painter's cap in his lap while talking softly to Eva, his dog. His white T-shirt strains at the armpits while, even sitting like that, his biceps flex like they can't help themselves. Soon he sticks his nose in his armpit, sniffs, and gets a look of wierd pride and elation. He doesn't see me. His bald head looks tender as a mushroom; I think of stripping naked, straddling his shoulders and licking his head, ear to ear in slow, continuing spirals.

FROM THE ROAD I can see my husband in communion with our pear tree; he circles it slowly, his fingers alighting on the tips of its branches now and then, his head cocked, his legs bent–mysteriously absorbed, he is like a tailor circling a dummy. The pear tree is slender and young, with trembling, budding extremities, just sparsely flowered. Petals drift from my husband's touch and come to light on the toes of his sneakers. Daniel is duck-footed; his splayed feet straddle the base of the trunk as he frowns and tends, tends and frowns. He might be toying with the secret, dewy recesses of his own soul, examining its negative spaces, its shapely apexes on which fruit is soon to grow. How tender he looks, from the sidewalk in front of our house, how grave and enraptured.

"This poor tree is so fragile," I say, coming up from behind.

"Bullshit," says Daniel, then kicks at the trunk with the rubbery toe of his sneaker; petals fly, I gasp, Daniel hops on one foot in a gesture of pain, yet the tree stands serene, its faint response over and done like the sigh of a house when its door has been slammed.

I step closer while Daniel resumes. Of course–how could I not have known?–he is hand-pollinating the flowers, choosing the healthiest, unblemished specimens to be plucked from the tree so the dust of their anthers may be applied to the receptive female counterparts, the blossoms of which he has not even paused to smell. That's the thing about Daniel: he's a scientist. For a living he follows bumblebees through glades and montane meadows, recording, with a clicking, hand held counter, the precise number of open flowers on which each bee feeds, and then, with a stopwatch, the number of seconds she spends probing each one. Often I've wondered, What kind of occupation is this? And what kind of man? Soulful? Eccentric? Adventurous? Or merely clinical, playing matchmaker on our fruit trees simply for the sake of a juicier F-2 generation?

The tree is shorter than Daniel, taller than I.

"When will it fruit?" I ask. "In August?"

"I *think.* I was just back from the field when it did last year. Remember? Or maybe early September."

I shake my head, no, although I do remember. Still I want him to tell me about it, because the things he recalls, however coolly, always make me nostalgic. These days, I crave nostalgia, because the present, somehow, seems vaguer than the past—less definite, less circumscribed.

"That was so crazy," he says at last, flicking away a fingerful of anthers, "to pick a fresh pear and wait a whole week to eat it."

"Go on," I say. So he tells me the rest.

How we had one pear, the sole product of our lawnful of fruit trees. The apple trees were sick, and the cherries half-eaten by blackbirds and sparrows before I noticed they'd ripened. The pear tree was smaller then, but the pear itself, mellow and golden brown, was of the usual size and so out of proportion to the thin droopy sapling that I thought Daniel had tied it to the branch for a joke. We watched it for days, waiting for it to ripen, wary it might drop, dreading all the while it would be stolen by students. It wasn't. We picked it ceremoniously, and deciding we wanted it cold, stuck it in a basket in the refrigerator and forgot about it. A week later when we found it, how sad it looked, no longer fresh, just an ordinary, brown-speckled fruit with no dewdrop remaining on its toughened skin. Guiltily we shared it. It tasted okay, a little mealy, just a pear. But, we sucked the juice from each other's fingers when we were done.

"What I mean is," I expound tonight at dinnertime, "that there may be other living, thinking beings existing simultaneously with us, sharing our space, but in another dimension, and in ways we can't sense. Think of your senses. Sight. Hearing. Smell. Touch. Who says there aren't other senses that we don't possess? And that therefore there are things, corresponding entities, that we *can't sense.* That we can't be made aware of. Whole lives, I'm talking about. All these daily lives going on around us that are inaccessible."

"So what?" says Ben, always glad to be the gloomy one.

"You left out taste," says Daniel.

"I did?" asks Leah, offended, chagrined. She ladles peanut sauce onto his shish kebab, sprinkles bananas, coconut, diced cucumber relish in a ring around his dollops of yogurt and chutney, then beckons, from the far end of the table, a teacupful of freshly ground *garam masala.* Ben was shelling the cardamom pods when we arrived, dropping them in with the other spices. Then, two cinnamon sticks and the whir of the blender.

"He didn't mean that," I say. "It's delicious. Everything. Absolutely." I finger a bowl. These are new, so thin-walled as to be nearly translucent, with cloudy tints of silver, turquoise, and aquamarine.

They look like mother-of-pearl.

"Are these raku?" I ask.

Stevie, our son, age one and a half, screeches from the other room. Something rips. I cringe, knowing it's the fish kite they've hung from the ceiling, its tail a cascade of red and yellow streamers.

"Simon!" yells Ben.

Ben and Leah's son, Simon, runs from the playroom, xylophone hammer in hand. Stevie follows, crawling, still screeching, pulling the xylophone upside down by its cord of yellow plastic.

"Did you take that hammer from Stevie?"

"Shish kebab," says Simon delightedly.

"Sooleybop. Jesus," says Ben, who refuses to acknowledge that Simon, precocious, is learning to talk.

"He said shish kebab," I tell him, as Stevie, forgetting the xylophone, climbs onto my lap. I pull a cube of beef from the end of my skewer, blow on it, touch my tongue to its surface to see that it's cool, pop it into his waiting mouth.

"How's work?" I say to Ben. He's a biologist, too. He studies a community of woodchucks who feed on the tract house compost heaps and make their summer burrows at the edge of the creek where it cuts past a meadow of fruit trees.

"I got the new zoom, at last," he tells me.

It's a hand-held zoom he must have ordered months ago.

"He got it on Thursday, he's out there till two in the morning, even though they keep bedtime hours," says Leah. "Those animals go to bed around nine, he sits there and zooms around hoping they'll sleepwalk. Three were pregnant this year. Just wait till the little ones come out of the dens. He's like a kid with a new toy."

"New toy, my ass," Ben says proudly. "That thing cost four hundred bucks."

"Banana," says Simon.

"Jesus. Anyana?" says Ben.

"I mean, there could be a whole other family like us, right in this room, eating their dinner," I say.

"God forbid," says Daniel, and strokes my arm.

"She's right" says Ben. "But it doesn't affect us. I mean, some invisible kid could be throwing up in my plate this very minute and I'd never know, I'd just eat my food, I'd say 'Hey, this stuff is really good.' That's what you're talking about, right?"

"Ben," says Leah.

"Simon said banana," I say, hurt, and remember my new friend, Emily. Emily would understand. Emily, whom I met at a party a week ago and haven't had the nerve to call up. It was the first time we met, but we understood each other completely.

"Careful!" yells Daniel a while later, because Stevie is kicking the table. Improperly braced, the whole thing sways. This happens every time we come here for dinner. Now Simon pushes hard against it, and Leah's beautiful bowls come sliding toward me. I catch hold of them frantically, two by two.

Stevie sighs, leans back into me, rubs a spoonful of yogurt onto my face.

WE TAKE the long way home because the night is so lovely, and let Stevie sleep in the stroller. His chin has fallen to his chest, his toes bob and sway an inch above the ground. From behind, my hands loose on the grips of the stroller, I watch the naked back of his neck, tendons taut beneath the skin. Darkened with sweat, a multitude of curls lie close to his skull.

Beside me, Daniel puts his hand on my back, hooks his fingers on the neck of my T-shirt and lets them hang.

"There's something I keep forgetting to tell you," he says, and sidesteps a hole in the sidewalk. Just ahead, exposed tree roots snake through a crack in the buckling sandstone and send up green shoots. Sidewalks are rarely repaired in our town, but when they are, the fresh, bland concrete clashes with the older slabs of sandstone whose porous surfaces echo the long-ago quarries. Here and there, the slabs buckle, split, and ooze. Pockmarks, filled with water and sprigs of moss, resemble small sinkholes.

"Yes?" I say, because he seems to have forgotten again. In a sense, I already know what he means to say. That is, I know it will make me unhappy, because those are the things he forgets to talk about.

"Who died?" I ask.

We go on in silence.

"Who's moving away?" I continue, and this time he tightens his grip on my shirt.

"Who already took off?" I ask, suddenly frantic, already feeling the loss. The front wheels of the stroller smash into a faultline. Pitched forward, Stevie topples face-first from the seat toward the ground, but Daniel catches him, rearranges him, sets him back in the seat. We're accustomed to this. Stevie opens his eyes, looks out at the night, closes them again, sleeps.

"It's a secret," says Daniel. "Nobody's figured it out, yet. Harley's gone."

"Harley. Oh, no."

"I went to his house when he didn't show up for a week."

"Oh, no," I repeat. Harley's the lab technician. He's awkward, shy, and the butt of Daniel's practical jokes. Daniel hid Harley's new bike in the cold room. He marked Harley's sneakers radioactive, emptied his bag lunch and filled it with chilled lampreys. Harley must know that it's Daniel who does these things; in return he visits Daniel in his office and they talk about Harley's rock climbing trips. Why Harley? I wonder, although the answer is clear. His wife left some time ago, as suddenly as this, taking only a backpack with rope and pitons. He thought she'd ridden to the quarry the way she sometimes did, to climb and relax at the end of the day. But her bike was still chained to the tree in their yard, and she never came back, and now, when we think of her, it's as a bright speck scaling a distant peak. Where can she have gone? And now, where's Harley? What's become of them, I want to ask, as if they have died. And maybe they have. No one knows, is the problem, about the people who've left. Hundreds. Sometimes they clear out their houses, sometimes they don't. They only rarely say goodbye and almost never come back. They don't seem to have planned it, actually, but one day they're here and the next day, where? It's the women, I've noticed, who vanish first. Or the women who pack, who arrange for the U-Haul, who surprise the rest, at dinner, with a bus ticket wedged underneath each plate. I haven't said this out loud, about the women being first, but increasingly I know that it's true. It happens mostly in summer; more this summer than last, and more last summer than the summer before. It's this excess of peace that scares them away: the fruit trees with their bruised blossoms hanging, hanging, the air barely stirring the tops of the grasses, those geese overhead with their silent shadow. Every woman wants peace, but not peace and quiet. Up one street, down another, U-Haul here, U-Haul there, amid cars with their tops buckling under the luggage. Some do it more secretively, like Harley's wife and then Harley—no preparations, no goodbyes—but the secrecy, we think, is only accidental. They can't help themselves, they can't take it any more, they have an urge–whatever–they pick up and go. Or just go. One neighbor left her television playing on the porch. She was sitting snapping green beans while her boyfriend trimmed the hedges at the side of the house. She owned the travel agency, was plump, blonde, and played the tv so loud we could hear people kissing on the shows she liked. Between one kiss and the next, she must have walked off somewhere. Several days later, on one of my routes, I stepped on a green bean lying on the sidewalk. It was the other side of town but it gave me the chills. I stood still a minute, listened and watched, then kept on going. It was no use getting excited. Everybody knows that. There's no logic in this, nothing you can explain. Before the travel agency closed, the boyfriend sat at her desk and wrote out the tickets for people who'd made reservations. He's left the television on, turned low, and spends most of his time outside in the yard, still trimming, pruning, mowing, and hedging. I've never told him I stepped on a green bean, of course. Maybe it was hers, but it could have been Harley's, for all I know.

"Did Harley like green beans?" I ask Daniel suddenly.

"*Does* he," says Daniel.

"Excuse me?"

"He *does.* Not, he *did.*"

"He does?"

"I don't know, Liz. Why?"

"Oh–" I shrug. "I thought Harley belonged here," I say after a minute, stung. "I thought he liked it. He *did.* Why the hell should he go? Because the video rental closed? Has it closed? Has it?"

Daniel nods.

"I thought they were trying to keep it open."

"They were, but they didn't," says Daniel.

"Maybe Harley's just sick, in the bedroom, maybe."

Just sick, I said. Just sick in the bedroom, not *gone.*

"I looked," says Daniel, and at that I take his arm and press it hard to my side. Harley was Daniel's, not mine, after all.

And then after a moment, "Maybe he just went away for a while. Maybe on one of his rock climbing trips."

I trail off hopefully, ready for Daniel's encouragement.

"Maybe," he says, which is what he always says, and I sigh and lean against him. Maybe, I think, and still my throat clenches up, unconvinced. In less then a minute, I'm crying. But not for long. A year ago this same process took months to accomplish. Then, weeks. Then, days. Now, only seconds, and I am resigned.

Bye, Harley, I think.

Then, silence.

Stevie twitches in sleep in his stroller.

We've crossed the bridge over a bend in the creek onto Morgan Street, closer to home. Adjacent to the road, a narrow, undulating meadow dips finally down to a strip of young forest where Ben's woodchucks live. Those woods are enfolded in darkness, while on the meadow the fruit trees are shot through with moonlight so that even their colors can be discerned. There are plum, cherry, apple – all reds, pinks, and purples. Throughout, the tall grasses bend over themselves beneath the weight of the perfumed air. From spring I remember an invigorating scent of pollen, exactly like semen, nothing like this. Harley's wife must have left, I realize, for the very same reason I stay. How daunting the air; so dense, so becalmed, the very pace of our breathing slows.

At home, Stevie in his crib, I sit in the kitchen at the darkened desk examining the moonlight on the telephone dial. I've found my new friend Emily's number, not a difficult chore at all. It was in the phone book just as she said it would be, an easy number to remember, the year and date of my own birthday. "Which only goes to show," I say to Daniel, "she and I are soulmates. I need to tell her how I feel."

"How *do* you feel?"

I sigh. "Restful."

"So call her already," says Daniel, swigging juice from the container at the open refrigerator, replacing the container, unscrewing a jar, popping a Spanish olive into his mouth. I reach out a palm, he throws me an olive, too. "Go ahead," he persists. I sit unmoving. He lifts the receiver, shoves it under my ear, sticks my finger in the dial in a spot untouched by moonlight.

"Dial," he says, and I begin to move the finger, but slowly, in trepidation.

"There's no need for me to call her," I say, withdrawing my finger. "It's an *insult* to phone her. She's thinking about me, I'm thinking about her, she understands me, I understand her, what's the point of calling?"

"What you're saying is if she wanted to talk to you, she would call you."

"Right," I say. "She's not interested."

"Tell me the God damn number."

"I'll do it," I say, and then dial not Emily's number but Danka's. What there is of my friendship with Danka is utterly dependable. We agree on nothing. When one of us phones, the other one is always in the tub.

Danka answers at once. I hear her husband in the background, shifting his position on the couch. He is papery gray, smokes a pipe, reads horrible autobiographies. Last I knew he was halfway through the life of William Kellogg, the one who invented cornflakes.

"Are you in the tub?" I ask.

"Not yet. But I am contemplating. . . "

I interrupt, "Would you like to go out for some pecan pie?"

"Oh, all right," says Danka.

"I'll drive," we both say, although we both know *she* will. Driving's her hobby. The other day I saw her drifting past a stop sign. There was a load of traffic crossing: U-Hauls, pick-up trucks, a bicycle coasting, and last of all, my Fiat. Had the cyclist not screamed, Danka would surely have hit someone. She slammed on the brakes, rolled her eyes, then winked at me when I went past.

"Liar," says Daniel, when I hang up the phone. "That wasn't Emily's number. It was Thank You's. You going out?"

"Yes. She's driving."

"Have fun." Floppy disk in hand, Daniel sits at the computer. When I've brushed my hair and teeth, changed shirts, and come downstairs to wait for Danka, I peek in for a look. He knows I am looking, but doesn't turn from the screen, just types away engrossed in his jewelweed, goldenrod, and phlox. I don't know what he means by, "Have fun." Maybe, "Talk long and hard so you can stop sighing about whatever you've been sighing about lately."

Probably he means, "Too bad you couldn't get up the nerve to call Emily."

Or, possibly even, "Have a good time," but that thought does not occur to me until later.

DANKA WEARS her black Audi like a little black dress, as if, were she to step out of it, she'd be naked. In fact, she does wear a little black dress most of the time, and this constancy of attire does seem a kind of nakedness. She looks frankly comfortable, understatedly sexy, elegant, and bored. We are of separate generations. Danka is older, voluptuous, short, but taller than I am, of course. In my jeans I could be Danka's waywardly precocious Americanized daughter rudely chastising her for smoking cigarettes. She favors a holder of slender black plastic with a filter cartridge, and tonight wears a string of pearls, perhaps in honor of our date, perhaps not.

Her English is nearly impeccable.

"This weather. . . " Danka gestures out the window with her cigarette at the quiet, dewy lawns with their overgrown violet shadows. "I don't know if everybody has been feeling restless, or if it's only me. You too, or only me?"

"Never. But that doesn't mean nobody else is. Harley, this guy who worked in Daniel's lab. . . "

"And I don't know how I feel about pecan pie," Danka interrupts. "There's a man I want to spy on."

"Who is he?"

We start driving around, aimlessly it seems. Danka takes the corners like a cat: rolling up on the curb, rolling down. Distracted, she turns on the windshield washer and then the radio in search of the cigarette lighter.

"Would you believe that I don't know his name?"

"That's the best kind."

"No. Really, I know his last name but not his first. Would you believe I peeked at his name in the library? He was there, and I was looking at the newspapers. He was signing out a book so I went and looked at the card, in fact I stole it. His name is Startup, unless he was joking. Maybe he knew I was going to do it. Oh, that's terrible. Oh Liz, I am really in need. I am soaking all the time. I should not have gone out with you tonight. It's too dangerous. You're too nice. If I drove to his house, and said, 'wait in the car,' and then I went and knocked on his door and threw myself into the room and made love to him, for an hour, an hour and a half, two hours, you would wait in the car, wouldn't you? With the radio on, and I have a book, I think. See? It's too dangerous. You would do it, wouldn't you?"

"What book?"

Danka reaches under the seat and pulls out one of her husband's books. The autobiography of Hutchins Hapgood. I pull it onto my lap, open it up and stare at one of the pages.

"I mean the book the man you're spying on took out of the library," I say. "What was that?"

"A woodworking book. He's very sensual. I knew he had a smell about him, from a distance, those oils they use."

"Linseed oil. Lemon. Mmmm"

"Rather musky, I think." Danka closes her eyes and inhales deeply while misjudging another corner. "Oh, God. We've got to be quiet," she says, and slows to a crawl. We've entered a parking lot behind two perpendicular rows of shops, one facing the square and the other, Main Street. On the far side of the lot, in the college conservatory building, a few practice rooms are still lighted.

"He might be sleeping," she says.

I wonder. In a practice room? Or does he live above the stores?

"The thing is," says Danka. "I don't really know where he lives, but I've seen him coming in and out of this parking lot so many times. How do you get up into those apartments? Are you supposed to climb the fire escape? Those are apartments, aren't they?"

"I think you have to go around to the front, where the stores are."

"I'll never find it. I shouldn't be doing this, Lizzie. But it would be so wonderful. I have a feeling he lives in this odd little building right here. What do you think?"

It's a single-story, square brick building that somehow I've never quite noticed, in the exact middle of the parking lot. The brick is yellow. All around it is planted tall shrubbery like the shade trees planted around farm houses on the open prairie. Outside on the cement stoop sit a couple of dented garbage cans and a mailbox with a number eight stenciled on it. Also, one of those tin boxes that milk bottles used to be left in.

"Looks promising." Inside, a tv flickers behind bamboo blinds. There are beer cans stacked on the window sill.

"He has a beer belly," says Danka. "How do I know there's not anyone in there with him? We'll have to sit, watch the windows for a while, see if we can tell."

"I'm going over to Lorenzo's for a second to get a Dove Bar," I say. "Do you want one?"

"Why didn't I just look up Startup in the phone book? Why didn't I think of that? That was stupid of me."

"I'll look in Lorenzo's. Want a Dove Bar?"

"Yes, please."

I climb out of the car, close the door softly, walk across the empty parking lot to Lorenzo's Pizza. In a way it seems unfair to me that I should be expected to sit in the car reading the autobiography of Hutchins Hapgood while Danka begins an affair. But then I think, no matter what I am doing at any time, there is always someone having an affair, somewhere, and if Danka's having one here and now would make me jealous, then I should be jealous always. Am I? No. My longings are sudden and transitory if fierce, like the one I have for Joe's bald head. It's like passing a pond on a hot day, thinking how good it would feel to jump in, then walking on by. Anyway, there's no Startup listed in the telephone directory. Danka accepts this news bravely, and seems content for the moment with peeling the wrapper off her Dove Bar. We both are. The parking lot is silvery, and some dogs trot across intermittently. Behind us in the conservatory the last practice room goes dark, and a few minutes later a girl carrying a cello crosses the lot.

"How do I know? That could be his wife," says Danka, and we watch the girl eagerly to see if she climbs the stoop into the low brick building. She doesn't, but disappears into an alley with her cello, which gladdens us even though we don't know if the brick house is Startup's or not.

"You are the kind of person who would consent even to knock on the door, so I could see if it is Startup who answers, at which point you could pretend you were looking for somebody else. Aren't you?" says Danka.

"Yes," I say. In unison we start on our Dove Bars. Both are coconut, but we go at them differently. I bite right in, while Danka peels oblong sheets of the chocolate coating and lets them melt one by one on her tongue. She turned the radio on while I was out buying them.

"And you could see if there was another woman in there with him, and if you couldn't see from the door then you could ask to use the bathroom in which case you could see if there was evidence of another woman, especially in the bathroom. Tampons and such."

Startled, I say, "In that case I may as well sleep with him to see if he's impotent, or if you want to know if he's circumcised. Then you can wait around and see if I get AIDS."

Danka sucks her chocolate quietly as if considering.

"But you *would* knock on the door," she says.

"Yes."

"But it really wouldn't do any good since I wouldn't know if there was anybody else in there."

"But at least you would know if it was his house or not."

"Yes. I don't want to know if he is circumcised or not. Why do you say that? Do you think it makes a difference?"

"I have this idea there might be more friction."

"Oooh," says Danka. "I'm going to look in the window." She hands me her stripped-naked Dove Bar, and gets all the way up to the stoop before turning around and coming back to the car.

"What time is it?" she whispers.

"Just about midnight."

She goes back to the stoop, stands there a couple of minutes as if listening, and returns to where I'm sitting.

"I can't tell if what I hear is the television or real people," she says.

"Is there a woman?"

Danka nods. I follow her across the lot to the stoop, still holding the two Dove Bars. Danka's, deprived of its coating, falls off the stick as we listen at the window. It's television, a laugh track, but that still doesn't tell us whether there's anyone else in there watching with him. Before leaving we open the milk bottle box, out of curiosity. There's a Barbie Doll dressed in a gold lamé jumpsuit. Danka stamps her foot, takes hold of my arm and leads me back to the car. Inside, she finishes off the remaining portion of the Dove Bar.

"Really, it is getting too late to do anything," she says.

"William might get a little suspicious," I concede.

"William is never suspicious. He is not imaginative enough to be so. William is probably sleeping. William says he's retiring after this year and that we'll finally be moving away, but he said that last year, too."

"I can't believe this," I say.

"What?" asks Danka, but I don't want to answer. Even the sight of a moving van loading up at the house of a family I've never met makes me feel abandoned. Sometimes I ask, "Why?"

and the answer varies only within the constraints of its unvarying theme. *There's nothing for us here, it's too slow, too quiet, there's nothing to do, the kids are just hanging out, there's no place to eat, no jobs, no place to purchase ethnic clothing, crafts even.*

"William makes me feel old just as I am beginning to feel like a teenager for the first time in my life," says Danka, starting the motor. The car purrs out of the lot, past the five parked cars and the stop sign, without pause.

"Come to think of it I don't recall ever seeing his car in this lot," says Danka, and spins around to pass through the lot a second time. His car is there. It's rusted through in places and has no side-view mirror. We have to sit for a minute while Danka smokes a cigarette and looks it over dreamily.

At last, we drive home. Daniel is not yet asleep.

"Your new friend Emily called," he tells me, rolling upright on his pillow. "She said she'd call back in the morning."

EMILY DOESN'T call back, but what choice do I have but to be as understanding of her as she would be of me? After all, we are soulmates, and were I in her place, I wouldn't call back either. Instead I'd be thinking, *Where could she have been when I called at eleven o'clock at night? She must not have wanted to talk to me, and told her husband to tell me she wasn't home. No matter that we were soulmates three days ago at that party. Now she's ashamed, embarrassed even, by our sudden, needy intimacy. Probably having caught sight of me the other day downtown she realized that I wasn't her type – my feet were bare, my toes dirty, and I was buying the wrong kind of toy. Oh God. She must have seen me on my way to returning those awful toy guns that Daniel's sister bought for Stevie. I was to exchange them for something summery and idyllic, a child's lawn-sprinkler in the shape of a juggling clown. Emily must have caught sight of me at a crucial moment, on the sidewalk right next to my car carrying my see-through plastic bag of Mr. Tough Guy Advanced System Machine Guns. She must have realized at that moment that she'd made a mistake, that the party had been a fluke and we weren't soulmates after all.*

"I know why she's not calling," I say to Daniel. "She must have seen me carrying those guns."

"She *did* call. Remember? You're the one that's not calling back."

"But she said *she'd* call back."

"Tell me the number," says Daniel. I tell him. He dials. The line is busy. When I dial again after less than a minute, it rings but no one answers. She must have phoned me last night only to to assuage her guilt about the fact that she could no longer stand the thought of being my friend. In fact, I conclude, very likely she knew I was out, she saw me driving along with Danka, and called at that moment perfectly assured that she would not have to talk to me and that, come morning, she would avoid me altogether by not answering her phone.

Built into the corner, our kitchen telephone desk forms a crescent of blonde oak glowing under the sunlight that falls through the evergreens outside the window. Like someone hiding under a sunhat, I sit in its semi-circle of protection, my private oasis of cool indifference. Our typewriter, for bills and business letters, is shielded by a dust cover of gray vinyl that I peel back just enough to slide a finger underneath and strike the keys.

I don't care, the finger types, but disconnectedly, as if the rest of my body *does* care.

These are the things Emily and I talked about on the day of the party: the overabundance of flowering trees; hallucinations; our mothers. Both of us are straight and pure, our hallucinations products only of our shared propensity for being awe-inspired. Hers featured moments of communion with inanimate objects, and mine, a centaur. I saw him standing very proudly near a railing spanning an overpass. Dusk had fallen; I looked up and saw him but he did not see me. His human half was hairless, with burnished skin the tone of polished chestnut. How regally he stood, as if his visit to our planet were only incidental, a stop-off at a scenic overlook highlighting the road to some far more significant destination. Indeed when I had passed beneath the span and turned back for a second look, the strange animal was gone; there was only a handsome black man walking a Great Dane. I had seen the man before, over the week I had spent in St. Louis.

"St. Louis?" asked Emily. "When?"

"Oh, '78 or 9."

" '79? When? Summer?"

"Early summer around June. The humidity was awful."

"I was *there.* In '79 in St. Louis in early June. For one day. There was a crafts fair under the arch, it must have been a weekend."

"The centaur was on a weekday," I recalled. "I know because I was coming home from work."

"Oh."

Collective disappointment. We felt it not just between the two of us but among the other people surrounding us on the lawn, as if everyone were momentarily chagrined by Emily's and my missed connection. The party was a potluck on blankets and lawnchairs, with two wading pools, a volleyball net, and music spewing from a corner of the patio. Looking back, there really did seem to be a lull, the beer cans held midway between lap and mouth, the hot dogs oddly silent on the grill, the volleyball pausing above the net. But then the watermelon seeds started flying again, and Marty Miller tripped into one of the inflated pools. Nobody laughed. We all knew that Marty had found a better job. He'd be leaving town. We could laugh about it when he was gone; his submerged eyeglasses, his drifting, floating hamburger bun, the pale undersides of his knees.

Emily and I decided to take a walk. We headed for the reservoir, and discussed what we liked about life in this town. "It's so easy to live here," we agreed. "Nothing ever quite happens. It's *comfortable.* It's like wearing old painted-up clothes."

We passed a moving van parked on the road near the reservoir, then turned and walked out to the gravelly edge to look at the view. It wasn't really a view, we agreed, but it was pretty. The sunlight made sparks on the water, and on the far side a dog nosed around in some Queen Anne's lace.

Soon we sat down on the bench and began talking about our mothers. Once, mine went with my father, a pediatrician, to see the movie, *Psycho.* Just as Janet Leigh stepped into her last, hot shower, my father was called to the hospital, leaving my mother alone. Emily's mother, far away in another dark theater, grabbed the hand of a stranger and clutched it tightly until the movie was over. She never found out who the stranger was. He wore a large pinky ring whose ghostly imprint she rubbed from the palm of her hand each time she related this story. Emily's mother is wistful, musical, and leery of showers. My mother's never wistful, but she's scared of showers too. Still, just to look at Emily and me, how opposite we are. My hair is a butch, and I come just about up to her shoulder. She's of average height, blonde and so wholesome I expect cheerleading pom-poms to materialize with every one of her good-natured exclamations.

We walked back to the party, split up, mingled. I saw her talking with my husband at the outskirts of the volleyball game. Hip to hip, they were sharing Bing cherries from a big, glass bowl.

"What did you think of her, anyway?" I ask him now.

"Who?"

"Emily. My new friend. The one who's not calling me back. You met her at that party. You were eating her cherries."

"Describe her."

I do. Daniel never notices beauty in women. Now he says, "Blonde? I don't know. She was nice. I mean, everyone I talked to at that party seemed nice. I didn't talk to anyone who wasn't, so she must have been, too."

"A cheerleader type," I say, redialing her number. "Don't you remember?"

"No."

"We have a lot in common."

"What you have in common with a cheerleader type I would really like to see."

Daniel grins, pulls up my shirt, clamps moist wet lips on one tiny breast, then the other, makes his way down my belly, has trouble, momentarily, with the buttons of my jeans, turns back for the nipples again. My breasts, he once told me, remind him of early frost; flowers trapped in the bud, unopened for eternity. Perhaps Emily imagines I am jealous of her talking with my husband. Perhaps that's why she hasn't answered the phone. If so, I have every right to be insulted by her inane speculation.

Still, I don't hang up the phone, I let it ring and ring and ring. It occurs to me that she might not be home, she might be out, playing tennis probably, or horseback riding. Emily must ride horses; she has bowlegs, she'd look perfect in a riding hat and jodphurs, carrying, in lieu of an ordinary riding crop, a gentle sprig of honeysuckle. Maybe I'm in love with a woman again, which is something that happens to me. Not a sexual love, but a hopeless, careless passion. Daniel already knows. He has pulled down my jeans, has parted my thighs. Through his tongue he feels the ringing of Emily's telephone like the purring of a cat.

THAT WAS the first week of summer. Now our town is caught in time as at the center of a whirlpool – all the days feel alike, all the mornings, noons and nights. The students are gone, the sidewalks and bike racks empty, the abandoned cats hungry for milk and affection. One brought us an offering; a mole half-alive on our doorstep, squint-eyed, belly quivering beneath the messy fur. With a dishtowel I shielded the mole, shooed the stunned cat back to the road. After an hour, when the mole had crawled off, I wanted the cat to come back; I stood at the door and called "Cat! Cat!" then listened for the padding of its feet along the sidewalk. Had it come I would have heard it; in the motionless air, small sounds thrived. Daniel was out conducting research in the field, Stevie had learned how to spin his new Astro-Top. On the hardwood floor, the toy made a cosmic whirring, while at the drop-off in town, the back doors of the airport limousine slam-banged shut. From so very far off, it made a sound like the shutting of a suitcase, a fastening of zippers, buckles, and locks.

Every time I hear it, I know someone's leaving. Hardly anyone visits; they say there is nothing to do. My own sister said, "No Tex-Mex? Forget it." She lives in Santa Fe in relentless sunlight crisscrossed by drunk drivers on whose pick-up trucks are strapped loaded shotguns. Here we have peace, and are drunk on air. Evening is redolent with dangling, overripe blossoms and with the songs of cicadas, a combination so dazzling as to displace the usual air with its own, unusual volume.

I tried enticing my sister with such descriptions.

"We take walks every night," I told her. "And we always run into someone we know who's just leaving town. The other night we had six people sitting on our lawn drinking beer and saying goodbye and listening to our neighbor Nikki playing her music, and we could smell the cherry trees a mile away."

"Where can you go dancing?" my sister inquired.

"In this town called Vermilion up by the lake."

"I didn't know there was a lake."

"Well, we never go there."

"And what if we felt like sightseeing during the day?"

"There's always Amish Country. You can get quilts and cheeses and have lunch and sightsee."

"Oh. Is it fun?"

"I don't know. We've never been there either. We like to take walks. The other night we walked around the reservoir and saw a real goldfish. You know, the Chinese kind. Somebody's left-behind pet, probably. Then we walked to the supermarket and it was gone."

My sister sighed. Apparently she had little desire to spend her yearly vacation in a town whose one supermarket vanished overnight. I told her I'd exaggerated. The building itself, with its brick exterior, its tape-scarred windows, its automatic doors, its L-shaped parking lot, even its gum machines, was still in place. But the doors were locked tight and the gumballs were gone. The food, too, was gone, the aisles dismantled. On the soiled linoleum floor lay half-coiled cash register receipts like limp albino creatures asleep in the twilight zone of a cave. On the far wall the Fresh Produce logo – a cut-out of grapes, bananas, and plums – loomed over bare, slanted shelving littered with romaine leaves. A few freezers were still lighted in what had been the ice cream aisle but cast only ghostly glows.

"Let's get away from here," I said to Daniel, surprised by the hoarseness of my voice.

But tonight we go back, perversely, needing to see it again. We had all known this was coming – the store was slated to close, but somehow I envisioned something less cataclysmic; gradual close-out sales, I tell Daniel, and maybe a farewell party for veteran shoppers, the cashiers handing out sample keilbasa on toothpicks. Nothing prepared me for this vast catacomb in whose sudden, closed-off reaches the butchers' helpers might still be de-boning breasts of chicken, ignorant of the store's closure like soldiers unaware of the end of the war. I press my face to the glass, peer in, bang twice on the door, give up, and press the lever on one of the gum machines. Out slide whole handfuls of pennies that dance on the concrete among the wheels of Stevie's stroller. I push the lever again; more pennies, and more. Hundreds. We have no place to put them, no pockets, no bag, no shoes, even, for we are wearing rubber thongs. Finally Stevie consents to be carried and we load the pennies in his stroller. The canvas sling seat swings rhythmically under the weight of the copper as we head home. Halfway there we find Simon, Ben and Leah scanning Plum Creek from the Morgan Street bridge, looking for baby woodchucks. All they've spotted are muskrats, so far.

"You can smell them," says Leah, wrinkling her nose and stepping down toward the sluggish water. "They smell bad, not like the woodchucks. They smell metallic, almost."

"You're smelling our pennies," said Daniel, who gestures at the coin-laden stroller and jokes, "The bank folded, and this is all they would give us."

"Jesus," says Ben. "Thank god we don't have any money saved up. Anybody seen Harley around, by the way? Gotta thank him for my zoom."

"Oh, Ben," I say.

"Excuse me?" says Daniel, feigning ignorance. But when he raises his eyebrows, Ben catches on. This is not a thing we like to talk about, if we can avoid it.

"Shit," says Ben. "When?"

"When what?" asks Leah, from her place on the rock. How tall she is, even sitting like this, her knees drawn up to her chin, her bony ankles bare beneath the loose, flapping hems of her pants. Between the spaghetti straps of her blouse can be seen the knobs of her vertebrae and the firm sinews of her musculature. Leah is, I have always imagined, stronger than any one of us.

"When does Harley get back from Bloomingham?" asks Ben. Bloomingham's one of Ben's jokes; whenever anyone disappears, he says they're sightseeing in Bloomingham. It's a town not far from here where hardly anyone lives at all. There's not even a cemetery. Just an old railway trestle and, underneath, a rocky stream bed where the teenagers gather to drink. Up a weedy slope and across the single road is a gas station selling sticks of beef jerky, and a dingy, mysterious storefront displaying God's eyes in its window. The God's eyes stare past the trestle into damp forest, and that's Bloomingham.

Now Leah darts a foot into the creek, quick as a waterbug, and withdraws it with a single plum blossom caught dripping between her toes. Ben doesn't see this; he's distracted by Simon, who appears suddenly from under the bridge.

"Hamburgers?" shouts Simon.

"Bugga bugga?" says Ben. "When will this kid learn to talk?"

"Not bugga bugga," I tell him. "Ham–" But something roars in the creek down below. Our pennies, like a sudden Niagara Falls. Stevie, gripping the handlebars of the stroller, has dumped it; he flops back down on his bottom, terrified, as the creek flashes copper. Twenty dollars for the muskrats. Stevie starts to wail, then stares past the railing, bewildered.

When we get home at ten p.m. there's someone swinging on our porch swing around the corner of the porch in a rectangle of shadow. The porch is wrap-around; it spans the whole, narrow front of our house before following the side wall all the way to the end, where the swing hangs perpendicular, facing the street.

Creak creeeeak, creak creeeeak, it swings, and we know it's not the wind; it sounds far too imperious.

It's my long-gone friend, Gail.

GAIL'S DEPARTURE from our town was especially protracted, and in those months, two years ago, when she was not quite gone but still moving from hideout to hideout, it was nearly impossible to find her. When you did come upon her, always at the door to some building–the post office, the travel agency, the bank–it seemed as unclear to Gail as to anyone else whether she had been on her way in or out, and her hesitant, somewhat breathless greetings all had the depleted, melancholy substance of weary goodbyes. She had just broken up with the man she'd been living with. Rather, George had just broken up with her. Rather, he had broken off with her long ago but had simply failed to tell her in as many words, so Gail, who was kind of spacey, hadn't picked up on things until George's new girlfriend moved in with the two of them. For a while after that, Gail stubbornly slept on the couch in George's living room within earshot of their shared orgasms, and later seemed to think that by lurking secretively for a while on the fringes of her ex-lover's awareness she might later find herself granted access to its center. Our town was once a stop on the Underground Railroad, and Gail seemed intent on excavating its desperate routes and solitary havens. Those days, she smelled faintly of mothballs and dust, or of cedar, dry leaves, and motor oil. I know some people whose attic she slept in for a couple of weeks, and someone else knows of a janitor who put her up now and then on the miniature cot in the infirmary of the elementary school, and when I pass a certain house on a corner in town I remember the time Gail led me inside to the room where she was staying that particular week. Then I followed her along numberless, dim hallways lined with closed doors. The house, pale green trimmed with darker gingerbread, appeared charmingly Victorian, the shutters on its narrow windows stenciled with fanciful cut-outs. Inside we might have entered a series of subterranean tenements whose intersecting passages pulsed here and there with obscure, seismic repercussions. Broken pipes, Gail said. Once, we passed a window, and there, surprisingly, was the yard I had seen from the street before entering, the sewer pipe exposed among the flipped, raw slabs of a still-flowering garden.

Tacked to several of the doors in these hallways were notes on scraps of paper that I longed to pull down and read. Instead I paused in my footsteps and peered over my shoulder when Gail had turned a corner up ahead.

The first was a sort of love note, I supposed.

"I came by, I came by," it read.

And the second, "Meet me at Tracee's."

Tracee's was a bar that had closed years earlier; the note on that door was four, five years old.

Gail led me past the bathroom she shared with eight people and up a tall flight of steps to a hallway lit with Day-Glo posters. Then she turned to me and said, "Well, I guess we'll go in here," as if talking about any old door, but it was the door to her room.

She was thin, too thin, with stooped shoulders, no bra, so her breasts dangled under her thin beige sweaters. For years she'd had ulcers, colitis, diarrhea, but she never complained. She never even complained about George. George the intellectual. When he removed his eyeglasses and perched them on the desktop, their wire frames mimicked precisely the stiff composure of his fingers. He wore caftans to work, in the bookstore, and made passes at someone named Candy who managed somehow to choose titles he admired. Gail didn't know. When Candy left town for a couple of days, Gail of all people was entrusted with the care of her houseplants and cats. I went up there with her once, and carried the watering can. The houseplants were herbs and the cats were affectionate sorts who slept peacefully on piles of antique clothing. When we entered the room, the cats rose and stretched, trailing lengths of black lace and white feather boas. In a way I couldn't blame George at all. It was cozy and sexy up there, like a movie set, with camp trunks and beaded throw pillows. There wasn't a bed. There was a velvet, fringed love seat, too small for serious loving, but on the floor under a table was a comforter scattered with books, so I suppose that's where they did it. Gail said, later on, that George sometimes made love while reading; when he came, the pages of his book slammed shut around his thumb, and he'd fall asleep holding it there. Everybody who knew him believed this story. He was selfish, cruel, and ridiculous. Gail had lost fifteen pounds by the time she moved out but still wore the clothing he liked on her, the beiges and buffs that made her look like straw. Those days she sighed even while riding her bicycle whose wheels clicked and spun with a tick tick tick that seemed to emanate from her rib cage. Her friends, myself included, became increasingly annoyed with her willful air of irresolution. If we met her for breakfast, at the diner where Gail ordered without fail one slice of toast, a cup of tea, a glass of orange juice, and a glass of milk, we wore our brightest, loudest colors calculated to elicit her famous reaction, a deliberate squint followed by a fit of helpless sneezing. Those were the Underground Railroad days. I saw her belongings, once: an ample straw bag stuffed with papers, recordings, books, clothing, and a ceramic canister containing wiry clumps of hair elastics and other toiletries including a razor on which she sliced her finger now and then while reaching in for a comb. When she led me to her room, it was to find a cassette that she wanted to bring to my house and play. That was the first time I saw Joe close up. I'd been noticing him a while, but only from a distance, and now here he was, on a flat, brown couch in a hallway, eating a deli sandwich whose second half he fed bit by bit to his dog. In Gail's room I asked Gail what she knew about the man on the couch.

"What man?" she asked.

"The one with the bald head. Wearing the painter's cap," I

said. *The one who looks like he never evolved,* I almost said out loud, but didn't. *The one who looks like an ape. The unmodified man. Pure, unadulterated testosterone.*

The one who makes me forget that I'm civilized.

"Oh," Gail said, and then said only that his name seemed to be Joe and that although he did not appear to live in the building, or to know anybody who did, he ate lunch on that couch every once in a while. Later when we left with her cassette, he was gone. The couch, when I reached out to stroke it, still held traces of his incredible body heat.

"SO THIS must be the All New You," I say to Gail when I find her swinging to and fro on our porch swing, her bare toes flexing and unflexing as they push against the rim of our geranium pot. On her lap is a spread of postcards depicting scenes of quaint landmarks, which after a minute I recognize as those of our town; the windmill on Route 58 on a day when the leaves of the corn stalks glistened with moisture, and another of the Chinese Missionary Memorial Archway on a day when the flower beds bloomed and there was nobody hanging out smoking, and another of the corner where the giant oak died leaving only a circle of international flags that on the day of the photograph balanced majestically on stiff, wide currents of air. Day to day, we hardly notice these things at all; they don't look important, they only blend in with the scenery. But the postcards look like photos from a boring history text. Gail is probably writing on the backs of them, "Now you can see why I had to get away from this place. Not too hip."

No longer limp, Gail's hair makes a spongy afro dotted here and there with corkscrew tendrils, and her clothing, although of similar but creamier browns and beiges, highlights her amazing green eyes and her new, amazing sexiness. The green eyes, too, are new (contact lenses) and I can no longer remember what color they used to be. Neither can my other acquaintances who knew her. Later on, we'll speak of Gail with awe because of all of the sex she's been having. "She doesn't use *rubbers,*" we'll say to each other breathlessly as if she's parachuting without a back-up chute or rock climbing without rope. "Did you hear about the guy from Haiti?" we'll ask, and each of us will have, and will try to duplicate with the palms of two hands the precise length of his penis as demonstrated by Gail, and then the circumference which she indicated with her thumbs and index fingers.

"Jesus Christ," I say involuntarily. And then, "Don't you ever think about AIDS?"

"No," says Gail.

She tells a story about a date she had with a man who wined and dined her one night after which they nearly made it on the dock outside the restaurant. When they rushed back to his apartment, a friend of his was there from out of town and, as Gail puts it, somehow she ended up in bed with the friend instead, in the spare room.

"Not real pleasant for the guy who took you out," I comment.

"He was kind of pissed off, I guess," says Gail. "I haven't seen him since then."

"Have you seen the friend?"

"No. He was from LA. I really missed him for a couple of days but then I met this actor in New York and we had an incredible weekend. We didn't even go outside."

"What were you doing in New York?"

"I was with this actor."

"But–"

"Actually most of the guys I end up with are kind of old, in their forties. I'm thinking about maybe going out with some younger ones, because the old ones are so weird. All they do is worry about performance even though some of them really know what they're doing, in fact some of them are absolutely stupendous, like there was this guy who could have written a book about it but still I had to tell him how great he was–like this Spanish guy I was seeing, I had to say 'magnifico' or else he'd get really unhappy–and then you have to get them to do it again and again so they know you really liked it."

"Sounds frustrating," I say.

"And I've also decided I definitely like the big ones better, although you can't always tell beforehand. Anyway it's okay to have a little variety once in a while. I act different, with different men. Don't you?"

"Well. . . "

"Can I spend a couple of days here, Liz? I really love this house, I've been thinking about it."

"Of course, as long as you wash some of the dishes."

"Come and see my portfolio."

What portfolio? I'm thinking. This is not the same Gail. This is not the Gail who, after George fell asleep on the bed beside her, pulled his book from his thumb and marked it with a feather so he'd know where he was in the morning. This is not the same Gail, who used to cover her mouth when she yawned. This Gail yawns with her body and soul. When it's over, she uncurls her toes from my geranium pot and takes from her suitcase a slick leather portfolio that she carries into my house. We pass the study where Daniel is already working, bare-chested, at the computer.

"He hasn't changed a bit," says Gail.

"Well, it hasn't been that long," I say defensively.

"Two years," says Gail, who flopping down on the bed in the spare room, unzips the portfolio and reaches inside. Watching her gives me the shivers. I never thought a person could change this much. Around here people stay pretty much the same. Whole months go by, and you still recognize people when you walk down the street, and they still recognize you. It's comforting. And I don't know about this new Gail. She's happier, for sure, but what's this stuff she's taking out of the portfolio? Photos, and sketches, and swatches of lace, and even a newspaper clipping or two; portraits of Gail, interviews with Gail, people talking about Gail. It seems she's a sensation. Fashion design, but she works only on commission, transforming old wedding gowns into negligees, lingerie, and even men's briefs.

"Can I see your old wedding dress?" she asks me.

I find it upstairs in its cedar-scented cleaner bag in Daniel's closet. "It was my mother's," I tell her. On my mother it must have looked regal. On me, trimmed down to size, it resembled the finery of a doll. At the bottom of the bag is the excess satin, yards of it, rolled up in tissue paper.

"Pajamas are the really big thing, these days. You know, loungewear," Gail says, fingering the pleats of the bodice. It was a risque dress for my mother's day: bare shoulders, the sleeves starting midway on the upper arm.

"I'm not the loungewear type."

"Turkish pants, how 'bout? A sash at the hips, a sash at each ankle. Real sensual."

"I'm not the type."

"You could be," she says, flicking a hair off one of the sleeves. The satin is cream, with a watery sheen that in certain light makes rainbows, and the lace is pearl-studded. "Better than letting it hang in your closet, anyway."

"It was in Daniel's closet, not mine."

"Or," she goes on, "I could make some maternity shifts out of it. A lot of women are doing that."

"What the hell would I do with a maternity shift?"

Gail smiles at me. "And that's another thing. Men's clothes. They can really get into the satin, once you make them feel, you know, that it's not going to make them impotent or anything. But which would you like? The loungewear?"

Shocked, I see she is already gripping a fancy pair of shears.

"I'll think about it," I say, taking the dress from her lap. I clip the dress back on its hanger, lower it carefully into its plastic bag. As I fasten the bag with a bread tie, Gail cuts the air with the shears. She does this with great care and fastidiousness as if the air were made of lace, snipping delicate shapes that seem to fall to her lap when she's done. Triangles. Hearts. Ribbons. Around the swish of the shears, we talk. After a while the computer stops whirring and the study light clicks off down the hall. Much later I go upstairs. Daniel has fallen asleep on our bed with his blue jeans on.

OUR HALLWAYS and rooms, when Gail has passed through them, resemble those paintings meant to suggest a tantalizing proximity of human experience, those still-lifes composed of telltale items – the empty hanger trembling on a rod in a closet, the just-abandoned rocking chair, the book still arousingly open, its single page free-floating. We find record albums turning silently in empty rooms, two half-drained wine goblets perching on the arm of a disheveled couch, and the tv still on to a late late show while on the floor beside it Gail's kicked-off sandals retain the narrow arches of her vanished feet. Then, in the hallway, a scrap of wedding gown lace that on closer inspection turns out to be an exquisitely stitched bikini panty, open-crotched, and in the bathroom at the edge of the sink, a contraceptive jelly applicator tube. Things like that. Once, we even find a man in a robe in our kitchen, spreading peanut butter onto a slice of bread. I don't know him, exactly, but he works for the local tree surgeon. Soho Trees. His brown hair is like feathers swinging over his shoulders, but you don't always see that part of him. Ordinarily he's up in a tree, suspended delicately among bleached-out limbs, in solitude and sunlight-dappled silence, while below the big truck whirs and chews, and the other, fatter, Soho men stand around waiting for the fruits of his labors, the shorn, leafless branches he keeps tossing down to them. He is splendid, graceful, inaccessible as an eagle. What did Gail do to get hold of such a creature? I wonder. Climb a tree?

One night, having followed Gail's trail to its end, I stand uncertainly at the guest room door, fingers outstretched for the knob. Daniel finds me and leads me away into the kitchen, kisses me, then turns for a cantaloupe melon that I understand we are to share on the porch swing in the dark as if this were one of the old days, the old familiar, patient nights, as if Gail weren't in our guestroom making love to the Soho Tree Man, as if, just this morning, she hadn't told me I was *quaint.* "It's nice to have someone you can count on when you need a taste of good old-fashioned quaint domesticity," she said, and kissed me gently on the cheek as if she didn't know she may as well have punched me in the nose. *I'm not quaint,* I think now, as impatiently I unzip my skirt, slide out of it, grind up hotly against my husband. Daniel's heartbeat stays relaxed, his whole body preoccupied, slicing the melon, scooping its hollows, tossing the fibrous, wet clumps in the sink and then turning on the water. He finds two plates, two spoons, one striped, woven dishtowel to be shared between us. I pull off my halter top, wrap it round his neck as if I mean to strangle him, and yank him onto the porch without the melon at all. Only then does he carry me down the porch steps and into the yard where our neighbor Nikki's music hums softly to the grass and to each damp blossom of our sour cherry tree, like a ghost sniffing perfume. The yard is all weeds beneath my spread naked buttocks as Daniel crawls on top of me and tickles my nose with his flopping pony tail. Our lovemaking is familiar as breathing: gentle and soothing, moist, uncomplicated, lengthy. Even Gail's flimsy guestroom curtains sleep at peace in the windows before we are done, yet still I watch with fresh longing as the moonlight climbs the chimney, filling it up. Daniel rises, goes into the house, brings the melon out onto the porch and eases onto the slats of the porch swing, naked, satisfied, the striped dishtowel unfolded on his lap.

I open my legs to a breeze. Daniel's spoon flashes as he eats.

NOT MANY NIGHTS later I am lying in the tub when the telephone rings. But I try to ignore it. I am in the downstairs bathroom which I don't often use but which I've chosen tonight for its residue of Gail; its candle, its glass jar of clear, amber bath beads. In the bath, Gail's forgotten body sponge, and beneath the sink a bottle of Gail's cheap wine, corked with a wad of pantyhose. The candle smells of musk, and the bath oil, too; it's like soaking in hormones. I've poured a mug of wine. Through the screens I hear the strains of Nikki's music: synthesized strings with some mild percussion.

Is it possible that Daniel does not hear the phone?

The last I saw Daniel, he was hunkered in the kitchen sucking home-made jewelweed nectar from a glass pipet in an attempt to regulate the sugar concentration. Gail left town yesterday having got what she was after, half an hour alone in her ex-lover George's apartment. There she rifled through his girlfriend's zippered clothing bags in search of antique wedding gowns. She found three, left the moth eaten one behind.

When she left, she kissed my hairline and asked sexily, “How was this visit? Was it okay?”

“Magnifico,” I said, and watched her breezy departure and remembered, the minute she drove away, the diaphragm she'd left hanging to dry on the shower nozzle and which I'd meant to point out to her while she was packing her bags.

Apparently Daniel does not hear the phone, so I climb out myself and answer it, trailing slippery beads of water amid frothy white clumps of shampoo. It's Danka, which I suppose I should have known, and which Daniel must have known all along. Who else calls while I'm taking a bath?

“I am dying,” says Danka. “Tell me something to distract me.”

Her way of saying, “What's up?”

I yawn, catch a ball of shampoo as it slips off my ear and flatten it into my palm. It's eleven o'clock at night.

“I was having a candlelight bath,” comes my response. “Daniel is sucking pipets and Nikki is playing Moon Songs on her synthesizer. She always plays those around *bedtime,* Danka, you know what I'm saying? Listen closely and you'll hear them.”

I prop the telephone receiver against the open, kitchen screen and slide down the hallway back to my bath where I finish drinking my wine, rinse off in the shower, towel dry, rub lotion into my knees and elbows before kneeling ceremoniously to blow out the flickering candle.

Then I turn on the light and comb my hair.

In the hallway I pause, listening for the angry, disconnected buzz of Danka's telephone. But there is nothing, just an isolated circle of unflappable patience floating in the spell of Nikki's music like a duck on a pond.

At the phone I ask, “How do you like it?” and soften a bit as I flop onto the chair. After all, I've phoned Danka during *her* baths as well, although she takes hers at all hours of the day. She eats breakfast in there on a floating tray, and once dropped a cinnamon roll in the water.

"Fantastic. But now tell me what is it you think you would like to do after your bath."

Around midnight, say.

"Oh, I was thinking about going out for a little spin," I answer sarcastically.

"That is amazing! Do you know that that is exactly what I was hoping?"

"I had this feeling."

"Naturally you did. You always do. Do you know you always know what I am thinking? Fantastic. When do you want me to come and get you?"

"THAT WAS Thank You," I say to Daniel in the kitchen. Bent over at the waist, I am batting my hair with a towel. Seen from upside down my husband more than ever resembles a drug dealer with his array of paraphernalia, his brown glass jars of assorted powders and concoctions, his slender scoops and measuring spoons and even, at his elbow, a plastic bag packed with syringes. He sits on a high stool at the counter, eyes riveted to the numbers on his Sartorious Balance. Soon he slides the glass door open again, taps the handle of the scoop, releases a gram or two of mercurium blue onto the circle of filter paper. No need for such painstaking exactitude, I've long suspected, but Daniel loves the little balance. How responsive it is; one breath, if its sliding glass door is not properly closed, is enough to send shivers along its dial. This is Daniel in a nutshell, this incremental striving toward perfect equilibrium. Now his hands hover tentatively over the scale, fingers spread like a conductor's sustaining a note. Finally he turns to me and asks, "Isn't it a little late to be going out? I mean, where are you going to go?"

"She wants to spy on someone, I think, and if I want to stay her friend I have to go with her, because she doesn't want to go alone. She needs a sounding board."

"And you *do* want to stay her friend?"

Pause, but the car honks outside. Danka's honk is like a strangled elephant; I have to soothe it before it wakes the neighbors. This happens, occassionally, all over town. It's the women who go out driving or strolling, and the men who stay home, patient and, maybe, a little bit scared–scared of holding so tight that when the women get loose, they'll stay that way. But Daniel feigns unconcern; he waves me away with a forceps, then turns and gently lifts the disk of filter paper off of the balance before sliding the dyes into a funnel. For a moment I watch him tapping the funnel, holding the beaker aloft.

"Have fun," he says. "Tell Thank You hello. Don't forget your seatbelt, and don't let her get you in trouble."

In trouble, I think, as I walk out the door. What constitutes trouble? Have I ever been in it? Danka has. But has she ever escaped? Trouble's her style, her definition, her history. She is imprinted on it, she follows its crazy shape. Crazy, because it can't contain itself. It's too big, too overwhelming. We were sitting drinking coffee when she told me about it. That was the purpose of our meeting, I remember. "I think you would understand if I wanted to tell you about some of my troubles," Danka had said when we first met each other, "How about coffee?" And we set the date and time. We met in the college cafeteria way past lunch hour on a brilliant day one November. Even the ivy had turned red and orange; sparrows clamored among it where it climbed past the windows. Still, inside, the room was dim as if submerged. A janitor was sweeping. He stood the chairs on the tabletops in organized rows, beginning at the far end but marching our way. Across the room sat a circle of librarians I recognized, but their words were inaudible; only the low notes carried. We heard the clatter of flatware from way in the back, and then a rush of steam before some lights flickered on near the door. Danka wore a black turtleneck, black jeans, and high-heeled black clogs with pointed toes. At the theater the previous Saturday night, where we'd introduced ourselves, many people had worn black but still I'd noticed that Danka's black was different. Hers was richer, more enveloping, scarier, somehow. During intermission, I was staring at her. She noticed, stared back at me and beckoned me close. We introduced ourselves, and then she led me outside. She drew a slender black filter from an evening purse, twisted a cigarette into its end and lit it with a pewter lighter.

"I've seen you around," she said, exhaling smoke.

People were always "seeing me around."

"I'm a mailman," I answered, nodding encouragingly.

"Yes," said Danka, "but that's not what I mean . . . "

I waited. She was older than I. My mother's generation. Maybe she would say, You are the daughter I have never had, in her faint European accent.

Instead, she started talking about the play.

"I have never understood the ridiculous notion that their backs shouldn't face the audience," Danka said finally. "As if they think we'd be insulted, when really what's insulting is when they must constantly stare out over our heads as if they don't even know we're here. Also, the set is many inconsistencies. They should never have – what? – fields of sunflowers and neon lights simultaneously."

"That's the point," I said.

Smoke in my eyes.

"Why didn't you tell me I was still wearing my apron?" said an elderly man just then. He had slipped up beside us and put an arm around Danka's waist. A paisley apron lay draped over his forearm.

"Because your fly is down," said Danka, who reached over and zipped it.

The patio lights blinked on and off, and people began filing back to their seats. We passed a table of Pepperidge Farm cookies, a quarter a piece, and glasses of wine for a dollar. Danka picked out three Lidos when no one was looking, and passed them around.

Later, after the show, Danka caught up with me and laced her fingers through mine, palms touching, square dance style. Her husband had just finished at the drinking fountain, and as he approached, made swipes at his mustache with the end of a rolled-up program. Drops of water flew around.

"I think you would understand if I wanted to tell you about some of my troubles," she said calmly, as if I were about to be hypnotized.

So we made our date for coffee. The cafeteria was two stories high and the unwashed windows, multipaned with a yellowish cast, arched all the way to the ceiling. The hinged arches were open, and threw beams of daylight down into the room. One shone on our table, too bright to look at. Instead we looked at each other somewhat testily, I thought. Danka resembled an aunt of mine, who wore skirts so tight she could hardly walk. But Danka was earthy in spite of the elegant clogs, and had beautiful deep crows feet on silken skin, like the soft tucks sewn into Gail's lingerie. Silver hairs made a shimmer on top of the black, and when she lifted her cup I noticed her ring, two gold snakes intertwined.

"Nice ring," I began.

"Shall I call you Elizabeth?" she asked.

"Liz, please."

"Oh."

She was disappointed. For a moment she busied herself with her jacket, purse, and coffee.

"Where are you from?" I asked.

"Austria."

"My parents had a housemaid from Austria," I said. "When I was growing up. She taught me to sing Edelweiss, and then brought me one pressed in waxed paper, but I peeled the waxed paper away."

"You were a sensitive child."

I faltered. I had lost the edelweiss. I had put it in a book, and had given the book to the library along with some others. Some other child must have come upon it and not known what it was; a circle of tiny rabbit ears, perhaps, of creamy, aged velvet that turned to dust when it was touched.

"I was the teacher's pet," I told her. "I once went to a friend's birthday bowling party instead of with my sister to Shea Stadium to see the Beatles first U.S. concert. I've never forgiven myself. That concert was history."

"History isn't so good."

We were silent, we drank our coffee, we felt the big room shrink around us while the janitor piled chairs upon the tables. The librarians filed out, replaced by a tall mathematician eating pears and cottage cheese while flipping through the pages of a textbook. Outside, swallows rustled the tendrils of ivy.

"How I love October," Danka said with provocation.

"This is November."

"I know. I hate November. You have your Thanksgiving."

"What's wrong with Thanksgiving?"

"Nothing. You Americans think nothing happens in November but Thanksgiving."

"What happens in November?"

"Happened."

"What happened in November?"

"I don't know if I should tell you," said Danka.

A twist of her head, a little shrug like the shrug of a child. Danka squinted hard, opened her purse, withdrew a silk scarf which she wrapped around her neck and knotted deftly and precisely as if preparing to leave the table. The scarf was a wisp of black smoke.

"I was in Skarzysko."

"I know," I said at once, surprised that what I'd said was the absolute truth. In fact I'd never heard of Skarzysko before but I knew at once it was a camp and that Danka had been in it. "There was no other explanation," I explained later on to Daniel.

"Explanation for what?" said Daniel.

"For Danka."

"I had a feeling you knew," Danka said, and played with the ends of the scarf. "So. What do you think."

"I think. . . " I paused. "I always see that time period in black and white, like photos, old film clips, you know? But it seems to me it must have *happened* in black and white. The Great Depression too. Not even the apples were red. No color would seem to make sense. I don't know. All the faces were gray, the sky was gray, the fields, everything."

A question, really.

"But, you know, that's absolutely true, it *was* gray, Lizzie, yellowish gray, and that's what saved my life, if you have to know the story. On the day–but maybe I shouldn't tell you. No. I will tell you. I will."

"You don't have to," I said.

Shocked, Danka glared at me and got up and left. Stalked out. I was too ashamed to follow. But in a minute I rose and went to look for her; in the lady's room, in the hallway, outside the front doors, in the stairwell, around the cluster of green vinyl couches, upstairs in the study lounge, in another bathroom and then out a window with a view from the fire escape down onto the courtyard and sidewalks. Wind blew in small spirals in the chilly, bright air. There was a goldfish pond out there that been drained for repairs, and some boys were skateboarding in it, up and around its concrete banks and then down into the middle where some wet leaves lay. Danka wasn't anywhere. I went back downstairs and into the cafeteria for my sweater. There was Danka sitting in the same seat, looking at me.

"I can't tell just anybody," she said when I got close, "because they won't believe me, not quite, they never believe it to the extent that is necessary, simply because they don't want to. They don't want to *know*. Someone once said to me, 'But what is so terrible about turnip soup?' But it wasn't turnip soup, it was liquid filth with turnip peels floating on top of it, and besides we had to use the same bowls we used at night in the bunk, when they wouldn't let us go to the outhouse. Where were you just now?"

"I was looking for you."

"What you said about the black and white, it really was that way although you didn't quite believe it when you said it, did you? You thought you were being poetic. I knew from the moment I saw you at the theater that you were innocent enough to believe anything, no matter how true it may be. Understand? I was seven. My aunt had to pretend that I was hers, because my mother wasn't anywhere, we didn't know where she was, or any of the others, but that was the first scary moment for me, when my aunt grabbed me and said, 'This one's mine.' Because I wasn't. You know? It was very confusing. Not that I objected to my aunt. I had always liked her. But suddenly everything was topsy-turvy. We weren't allowed in the barracks during the day, so on that first day we sat in the mud where it was chilly. Our heads were shaved and we wore our striped pajamas. We hadn't eaten in twenty-four hours and when we did it was that soup with the turnips floating in it that tasted like ashes. Someone spilled hers on the mud and three skeletons appeared out of nowhere and licked the soup off the ground. There was a lot of lice and we were all covered with it. After several weeks I caught some illness and became feverish, although my aunt tried to hide this terrible fact. But I was very, very pale, and one day during selection – my aunt was working on the day shift in the munitions factory at the camp – I was picked to be transferred. My aunt returned to the barracks at nightfall and was told what had happened. She had become friendly – well, that is an odd term under the circumstances but it was true – with one of the guards at the place where they took sick people to be shipped off to be killed. This guard had been a prostitute before working in the camp. She had a daughter of her own. But she wasn't going to get me out of there, oh no, but she was kind enough to let my aunt go inside to say goodbye to me. But my aunt brought a bowl of water, and a comb she had borrowed from another inmate, and while she was visiting with me, in the few minutes that the guard had given us, she washed my face and combed my hair and even gave me a clean shirt to wear. I don't know where she got that. But the really important thing – she had a little slip of red paper she had taken from the munitions factory, and she dipped it in the water and rubbed the dye onto my cheeks and lips until I looked healthy. Then you should have seen me. That was probably the loveliest I have ever been, my aunt has told me, and I be lieve her. I was lovelier then, than on my wedding day. All the people all around were yellow gray, like parchment, they were drying up, shriveling, dying. And I was looking like a rose in a field of dust. So I was saved, they didn't put me on the trucks after all. Do you believe all of that?"

"Yes."

"I don't. Not a bit. It's my aunt's favorite story. My aunt was plump – that is, before the camps and after. Not like my mother, who was fashionably slender, slinky, even. I've turned out to be more like my aunt. Isn't that interesting?"

"What happened to her?"

"My mother?"

"Your aunt."

"Why don't you ask me about my mother? Everybody is always afraid to ask me that."

"What happened to your mother?"

"I already told you: nobody knows. She died, that means. My aunt lives in New York. She was recently widowed. We lie to each other whenever we can. My mother has never been heard of, or anyone else. When I married William I thought I would get away from it all and that is the problem. I *have*. Too completely. You might ask, 'So what is the harm in forgetting such a place?' But it was my childhood. How can you ask me to forget it? How can you expect me to wonder around believing that I never came from anywhere. How can you expect – "

"But I don't – "

"How can you live in this town? It's so smug. I no longer trust it. It's the calm before the storm. It's like living in an egg about to crack, and then it doesn't. It never does crack, it just sits here in peace. It's enough to make you scream."

"I have my *life*," I said. "I like this town." I was feeling defensive. Unworthy. What could be said? Then the janitor approached with his army of chairs close behind. He winked at me flirtatiously as he hefted another one onto a table.

"It's getting late," I said. "You said 'wonder around'. It's not 'wonder', it's 'wander'. Wonder is thinking. Wander is walking."

"I suppose you have to wonder home and cook dinner," Danka said.

"We make sandwiches," I said. "Or spaghetti or tacos. That's not really cooking, it's just doing things."

"But you do them together."

"Most of the time. How about you?"

"William is a fastidious cook."

How sad I felt for her, all at once. I pictured him wearing the paisley apron, circling the kitchen with his spoon in his hand, reciting the names of fresh herbs.

"IS THIS a Dove Bar night?" I ask Danka when we've been moving for a while.

"Dove Bar? Oh. Those big ice creams. No. Why do you... why would we... "

"That's what we ate last time. In the parking lot. Remember?"

"That? That's all over with. Nothing's going to happen with him. I have not even run into Startup in ages. Why would you suppose we were going there again? Don't you suppose if anything were developing I would at least have mentioned him? Besides, I don't even know his name, and besides I have a feeling he stays occasionally in Bloomingham of all places in the whole wide world. I don't think I've given you any cause to think–"

"I just thought we were heading sort of in that direction, Danka. That's all."

"Well, it wouldn't kill us to see if his lights are on."

We slowly enter the alley leading into the parking lot. Danka switches off the headlights, scooting forward on her seat. Her chin is inches from the top of the steering wheel.

"Ooomph," she says, and swings left to avoid ramming into a tree. "I cannot understand why they have trees in a parking lot, for goodness sake."

"Probably the same reason they have his house in the parking lot."

"But we don't know if it's his house. We have no way of knowing unless you knock on the door. There might even be a woman in there with him, for all we know."

"Or a man."

"No. Not a man. If you had seen him even once you would know that. It's the way he looks at me. I can't see the house anywhere."

"Over there." I point.

"But the lights aren't on. That bastard. I'll be damned if we hang around here. He is probably watching. Don't you think? Can you see him in the window?"

"No."

"Well, that tops it."

On Main Street, she speeds up and heads out of town past the windmill to the fields where the private air strips are. The corn is flowering now; the tassels make a nimbus on the surface of the fields although the moon is just a sliver, the sky starry, indigo, and streaky from so many planes. Slash here, slash there. Far ahead is a glare, but that's only the steel mills up by the lake. We'll turn off the road before then if we go where I think we are going. I turn the radio on to a talk show and get homesick all at once, for a drive I took with Daniel out here last year. That was late at night, too, and the show was a matchmaking one. All the people who phoned in were sixty years old or older, widowed, wanting company. Daniel and I held hands as we listened, hoping they'd find each other. But tonight's show is fuzzy, all the way from Chicago. I switch it off, and Danka tells me she's considering getting a job, she's put her résumé on file with the personnel office at the college. She's an expert typist, she says, and adds, "It's no wander when I have been typing all of William's papers for him all of these years since the children left home. William doesn't know how to type. He is worried about me getting a job. He said to me, 'Why go to the trouble of typing for somebody else when the only difference is that they will pay you?'"

"He makes you type all his papers for him?"

"No, he doesn't *make me,*" says Danka, stung. "I do some of the research. I make suggestions now and then. He depends on me."

"Sounds interesting."

"It isn't. Not to me. Right now he is trying to track down a city he somehow managed to read about, the City of Repose. He can't find it. The place does not even exist anymore. Well, no, that's not true, but the name has changed. It's a town eight miles north of Jerusalem of all places in the whole wide world."

"I thought you said he couldn't find it."

"He can't. *I* did. I'm afraid he'll want to go there if he finds out where it is, and be reposeful. Do you know he wears a toga sort of thing, before bed? For a bathrobe, you know, but with pockets, for after his shower, just before he goes to – Oh my God, what is this –"

Danka swerves to avoid a pick-up whizzing toward us in our lane, its brights on, horn blaring. We miss it by a foot, but now we're following the left lane on a two-lane highway, a circumstance which appears not to worry Danka at all.

"Danka," I mention after a while. "We're driving the wrong way."

"How would you know? I haven't told you where we are going," Danka answers contentedly.

"We're going to Bloomingham, right?" I ask.

No answer. Just a shrug, a shifting of her foot on the gas pedal, a decrease in pressure. Overhead a small airplane floats into the night, blinking red at the tips of its wings. How gently it rises, like a balloon. We haven't crossed to the proper side of the road, but I won't raise the issue again. Such impasses are Danka's way of reminding me of what she told me about in the cafeteria – she has suffered in life while I haven't, she knows about things I can hardly begin to imagine. This fact is like a thick pane of glass between us, but if we ever break through it, we'll stop being friends. We have nothing in common. My life has been perfect and hers has been hell, and that's why we need each other.

Besides, I realize, leaning back in my seat, there is not a car in sight, and the road is flat and straight. To either side are black fields and scattered here and there the darkened shapes of farmhouses at peace in their circles of trees. From one tree hangs a swing mysteriously swaying, a faint tremor passing along its ropes. Two women stand nearby in nightgowns. We are coasting now, enjoying the nighttime scenery. Danka is smiling when she suddenly pulls over to the wrong shoulder, stops the car and climbs out. Up ahead, the old train trestle spans the road. To the right climbs a forested hillside broken here and there by narrow lanes, and to the left is the drop-off, a rough, graveled slope ending fifty feet down at the edge of the river. I've met several elderly people who were born in this town, but no one who lives here now. I think of something I once learned: if you are walking in woods and find daffodils growing, or irises, then there once was a house in that spot. Search, and you'll find the foundation, a few crumbling slabs of limestone, a threshold, a small pile of bricks. Bloomingham is different; no daffodil, no iris, just thistle, goldenrod, black-eyed Susan. Just the rusted railway trestle with its loosened nuts and bolts, and up ahead is where the God's eyes hang in the window. Behind them is a freezerful of ice cream novelties. That's it. Near the store a dirt lane begins and disappears among some hickories, the shag bark rustling with the start of a breeze. How quiet it is. Danka says there are houses hidden up there but that's not where we're going. She takes my arm, leads me to the drop-off over the river. When we've followed the shoulder a while, we come to a path lined with tall brittle, flowering weeds. Their pollen tickles my nose and I sneeze.

"Shhhhh," says Danka, pinching my arm. "Be quiet!"

"Why?" I whisper in return.

But Danka doesn't answer. We continue down the path, sideways, because the gravel underfoot is slippery. Soon the path is no longer; there is only a slope heavily littered with beer cans and fast food bags. Across the river the trees are tall and dark, layering the hillside. Something hums. Powerlines. Something gurgles just ahead, but that turns out to be the river parting for a hunk of concrete. Danka picks her way along the bank as I follow until we've reached the shadow of the suddenly looming trestle. There we pause, and Danka cocks her head.

"Listen," she whispers. "Hear that?"

"What?"

"You listen, and tell me what it is that you are hearing. Then if you are hearing what I am hearing, then I will know for sure that that is what it is."

"I don't hear anything," I say.

"Shhhhh. Just *try.*"

I listen so hard that I believe I hear the insects walking on the river.

"Nothing," I say after a minute.

"That!" says Danka. "Hear it?" and at once I hear a can skidding on the rocks.

"Someone kicking a beer can. Probably a rat," I add, looking around.

"Not *that,*" pleads Danka. "Come on. Can't you hear anybody snoring?"

"He sleeps here?" I ask, astounded. We are no longer whispering.

"Who?"

"I thought he lived in the house in the parking lot."

"*Maybe* he does," Danka answers. "But sometimes he sleeps here on an old mattress under the trestle."

"How do you know this? You don't even know his name."

"What does his name have to do with it? If I thought his name was so important I would have asked him."

"You've spoken to him?"

"No. Not really."

"Danka. What are we doing here?"

"It was just a possibility. I thought, if. . . "

"If what?"

"If you were homeless, where would you sleep?"

"In my car. Besides, he's not homeless. He lives in that house in the parking lot."

"He does? For a fact? When did you see him there?" asks Danka eagerly.

"I didn't, but–"

"I can picture it so clearly, him lying on the mattress with his hands on his beerbelly, snoring."

"Oh, Danka. You are really in love."

"I know. What should I do?" she asks, as we reach the road again. We make our way gingerly back to the car. "Maybe he doesn't snore," Danka says as we climb inside. "We should have listened more closely."

"Danka."

"I know."

I buckle my seatbelt. She starts the car. At once, the same pick-up truck we passed earlier appears from a lane in the woods. It pulls into the road behind us, revs its motor and passes, then slows down so suddenly we are driving bumper to bumper. Danka passes but the truck squeals ahead of us in return. The truck's cab light is on and we can see three teenage boys drinking out of a bottle, laughing at us.

"Lock your door," I say.

But Danka reaches into her purse for her filter and cigarette, then finds her pewter lighter nestled in the space between our seats. When she gives me the cigarette to hold, its bright ash shakes with my sudden fear.

"Those boys are my son's age," says Danka, and takes the cigarette back as she makes a U-turn and applies more gas. Seventy, soon eighty miles an hour, but it's no use; the road is too flat, too straight.

"They're following us," I say, terrified.

"No, they're not. They're chasing us," says Danka. But Danka is calm, happy. She slows down until the truck is nearly upon us, then does another U-turn, and waves as we shoot past the boys.

"What do you think this is?" I ask frantically. "A game?"

"What do you think it is?"

I almost reply, "I think they are going to rape and murder us," but find myself unable to say such a thing to person who survived her childhood in Skarzysko. She used to hear the inmates joking, "Tomorrow you'll be soap". Surely Danka would know better than I. I take her cigarette and put it to my lips, not breathing. The truck whizzes by us again, honking its horn, and disappears up the same lane from which it appeared.

"They're gone," I whisper.

"Don't worry," says Danka. "They'll be back. But all you have to do is beg them to kill you. Then they won't do it. They'll be suspicious. You'll see."

I unbuckle my seatbelt, having decided it would be better to die in a car crash than be stuck on the seat with three teenage boys and Danka.

"Please lock your door."

"What difference does it make," says Danka, crossing her legs in their black hosiery. "You think three boys won't smash a window? If they were women, I'd be trembling, also. Mean women are meaner than mean men. Say that fifty times. It will make you feel better."

I'm still saying it as, alone, we make our last pass through Bloomingham into the fields, where the night has reached its coppery turning point. Having never been so alert at this hour before, I can see its allure. It's as tranquil as no-man's land.

"Mean women are meaner than mean men," I recite. "That's fifty, I think, but I still don't know if it's true or not."

"It is," says Danka. "Men puzzle more easily, right in the middle of things. You'll see. I'll slow down. I'll give them something to wander about."

I whip around in my seat. The truck is tailing us again; how could I not have noticed? One of the boys is asleep, his head slung back against the window of the truck, but the others are only bleary-eyed. The one in the middle is staring at me. To look tough I stare back, but I'm quaking inside. His gaze is as blank as a bull's, drained of energy by the live wire that is the rest of his body. Danka slows to ten miles an hour, opens her window and waves with a flutter of fingers. Is she crazy? Or does she know what she is doing? Maybe she has a plan. Still driving, she reaches into her handbag, finds a bottle of nail polish, unscrews the top, applies the delicate brush to a run in her stocking. Now I know she is nervous, too; she had meant to use clear polish, this polish is plum, a wet purple bruise.

"If you beg them to rape you, too, does that mean they won't do that, either?" I ask.

"Whoever said such a thing? I can't imagine – but watch this."

Danka lightens her foot on the gas, lets the car glide to a halt. Smack. The truck rear-ends us, the three boys yelp, and in a second we take off like a rocket.

"You see what I mean? They're stupid," says Danka, calm as can be when enough time has passed. "That's out, I see."

"What?"

"That cigarette."

Ashes litter my blue jeans, the dashboard, the tops of my feet. Now I practice composure. If I could be like Danka. . . . I twist the cigarette free of its holder and drop it elegantly into the ashtray.

"Breakfast?" I ask casually. "We could go to Bob's Big Boy for bacon and biscuits. Say that fifty times."

"You've got to be joking," says Danka. "It is nearly five o'clock in the morning. No, thank you. I am going to bed. I need my rest. Besides, William will be having bad dreams. Do you believe that? He grades papers in his toga, and has bad dreams. I have such an old man for a husband. I always know what to buy him for his birthdays – lined slippers, reading pillows, one day I will buy him a lap desk."

"Why not cooking tools?" I ask, my mouth still dry, my voice still unsure of itself. "Like cookbooks, aprons – "

"Aprons!" yells Danka. We have started to laugh. "Tea cozies! Oh, God. The man I have married!"

"The father of your children!" I say.

"Well, not exactly," says Danka.

We glide back into town, feeling safe again. There are trucks on the highway, headlights on, and a woman rocking on a porch in a bathrobe, reading a map. It's a steamy dawn. Danka titters, then goes silent and still all at once.

"God, I am sleepy," she says. "Why don't I drive straight to my house, drop you off, let you walk home? You're the hungry one. You can stop on the way home for breakfast."

"Why don't you drive me home." I say.

"That's all right. You'll have a nice walk, feel refreshed when you get there."

"If you don't drive me home, I will tell William what you told me."

"What?"

"About your children."

"What about them?"

"They're not his."

"They are, too. They're not *mine.* You must be shameful telling me I would lie to my husband about such a thing."

"All right," I agree. "Just stop. Let me out." She does. There's a U-Haul parked at the curb, the backside open, chairs on a ramp. I have a terrible urge to sit on one. It's velvet with covered buttons and gleaming mahogany legs and arms. The velvet is cranberry mostly, with blues and pinks. If I weren't so spacey, I'd do it, I'd sit. Instead I simply gaze, half asleep on my feet, until someone says, "Liz, you all right?"

"Just tired," I say. It's a history professor whose class I sat in on a couple of years ago. Her husband's a lawyer.

"You moving?" I ask.

"We're blowing this popsicle stand." She laughs, drops a box on the velvet seat of the chair, carries both into the shadows of the van. Lonely, I walk away before she comes back out, and when I reach home I sit on the porch swing awhile sipping cold water and eating a shoelace of black licorice, not wanting to wake up Daniel. He's upstairs in our bed; I hear his sighs escaping through the window. He left the kitchen nice and clean; the jars of powders aligned on the counter, the balance wiped and covered, three spoons, one pipet, and several spatulas drying in the dish rack.

But there is no place to lay my head on this swing, all hard wood slats and one saw-dusty pillow. And the yard is slick with dew. I lay my head on my knees, rock for a minute and decide to take a nap in the spare room on Gail's old sheets that must smell of tangled bodies. Down the hallway I go, removing my clothes, and open the guest room door. The blinds are drawn, and the room does smell of bodies, but clean ones, sweet and dreamy. On the bed the sheets are velvety but won't cover me up; I tug and tug, but the other side of the bed keeps tugging them back. Odd, how it takes me so long to realize I'm not alone. There's a naked person here, murmuring in sleep. It's not Daniel, I know, because he's upstairs, and it's not Gail because the hand suddenly on the pillow is unmistakably a man's. I won't scream, I think. Better to sneak out and lock him in the room before calling the police. But the sight of the fingers stops me, and in a minute I know whose they are. They are sun-browned and callused, but the backs are black fuzz, so soft on the eyes I almost drift off to sleep. The knuckles are smooth, the fingernails rimmed with dirt. I place my own hand on top, give his knuckles a squeeze.

"Wake up," I whisper, and he sits up, terrified. It's him, the Soho Tree Man, bare shoulders shaking, hand on his throat. He's not naked, after all. He's wearing briefs of creamy satin, slick as can be, with a watery, rainbow sheen.

"Where's Gail?" he finally manages. "I think you got the wrong room."

"Nope."

"Oh," he says, looking me over apologetically. "I've seen you around. Nothing personal. It's just that I want Gail, you know? And if she came back and found you in her . . . "

"In her what?"

"In her bed."

"She won't. Believe me. Don't you know what's going on here? Do you know you're in my house?"

"This is Gail's house," he says.

"My house."

"But this is Gail's room."

"My spare room. My guest room. Gail was my guest, for a couple of days. That's all."

The Tree Man shakes his head. His hair is down around his shoulders, feather upon feather.

"I could have you arrested," I say to him gently.

He shakes his head again, grinning nervously. How surprisingly frail he looks. I had thought he was an eagle, but he isn't, he is only a wren.

"You might let me go to sleep in my own house," I recommend.

Shocked, he hands me a corner of sheet, then drapes the folds over my chest.

"Seriously?" he whispers after a moment.

"Seriously what?"

"Everything you told me."

I nod.

"So I guess I better get my ass out of here."

"My husband's upstairs," I tell him.

"Where's Gail?"

"I don't know, exactly. She left. She's a real sweet potato."

"I know," he says sadly.

I lay my head on the pillow, and on the verge of sleep I realize what it was I'd meant to say. Not *sweet potato. Hot potato. She's a real hot potato.*

But when I open my eyes to tell him, he's gone.

I N T E R V A L O N E

THE STAIRWAY leading from the front hall to the second floor of Ben and Leah's house consists of six steps, then a broad, bare landing where a window looks out, then five more steps climbing to a corridor always littered with stray bits of laundry. At the landing the stairs jackknife, and the window frames a view of a lawn sloping down to the creek where some saplings are planted. On the ground floor just behind the front hall, beneath the six ascending steps, is a cubby lined with coat hooks and high, narrow shelves where Ben and Leah store an assortment of items: boots, gloves, hats, binoculars, even a set of barbells. Hanging among the coats are several net bags and leather-handled baskets, one–Leah's favorite–with a purple stripe woven into the straw. On the floor is a mess of shoes and toys, also the telephone. The oddest thing is a medicine cabinet hung on the wall, mirrored door and all. Inside on the flimsy glass shelves is where they stack the bills.

Tonight Ben pulls handfuls of bills off the shelves, then sits on the floor to sort through them for clues. Simon is quiet in his father's lap, one torn envelope balanced on his knee. He is picking his nose. First, Ben scans the long distance calls on the telephone bills–her mother, his mother, her sister, her glaze-supplier in New Jersey–but finding only the usual begins shuffling aimlessly hoping for letters from travel agents, from airlines, even sweepstakes announcements. There's nothing, though, and that's just it, because whatever it was, she would have taken it with her. Daniel has a plan; we listen, we nod, and pretty soon we're all busy looking for what's gone. At once, I find a missing pair of canvas platform sandals; that is, they are not on the shelf where they are ordinarily, and Daniel finds a raincoat missing from the second coat hook. The purple-striped basket is gone, as well, along with a twenty pound barbell and a wide-brimmed hat. Leah's sunglasses are not on the dining room table, but then again, they often need to be hunted. So, we hunt, and give the hunt seven minutes, which is how long it usually takes Leah to find them.

Afterwards we gather at the wobbly table, empty-handedly bearing our hodgepodge of clues. Leah, it seems, was not taken entirely by surprise. ("Taken by surprise" has become, in this town, a horrifying pun, as if "surprise"–winged, taloned–might swoop down at any moment and take any one of us.) Clearly Leah had a plan, as the things she brought with her add up to a kind of forecast–sunshowers, we agree, and we identify a few possibilities. Vancouver, Mississippi, Seattle, Maine, really anywhere damp as long as it's far enough away, because she took the whole stack of Sunday *Times* magazines as if for reading on a train. She chose a cookbook, too, although it takes us a while to figure out which one's missing from the shelf. It was a present from Ben, a book of international sweets. For a minute we imagine her preparing those foods–the pastries, the syrups, the delicate custards–for a tableful of guests whose faces and names we don't recognize. Once, because she found it amusing, she read to us a passage from a recipe for Indian *jamuns.* "Display the sweetmeats on a serving platter of unusual beauty," Leah read, and recalling this I quickly open the cabinet where she keeps her serving platters, but all of them are there; the raku, the stippled pastel, the hand-painted floral.

"She must be headed someplace where she can work on pots," I say, and Daniel stares at me as if I've said something really stupid, which of course I have.

"She can work on pots here any damn time she wants," says Ben, bewildered, wounded. Simon pulls a platter from the open cabinet, distracting us, at which we notice all at once that little Stevie is not in the room, we haven't seen him in a couple of minutes, he's gone, he's missing, and we stand unnaturally until hearing the thump of his crawling.

BEN CONSIDERS the presence of Leah's winter jacket still hanging on a coat hook to be an encouraging sign, suggesting that she plans to return before winter if only to pick it up, but I don't tell him Leah mentioned to me recently that she was due for a new one; the armpits on that one have always been tight. She told me this as we were strolling to the reservoir a bit behind the men, talking about *possessions*. About how much *things* mattered. I commented on the men's cut-offs, so threadbare and torn we could peek at their bottoms.

We did, for a moment.

"Men's bodies never change," I remarked. "Any clothing a woman had that was that old wouldn't fit her anymore." It was a fact to which I alone am an exception among the women I know.

"Really," Leah said. "Anything pre-Simon, forget it, it doesn't fit me under the armpits these days. Across the back."

Then, the thing about the winter coat. Which seems portentous, now, as if she'd known we three would be sitting here. She didn't, though. Not in advance, and I believe that with all of my heart. She must have realized all at once that she was leaving, too late to stop it from happening. The straw basket over her elbow, the rain hat crammed into the sleeve of the coat, the sunglasses askew on the top of her head amid haphazard strands of hair. Then a second later she was gone.

"I have this feeling she couldn't possibly have known what she was doing," says Ben after a while. He looks at us questioningly over the mute top of Simon's head, and Daniel and I nod, both of us thinking, At least she didn't take Simon; she left him for Ben to hang on to. Most women do this, I've noticed. Later the three of us agree: naturally she must have been in some kind of a trance, because otherwise why would she have taken the barbell? Just to keep her arms in shape for throwing pots? Well, maybe.

And that's how it goes; we sit there three hours, four, talking, not talking, never ever alert to the possibility of Leah's step on the front porch because we know we won't hear it. What's possible is that maybe she'll write Ben a letter, either soon or not, and tell him she misses him, because that's what they do, usually. Certain people do. I know because I've seen quite a few such letters. That's the thing about being a mailman in a town like this; people stand on their porches, open their letters, exclaim over them, and then, sometimes, they show the letters to me. It's the uniform, I think. I fill the same need the hairdressers filled before the hair salon closed—a confidant, but anonymous, and never judgemental. I'm just doing my job. I take the proffered letters, look them over, hand them back sympathetically. The letters say: "Missing you. Come see me soon," but then say neither where, nor when, nor how. All are postmarked in Erie, Pennsylvania, but Erie's just a decoy, everyone knows. So I'm thinking, if Leah writes such a letter, do I deliver it to Ben, or should I spare him the grief?

Spare him, I think.

"Deliver it," says Daniel, later on in bed. How innocent he is. He is truly astounded. "You don't have a choice. You're a *mailman.*"

"I'm a TLC," I argue. Temporary Letter Carrier.

Daniel sighs, rolls over on his stomach, reconsiders, migrates, lays his head on my belly. Case closed. I don't know. But maybe Leah won't write Ben a letter. And how terrible *that* would be. It's not impossible, considering the sunglasses and raincoat. An odd combination, more suitable for subterfuge, I've begun to realize, than for Oregon or Maine. The rain hat, too.

Ben was sitting on the couch when he got his last glimpse of her. She was climbing the steps. Going up. She was crossing the landing. It was half-past eight. Ben was reading Simon a favorite bedtime book–cartoons about slugs–and Leah went upstairs to get Simon's pajamas. Simple enough. Through the living room archway he could watch her climb the stairs as usual. She was barefoot. Leah's ankles are strong, erect, broad-boned. She wore a dress to mid-calf (I know this although Ben didn't say), and the wood creaked under her step. Then the creaking ceased. Ben thought, She's in the bathroom. Then he thought, She's looking out the window in Simon's room at some kids playing under the bridge in the creek. Then he thought, She's reading something at the desk, some newspaper or something. She's on the phone, he thought. She's steaming her face. She can't find any matching pajamas.

But Leah had never cared about matching pajamas, before.

He thought, She hit her head.

And he went up to take a look.

There's a closet in their bedroom, under the eaves. The door is child-sized. The interior, slant-ceilinged space extends straight across the width of the house with room enough for boxes, crates, camp trunks, the floor rough-hewn, the rafters showing in the sides, no insulation, the air close and smelling of bats. After looking upstairs and finding no sign of Leah, and after looking downstairs, in the kitchen, in the basement, in the backyard whose barbecue still smoldered from dinner, and in the playroom, and then checking on Simon, and then checking the front porch and up and down the street and even over in the creek where the boys were still tossing stones, and after checking upstairs in the bathroom again and in Simon's room behind the crib where she kept some of his clothing, Ben opened the door to the eaves and looked in there, first without a flashlight, then with. He showed the flashlight beam around and called, "Hey, Leah," in what he described to us as a perfectly natural voice, because at the time it seemed entirely likely to him that she was in there. Then Simon started crying downstairs, and the telephone rang. It was me. I was calling to see if they wanted to go for a walk.

"I think Leah already went for a walk, or something," Ben said.

"Oh. Is she headed this way?"

"She is?"

"What?"

"Is she headed your way?"

"I don't know, Ben. How should I know? Let me see. . . " I took a look out the front door.

"Call me if she gets there," Ben said. He sounded pissed off. I figured they'd been having an argument. Daniel and Stevie and I went out for our own walk, around the reservoir. The evening was humid, and there was still enough light that the turtles were basking, their small heads blindly lifted toward the sloping rays. Nobody was sitting on the bench, but there was popcorn scattered round it and pigeons eating. The pigeons roosted high up on the stone water tower, and we had seen them flock down on our way over.

We kept walking until it was dark, then started home along Plum Creek past Ben and Leah's. Their porch light was off, but we could see Ben standing near the railing among the hanging spider plants, holding Simon in his arms. That in itself was a frightening sight, because Simon doesn't like to be held in such heat. He's a rambunctious baby. But he was not so much as tugging at the fronds of the plants, so the pots hung motionless. We were climbing the slope, slowly, pushing Stevie in the stroller, when Ben turned around and went inside. When we got there Simon was under the table with a cookie and Ben was washing dinner dishes. He had put on rubber gloves, but I could tell that the water was cold. I brought Simon upstairs, dressed him in his pajamas, ran a washcloth round his face and the palms of his hands, and put him in bed. I found a night light on a shelf and plugged it into its socket, but the fan on the dresser had already been switched on.

WHAT HURTS us most, I suppose, is that she left with the mystery still intact. Somehow we must all have believed that if the secret were revealed to one of us, it would be shared, or at the very least, suggested. A bus ticket stub might suffice, a canceled check, even a door left ajar might point us in the direction of understanding. As it is, we can't be certain that she even *used* a door.

Which leaves me contemplating the very scariest possibility of all; that not even Leah can pinpoint the method of departure. Of transition. She might simply have ended up somewhere. In the Southwest, maybe, throwing pots in an adobe studio. She might be longing for us – for Simon, for Ben, but unable to draw herself away. A prisoner of desire. Of her own heart's content.

Later on she'll be wearing that trench coat, its collar turned up, her head erect inside it, her long legs scissoring under the hem. The day is sunstruck, the sidewalk leads her to a bank, a utilities office, and then, further north, along a roadside mall whose pay telephones she'll pass without slowing, without thinking, even.

She's not thinking about us. We can't fault her for that; there's no malice involved, no neglect, even. We don't occur to her. That's all. She'll feel, as she passes the telephones, a little buzz of indecipherable concern.

And if it happened to Leah, what's to stop it from happening to me?

I mention this to Daniel.

He doesn't want to talk about it.

But he says, "That's ridiculous. It's not something that *happened* to her. It's something she *did*."

"Well," I say, "What's to stop *me* from doing it, too?"

"In spite of yourself?" says Daniel.

"In spite of myself," I say.

I am holding Daniel's hand. I give it a squeeze. After that we don't move a muscle.

P A R T   T W O

Danka's Soup

SEVERAL YEARS AGO on the railroad tracks I found what I'd long since given up looking for; I'd searched at garage sales, flea markets, in newspaper classifieds, and finally drove out to a strip near the mall where there were some lighting stores. It was a pole lamp I wanted, standard and practical, floor to ceiling, the three lamp shades cocked at complementary angles so the beams of light might commingle in the center of our living room. We'd been sitting in darkness, our reading illuminated only by a small table lamp handmade by one of Daniel's brothers; the base a tree trunk, the shade, foliage. At the lighting stores I was told matter-of-factly that pole lamps were "out of stock", "out of style", and at the last store I visited, "out of season."

"Out of season?" I asked.

The salesman was deadpan.

"Pole lamps start coming in around May," he said. He started flipping through one of his catalogues.

Next day I found my pole lamp standing near the railroad tracks like someone waiting for a train. The trains had stopped passing through around 1949. Now saplings grew here and there among the ties, which followed a high ridge bordered by woods and tall brambles. There was a narrow plateau where the lamp stood waist-deep in grass. How serenely it stood, its three heads inclined to the east and west. A breeze started and stopped, and in the distance, from the far side of the brambles, came a frantic barking of dogs. The dogs were usual. There were tract houses back there, and then a highway, and then farmland, and the people kept hunting dogs penned in their yards along with pick-ups and old school buses. The pole lamp was burgundy, with a matching cord neatly coiled around its ankle. I carried it home, first on one shoulder, then on the other. In the living room I screwed in three bulbs, unwrapped the cord, plugged it in and flicked the three switches. It worked perfectly.

Today I'm looking to replace our Fiat's right, front axle, which snapped in two several days ago. The Italian makers of Fiat no longer ship to the United States, and dealers here have gradually stopped servicing their models. Until now the car has handled well enough, and it's been only minor parts – windshield wipers, gas caps, head lights – that we've had to special-order from Pittsburg through a parts store in town. Now the parts store has closed, and the dealer in Pittsburg has cut ties with the parent company, so we don't know where to go. Overseas, maybe. I didn't come to the ridge with the axle in mind, but when I've followed the tracks to the grassy plateau I find myself stopping, then spinning in slow circles all the while peering here and there among grasses and weeds until I realize just what I am doing. Stevie likes turning in circles. He's on my back in the baby pack; his wide-brimmed sun hat throws its laughing shadow every place I look. No axle, though, and I am truly, confoundedly surprised. But then I see something else, something waxy and pale, up ahead where the train rails meet the horizon. Not far. There's a hill, and at the crest is – what – the head of a doll, red-curled, blue-eyed, with eyelids that flutter when I pick it up, then close resolutely. Inside the head is a pebble; I shake it loose and hold the head upright again so the lashes pop open. The doll's body is thirty feet or so down the tracks, half-buried in a pile of splintery woodchips, its little crotch-hole clogged with dirt. I rub it clean with a moistened finger, than spit on the finger again and try wiping the smudge off the knees. The fingers and toes have been chewed somewhat, but the head is a perfect fit.

"Hello," I say. "Say hello to our new doll, Stevie."

Stevie is quiet.

"Well," I exclaim. "This is the kind of doll I've always hoped to find."

"Why?" asks Stevie. It's not a word exactly, but Stevie's all-purpose squeal. Sometimes it means what he wants it to mean, and sometimes it means what we want it to mean, depending on who cares the most.

"Oh, I don't know why," I answer, and then, "She's hollow. Now we can pick berries. We can fill her up with them."

The berry bushes are back where we'd come from, behind the tract houses where the hunting dogs are barking. Mosquitoes are everywhere, and tiny spiders crouch among the cushions of the berries. The berries are sun-baked, their juices warm and explosive, and there is always a plumper one farther in, low down where the birds don't see it.

Soon the doll's head is heavy with fruit, and so is Stevie's big sun hat, and so is Stevie, but I can't find the rest of the doll.

"Stevie, do you see it?"

But Stevie is sleeping, suddenly, his purple mouth adrool on my shoulder. How long have we been picking? Half an hour, maybe, my gaze riveted upon berry after berry like a trucker's upon the vanishing point of the road. I figure I am west of where I started, but if so I am facing the tracks from the wrong direction. Somehow I must have spun myself around so now I don't know where's east and where's west, a fact that matters at the moment only because I want to find the rest of the doll. I'd placed it, still empty, gently on a rock and made my way gingerly through the brambles, always careful of the top of Stevie's head among the thorns, and of his bare, tender ankles and flopping wrists. How heavy he is, almost twenty-three pounds, like a sack of mail. But I'm strong-backed, strong-shouldered, strong-hipped; I set off on my search with aplomb, thinking hopefully that if I don't find the body then I might at least stumble unawares on a Fiat axle or something else I've been needing.

In a way, I do.

It's Joe with the piercing eyes.

Having caught sight of him from a distance, I manage to back up into the shadows of some bushes so that he won't catch sight of me. He's not wearing his cap, but his head is still pale as a mushroom. He is carrying a slingshot and, knotted to a thong around his neck, a drawstring pouch of bulging leather. Stones, I guess. The slingshot is crude, just a forked stick fitted with a wide rubber band, but Joe grips it possessively by its straight end. Eva, his dog, leads the way down the tracks chug-chugging like a locomotive slowing for the station. Following, Joe steps carefully from railroad tie to railroad tie, and at a spot where the ties are missing, from imagined tie to imagined tie, always staying dead center between the rails. Eva's not so sensitive; she weaves, trots sideways, sniffs, follows the scent, whatever it is. They are looking for something, too. Maybe a rabbit, or some tracks or droppings.

But Eva's not a hunting dog; she looks nervous, confused, and keeps wanting to heel, so Joe has to shoo her away with the slingshot, first grabbing her collar and pointing her nose to the ground. He looks good in his T-shirt and cut-off sweatpants low slung under big love handles. He's fat and unmindful of cleanliness. When he bends to pet the dog, the pants slide free of the small of his back, revealing the top of his crack amid a pattern of stretchmarks by which I can guess his bathing habits; the creases are dirty, the surrounding flesh healthy and pink. So, Joe washes, but doesn't scrub, and it's the dirt I want, suddenly, as much as the man himself. A piece of the ground he sleeps on, if, in the summer, he sleeps on the ground at all, and not in his car. Probably he does. Probably when it rains he stands naked with a bar of soap, yelling at the sky, which is what I'd like to do next time it rains – yell crazily right along with him, then lather his back with the hard, lardy soap. Soon I'm following him, secure in the belief that I can jump off the tracks should he mistake my footsteps for a rabbit's and whip around to kill me. Besides, I'm downwind; I can smell Eva's panting. She pokes her nose here in the grasses, there in the weeds, then turns to sniff under her tail, snarls, lies down on a cleared spot of earth, and, puzzled, snaps at her own rear paws. Joe bends over again, lifts Eva's floppy ear and whispers something into it. Up she jumps ecstatically and at once finds something–what?–near a cluster of flat rocks. Sits down, thumps her tail, paws at the thing with her foot. It's the body of the doll. Joe picks it up, examines it, sticks the slingshot in his waistband and carries the doll touchingly by the hand, the pad of his thumb nestled snugly in one chewed palm. Now man, dog, and doll continue on their way, from railroad tie to railroad tie, barely missing a beat and apparently not looking for anything else, as if the existence of a doll's body might not necessarily indicate the possibility of the existence of a head. Joe's big work boots, without laces, flop and wobble as he goes, revealing naked ankles. He is solitary-looking as a tree trunk, self-sufficient, barely touched even by the moody caress of the weather–his neck toughened, his knuckles chapped, but the backs of his knees below the unhemmed cut-offs tender as new asparagus. No mosquito bites, even. Drawing closer from behind, I intend to catch up with him and bargain for the body of the doll–in exchange for some raspberries, maybe–but at that moment Eva veers off the train track through an opening in the brambles onto a trail I've never noticed that cuts to the right before dropping down steeply into some woods. Joe follows, then swivels abruptly to face me head on, one hand darting under his waistband and withdrawing his painter's cap, which he puts on before looking me appraisingly up and down. After a minute, he grins, and shows his bad teeth. No surprise. In my imagined kisses I've often poked my tongue into the gaps in his mouth. He's a Cro-Magnon man, about three-quarters civilized, tipping his cap, then cooing and wiggling his fingers in Stevie's face.

"Hey Pebbles," he says. "Your mom married?"

My spine tingles. He might drag me by the hair into a cave in the woods, show me the bisons he's drawn on the walls.

"Sure am," I say, and he's off down the hill with his dark eyes aglitter, his unlaced boots flop-flopping along with the jingle of Eva's collar.

Neither of us mentioned the doll.

AT HOME I say, "Look what we found," and thrust the head, dripping purple berry juice, under Daniel's nose. He reaches in through the neck hole, finds the one firm berry among the squashed others, pulls it out, bites off half of it, and puts the rest between my lips. I dump the raspberries into a bowl, shaking the head by its curls to get out the last of the seeds, then rinsing it clean in the sink and even sponging the soiled cheeks, the chewed nose, the matted, fluttering eyelashes, before laying it on the dish rack to drain. I spoon some dry tapioca into a bowlful of sugar, mix it together and stir the mixture into the berries to thicken. Only then do I find we have no shortening for the crust; we have flour, salt, but nothing to bind it together. So, leaving Stevie with Daniel I take my bike downtown past the vacant supermarket to the Epicurean, a cozy place with a European flair; around the few small tables are shelves laden with imported foodstuffs and barrels of flavorful teas. It's expensive, of course, but the remaining supermarket is sixteen miles south on a truck route, too far to reach conveniently on our ramshackle bike. There's a small cooler near the cash register in the Epicurean's tea room, and in its depths, behind some wheels of Camembert, I find a tub of sweet creamery butter stamped with pictures of sailboats.

"It's all because you refuse to understand that we need a new car," I say to Daniel when I get home. "No one short of Italy has the axle we need. We could be stuck in this town forever eating Stilton and Carr's Water Biscuits."

"What's wrong with this town?" says Daniel, pulling the butter out of the bag. "Besides, these aren't sailboats. They're *sailing vessels.*"

He's right: they're majestic as Mayflowers, each different from the next but with a uniform, easterly wind stamped into their billowing sails. I touch the crest of a wave with my finger, hold the fingertip of butter to Stevie's tongue as Daniel sets the other groceries on the countertop. Our dinner. Six croissants, a tin of goose liver paté and a squat jar of strawberry jam from England.

"We'll have the pie, too," I say worriedly, already cutting the butter and flour. "And maybe Nikki will trade a zucchini for a croissant. Set the table, please?"

"Okay," says Daniel, but as soon as he starts, he's doubtful. How does one eat a fancy meal like this, he wants to know. Cloth napkins, or the usual Kim-Wipes pulled from their dispenser near his microscope? And do we need good silver?

"We don't own any silver," I remind him.

"Let's just eat on the porch swing, again," he says, then holds up the tin of paté and stares at it disbelievingly. "Do you think this is real goose paté?" he asks. "Or imitation?"

"I've never heard of imitation goose paté."

"Do you know how they make this stuff?"

"Yes."

"They take the goose, and they–"

"I know, I said."

"and they force feed it mush till it–"

"Daniel. I *know.*"

"practically keels over, but it's penned up, or tied, and they–"

"Okay, Daniel," I say, and take the small, oval tin from his hand and drop it into the trash. It's the only thing in there. It thunks when it strikes the bottom.

"Is that better?" I ask.

"You mean, will the goose feel better if we don't eat it?" says Daniel. "Wow."

"It's already dead, Daniel. It doesn't have feelings. Forget it, Daniel."

"What are you talking about?" ask Ben, who is standing at our screen door, looking in at us through his hand-held zoom. Since Leah disappeared, he brings it with him everywhere he goes, as if it might help him find her.

"A goose," says Daniel.

"You're going to slaughter a goose?"

"It's already slaughtered," says Daniel.

"A goose liver," I tell him.

"That stuff's wicked. You know what they do to–"

"Yes," says Daniel.

"We threw it in the trash," I say.

"You threw out a goose liver paté?" says Ben. He opens the door, bends over our trash, peers in at the tin while twisting the focusing knob of the zoom. "Maybe it's that vegetarian goose liver paté," he says doubtfully, and reaches in to get it.

"Have a beer," I say. "And stay for dinner, please. We have croissants, jam, and a big raspberry pie, if I ever get to put it together, and I'll invite Nikki over with tomatoes and zucchini from her garden. But sit on the porch and drink your beer, please, while I make my pie. Where's Simon?"

"SIMON!" yells Ben, and he and Daniel are out the door, beers in hand. Both children are out there too, in the sandbox banging on the pie plates. Being alone feels strange and sad, because Leah is not in the kitchen with me although the men are on the porch swing as usual. My invitation to Ben was a kind of white lie; he's come for dinner every night since Leah disappeared, but I don't want him to know that I know this. Now he flips through the notebook he keeps in his T-shirt pocket, filled with the names of the people who have said they'd get back to him. Long distance friends, relatives, missing persons bureaus, police. Also in the pocket, two pens, in case one runs out of ink the very second he gets the news he's been waiting for. He won't, I think, and set to work on our dinner. I dust the desk top with flour, all ready to roll out the dough. From here I can look right into the pine where a blue jay is scolding the air.

"Be quiet," I say, and dust the rolling pin as well, but the blue jay keeps scolding, chattering, hopping from branch to branch.

When I tap the window with the rolling pin, flour explodes from it onto the telephone. At that moment, the telephone rings. Expecting Danka, I pick it up and say, "Not now, I'm taking a bath," but after that there is only silence, and I listen to it breathlessly as if absorbing it, three seconds of silence, of absolute peace. Four seconds, maybe even five. It's like holding your ear to a conch shell. Even the blue jay cocks its head, closes its beak and is quiet. A car rolls down the street, parks on the drive between our house and Nikki's, behind our Fiat. A tall black man climbs out, carrying a trombone case.

"Shit," says a voice on the telephone. "He brought his damn horn."

"Is that you, Nikki?"

Silence.

"Nikki? You all right?"

"I guess."

"Good. Come to dinner?" I ask, and noticing flour on the telephone receiver, blow on it hard, to clean it. Next door, Nikki drops her telephone; I hear the clatter and thump as it hits her floor. This same thing has happened before. I was on the phone with Nikki, I sneezed, and she dropped her receiver.

"Liz?" she asks.

"Yes, Nikki."

"No dinner tonight, but I was hoping maybe you could use up some of my garden. You can come back there and take as much as you want, okay, honey? I can't eat so much. I got to go now."

"Thanks, Nikki. That's just what we needed. Our car broke its–"

But she's no longer on the line. Already she's out of her house, her arm linked through the arm of the tall black man. They're taking Nikki's little yellow sportscar. For a moment it looks like the horn won't fit through the door, and when that slides in finally, I wonder about the man. He has to fold himself up like a pocketknife, then slowly resume his original shape. He sits with his knees pressed into the dashboard, his long fingers delicately at rest on top of them. He is Nikki's younger brother, but when she told me that I didn't believe it. He looks reverential, adoring, insistent as a lover. When he comes to get her, she tells me, usually they're on their way to meet some of his friends in a club. Nikki always comes back alone, and wakes us with her late night music, not a bad way to be wakened at all. It's like waking to a breeze, listening a minute, then losing track of the sound as it blends with the rhythms of dreams. Nikki doesn't dream, she claims. Nor does she seem to have lovers. She likes being alone, and what puzzles me most is who does her hair, in cornrows, the dangling braids heavy with beads. Could she possibly do it herself? And she always looks romantic. Tonight she's wearing a sarong. She's barefoot, with a wide brass bangle around one ankle. When they've driven off, the blue jay starts scolding again.

Nikki's carrots taste like onions, but her onions are sweet, and with the pie on the table it looks like a feast. The pie is beautiful, really; the very edge of each ribbon of lattice is golden, and the sweetened juices bubble furiously among them. I set it still boiling at the center of our table amid the wedges of tomato, the croissants, the paté. We pop open the tin and eat, a little of this, a lot of that, a wedge of tomato, some sautéed zucchini and onion. Ben is distracted, of course. Every once in a while he stands up suddenly, then either sits back down or makes his way to the window with the hand-held zoom. Daniel and I keep the conversation moving. The talk is familiar, about July Fourth approaching, and will there or will there not be fireworks this year, and will there or will there not be a band to play along with the fireworks.

"More pie!" yells Simon, reaching across.

Ben grunts and mimics. "Muppy," he says, "What the hell is this kid trying to tell us?"

I cut a narrow slice of pie for Simon, a wider one for Ben, and lay them side by side on a single plate. Stevie wants some too, although he'll only suck the fruit before spitting the seeds back into his hand.

"Here, Pebbles," I say, handing Stevie his spoonful of steaming berries.

Daniel looks quizzical. "Pebbles?" he asks.

"Pebbles," I repeat, and smile happily at Ben, who looks sadder than before, so that I wonder if he knows what we all are doing: going on with our lives, the way you have to when somebody dies.

When he doesn't eat his pie, I decide to talk about it.

"You know," I begin, glancing at Daniel, "we've been avoiding the issue. We're so very sorry. We wish we could help. We just don't know what to say."

"What issue?" asks Ben.

Daniel is silent.

"What issue?" Ben repeats. "There's no issue. She's not an issue. I'm not making an issue out of it. I'm not making a big deal out of it. It's not like I'm losing my mind. It's not like I want to kill myself, or anything. I'm just keeping things moving." He taps a spoon on the rim of one of my pie plates and then on the seat of the empty chair.

"Come with me," I tell him, and with a little more prodding he follows me outside to Nikki's, both sneakers untied, laces flapping. Her door is kept unlocked, like mine, like Ben's. I knock, just to be sure, and when no one answers I turn the knob and slip in, motioning Ben to wait in the front hallway along with several bongo drums and potted avocado trees. Last year I bought Nikki one of Leah's covered bowls that with the lid in place resembles the planet Jupiter.

"See this?" I ask Ben in the hallway. "I bought this for Nikki on her birthday, when she turned thirty-six."

Ben's face turns red when I've set the familiar object in his hand. He has cumbersome fingers; nestled there the bowl looks as fragile as a bubble. Like all of Leah's pots, it's so thin-walled it's luminous, the glaze a wash of burgundies, purples, and grays. It is the size of a grapefruit. To raise the lid, which has no knob or indentation, Ben must flip it gently onto the palm of his other hand, then hold the two halves as he'd hold open a book. Everyone does this with Leah's bowls, but simply for the feel of it, not to see what's inside.

But at the sight of what's in it, Ben jumps and drops the bottom of the bowl, which lands upside down, unbroken on the skin of a bongo drum. The contents are spilled with a noisy clatter, and on our hands and knees we search the hallway floor among the bases of the drums, then feel in the soil around each avocado tree, then crawl into Nikki's living room and search in there as well.

"I don't know if they're Nikki's," I say after a minute. "They might be her grandmother's. No. Her grandmother's dead. I can't imagine she'd keep. . . . They must be Nikki's. This is too awful. This is horrible. I'm going to laugh."

"Not me," says Ben, so sharply I feel I've been slapped. He lifts the edge of a beanbag chair and slides his hand underneath it to feel. I toss another three teeth into the bowl, where they skid grittily across the glaze like pebbles on glass. That makes seventeen. They're like fragments of a mummy left behind in a cave. Together we gaze at the worn-down shapes, so for a minute I imagine we are doing what I intended for us to do – staring hard at Leah's absence as if it were a thing that could be handled and understood – but then I know that we're not; we're not staring at Leah's absence, but at Nikki's pulled teeth, at the stain of dried blood and clinging nerve. It's impossible to look at what's not there. Besides, the whole town is adept at not-looking, at not-wondering, even. After a while, you take things in stride. Stores close, and the newspaper shrinks down to practically nothing. No news. No births, no deaths. There was an editor who talked about listing the names of the people who had moved, week by week, but all the hangers-on objected, and then the editor herself moved, too, to Las Vegas, people say, although nobody knows for sure.

I set the domed lid in place on its ludicrous cargo and carry it back to its table. Leah's bowl has no base; it's a perfect sphere. It wobbles a little, then balances exquisitely.

LATE THAT NIGHT, perched on the edge of the bed undressing, I find one of Nikki's molars lodged in the toe of my sneaker. Not wanting Daniel to see, I slide it under my pillow and, still later, fall asleep with my hand cupped over its rotted peaks. I dream of an abandoned quarry we sometimes visited: Daniel and I, and Leah and Ben, the two children strapped into packs on our backs. In the shade of the woods are huge boulders slick with moss. No matter what time of year we went, the quarry was always murky and damp, and once there we always wondered why we'd come at all. Then we'd find some wild ginger growing among the detritus, exclaim over its heart-shaped leaves and go home, all four of us feeling romantic.

We do this in the dream as well, and when I wake in the morning, the tooth is gone.

ORDINARILY in summer the college opens its swimming pool for several hours a day and again at evening, so that the faculty hangers-on, as well as members of the public who've joined the athletic club, can bring their families to swim and cool off. It's an indoor pool, but the doors to the outside – two sets of wide, double doors – are propped open, so a fragrance of mown grass and pendulous honeysuckle makes its way into the space where it mingles with the smell of chlorine. There is no kiddie pool, but there are life jackets, kickboards, and bleachers for restless children. The youngest of these dress in the women's locker room and gaze interestedly at our bodies as we pamper, shave, and comb. How unconsciously familiar we become in that room, unclothed, the old with the young, the fat, the thin, the plain, the lovely, our pubic hairs beaded with moisture, our imperfections awash in a bluish light that seems to bless us equally. Every summer in the locker room I make some new friends, to replace those who are moving away. At some time each day the hot water runs out so the showers turn warm, then lukewarm, then cold, then icy, and we complain or holler jokingly in the spirit of our communal nakedness, swapping shampoos, cream rinses and lotions, borrowing razors, tampons, and deodorants, losing towels, hair clips, beach thongs and caps, but keeping track of each other's slippery children, each other's names, each other's telephone numbers.

But this summer the recreation center is closed; the college, we are informed by its apologetic mailing, is experiencing "a season of sacrifice" owing to the cost of liability insurance.

Nor will the library be open, nor the snack bar, nor even the credit union office. The summer conference season as well has been canceled, a situation that, like the recent closing of the local movie theater, leaves us dazed and bewildered; pausing to examine the coming attractions we found ourselves staring instead into our own eyes reflected by the black glass facade. Although the conferences themselves were closed to the public, their very presence in our town changed the pace of our affairs; our parking lots were filled, our streets and stores crowded, our newspaper vending machines emptied early in the day as did the bakery of doughnuts, fresh breads and half-pints of orange juice. Every week brought streams of new faces – whole sidewalks of young socialists, squadrons of practicing cheerleaders, bagpipers parading in kilts, the monotonous whines of their instruments invading even the insides of our houses. Our favorites were always the Quaker Friends with their monkish smiles, their leather sandals worn with coarsely knitted socks, and their aura of pastoral benevolence that made us feel, in contrast, frenetically cosmopolitan.

Now that the college lawns are empty, we go swimming in the west reservoir, which is larger than the one close to home and set on a balding rise from where the distant golf course is visible on the far side of some open fields. At the base of one steep incline are several targets for archery practice, so ancient and worn that the sawdust stuffing, long exposed, has all blown away. In past summers, teenagers hung out on the ridge, partying, so that now, broken beer bottles litter the reservoir's bottom amid sharp rocks and hunks of concrete, making swimming risky. A few days ago, Daniel cut his foot. A lot of people do. Nobody seems to care; we are as hardy and inured as soldiers in a war, carrying in our picnic baskets rolls of bandages and bottles of Mercurochrome. As the summer progresses, more and more of us will be seen limping along the sidewalks in town, and limping while crossing the streets, and limping while strolling lopsidedly arm-in-arm at dusk, like the summer several years ago when it became popular to strew tacks along the roads leading into town so half the cars had flat tires.

Therefore it's not surprising that my own limp should go unnoticed even though I didn't get it at the reservoir. No one offers a hand or asks how it happened. Not even Daniel asks, when I've limped demonstratively home from an early morning route. I have to say, "Look at me, I've been crying," before he notices that anything–everything–is amiss: the leather strap of my mailbag snapped, one leg of my pants split down to the ankle, my face tear-smudged, my hands still trembling.

"Guess what's missing?" I say, when Daniel embraces me and asks me what happened. "Guess what's gone," I say, sniffling, suddenly more upset than I thought I was. "What do I *not* have that I had before?"

Nervous, Daniel lifts my hands, counts my fingers, then bids me sit down and unties my shoes. My toes are all there, my limbs whole and in place. Still kneeling, Daniel touches each leg, reads them with his fingertips, taps my knee for the reflex, and says he can't guess. Soon he rises, checks each ear and examines my head from above.

"Your earrings are missing. I don't know," he says guiltily.

I wipe a tear from my eye. We both know I don't wear earrings when I'm working.

"I'll give you a hint," I tell him. "It's broken."

Daniel shakes his head, squints, makes a face, and disappears from the porch for a minute, into the kitchen. He returns with his magnifying glass, examines every button on my blouse, and says, "If you don't tell me, then I'll have to call the post office and ask *them.*"

"My can," I hint.

Daniel spins me around, squats once more for a look at my backside. I'm crying, again, suddenly.

"Not that," I wail. "My *can.* My *Mace.*"

"Oh," says Daniel. "Your Mace. Shit."

"It was a Doberman."

"Poor baby."

"It didn't bite me, I swear." I'm crying again.

Daniel enfolds me, lifts me, lays me down on the porch swing on a scant nest of pillows.

Ashamed, I add, "No stitches. No broken skin, even. No anything."

Daniel kisses my leg, then fetches a flask of fresh iced tea, stirs it with a pipet, pours it into a beaker and puts the tall, cold drink in my hand. The beaker is graduated; the iced tea hits exactly the two hundred and ninety milliliter mark. I sip it through the pipet. Two hundred and forty-eight milliliters. I sip again. Two hundred and forty-three.

"It was the funniest thing," I say to him.

"Sure."

"Where's Stevie?" I ask.

"At Simon's."

"Oh."

"What was?"

"What was what?" I ask, sipping my tea, still rationing. We have finished all our ordinary leaf tea. This is a potent licorice tea from the shelves of the Epicurean, where I'd also purchased a baggie of jasmine tea and one of chocolate flavored. The jasmine makes us woozy, and the chocolate makes us high, but the licorice is fine. Sharp and mysterious. I play the usual game with the pipet – sipping, letting it fill up with liquid, then aiming it at Daniel and threatening to squirt him in the eye.

"What was the funniest thing?" he asks again.

"Oh." How patient he is. "How is your foot?" I ask after a while.

Daniel wiggles his toes.

"That was the most awful part of it," I say finally. "It was in that part of town at this house that didn't have a door, there were only shower curtains hanging in the entrance way, and in the front yard was a coffee table with a bottle of Alka-Seltzer sitting on it. The mailbox was outside the gate, but I opened the gate anyway because. . . "

"Because why."

"Because I wasn't paying attention. I was trying to read the letter."

"What?"

"Through the envelope. I didn't *open* it. It was from *Gail.*"

"Gail wrote you a letter. That's nice. What does she say?"

"She didn't write it to me, Daniel. That's what I'm trying to tell you. I thought it was for the Tree Man, because I don't know his name, you know, I only think of him as the Tree Man, and he's the one in love with Gail, so I wanted to see if she said anything worth congratulating him about the next time I ran into him. Like, if she told him she loved him or anything, or if she invited him to come live with her, or if she was having a baby or something. So I was just trying to get an idea, and then I figured I'd just go right up to the door and hand it to him and wait while he read it through, in case he started crying or anything, in case she said something careless. You know Gail. Something mean. I wanted to comfort him. I was a little confused – sad – really, because I didn't think that that kind of house was the kind of house the Tree Man should be living in, with carpet remnants overlapping all over the front yard and a bottle of Alka-Seltzer on a coffee table in the middle of it, and anyway it wasn't his house, it wasn't him, it was the sweaty guy who drives the taxicab. You know, the guy with the bushy white hair."

Daniel nods.

"But before he got to me, his dog did, and the Mace can was out of date or something. It didn't spray."

"And then what?"

"Then the letter blows away, and the dog starts . . . it was a Doberman."

"Yes."

"It doesn't hurt."

"You already said that." He puts the tip of his finger on the hole on top of the pipet, raises it out of the glass, inserts its end between my lips before releasing his finger so the fluid slips down to zero and I swallow. He lays a hand on my brow, strokes my temple, lets his finger slide down to my neck while giving me butterfly kisses, then pulling back to stare at my pupils. He's sneaky for sure, but I know what he's up to; checking my vital signs – heart and respiratory rate, muscle tone, skin tone, and whatever other reflexes he chooses to arouse.

I blink at the kiss and stick out my tongue.

Momentarily satisfied, he gazes at me and says carefully, "I'm still not exactly sure why you were trying to read this letter."

"I told you. Because I wanted to see what it said."

"Maybe I should rephrase this." Daniel hesitates. Then, "I think you would agree that it's not all right for a mailman to read other people's mail."

"I'm not a mailman. I'm a TLC."

"All right. Would you agree that a Temporary Letter Carrier should not read other people's mail?"

"It was Gail's mail, Daniel. Gail doesn't *believe* in privacy. And I only wanted to be there for him if he needed me, in case she said something terrible to him. You don't know the Tree Man, Daniel, but he's surprisingly fragile. He doesn't know himself how fragile he is. He needs support. He needs reassurance. That morning I was in bed with him – "

"That morning you what?"

"I didn't know he was in there. He thought I was Gail."

Daniel eyes me warily, just as I begin to laugh. It comes on rather gradually. Deceptively, really, so in the beginning I think I can stop it whenever I want. I can't, but I don't want to, either. Tears roll down my face and in less than a minute I'm doubled over, my hands pressed into my belly. But inside I'm calm, the way I get when I'm watching the approach of a thunderstorm. Sometimes we sit on the porch swing, Stevie and I, gently rocking as the darkness and rain roll in and the big drops pick up weight and speed. Still, when the thunder and lightning break directly on top of us, we know we'll stay cozy, sheltered, untouched.

"Liz, what doctor did you say you think you saw in the emergency room?" Daniel asks diplomatically. Diplomacy has a way of making him awkward.

I keep on laughing.

"Liz. . . "

"I say I think I saw nobody. I say I think I didn't go to the emergency room, Daniel. I say I think the dog didn't break any skin." Mouth twitching, I double over again and laugh. It doesn't feel anything like hysteria. It feels wonderful. I try explaining this to Daniel but can only sob.

"Just a minute," says Daniel.

He takes the glassware away and walks into the kitchen, picks up the telephone, dials. I hear him asking for the doctor, introducing himself, then all of a sudden his voice gets low. Poor Daniel, I think, he is always so determined, so *at pains* to do the right thing. I climb off the swing, poke my head in the room, accustom myself to his whispering, hear the word *frightened,* hear him asking the doctor if he should put me to bed. But I won't go to bed, I don't want to sleep, I am far too excited. Besides, I was frightened only for a few minutes, at the beginning. The dog dragged me to and fro by the mailbag, flailing and growling while I pulled the can of Mace from its loop on my belt, aimed and tried to spray. No Mace, no weapon, and in the end, no blood, just the same dog chasing Gail's letter as it floated across the yard, catching it, then holding the envelope between its paws and ripping it open.

"There's your letter," I sobbed to the cab driver, who was trying to comfort me and paid no attention to what I said. He was grasping my elbow and helping me up solicitously.

"It's from Gail," I added, and the driver let go of my arm at once, dropping me onto the carpet remnant. Red shag. I had already noticed that Gail's letter wasn't only a letter, there was something else included, a pair of cream-colored satin briefs with a special flap sewn in the crotch. The cab driver lunged for the dog but was far too late, Gail's letter was ruined, half-chewed, ink-smeared, and the briefs were in ribbony, pearl-studded shreds.

"You bitch," the driver screamed, at me and the dog at once, before stomping off through the entranceway of his house, pausing only to grab the bottle of Alka-Seltzer from the coffee table in the yard. I had to pull myself up, but as I did so the dog lunged again, straddled me, and stared into my face, its wet nose tensed, not twitching at all. It put its nose on my nose and, that way, pushed me straight back to the ground. After that it raised its head and for a moment only stood there listening, to what I didn't know. I didn't make a sound myself, for a moment, and then I heard myself say, "Don't touch me." That's all. Two or three times I said it, I think.

Should I knee it? I wondered.

The dog was a male, it smelled of cooking grease, the very tip of its tongue protruded out of its mouth. I detected no whiskers at all, and no collar, and on the taut curve of the throat a few desiccated burrs, the shells split apart, the seeds already dispersed. I studied the fur on its muscular chest; how close-cropped it was, the pink skin just visible underneath.

Should I try to poke my fingers in its eyes? I wondered, at which it lowered its head again, bared its teeth, sniffed me again, took hold of my wrist with its jaw, but gently, ever so gently, and began to lick my arm. It licked meditatively in sopping-wet whorls from wrist to elbow. Then it pressed the tip of its tongue in the crease of my elbow and let the tongue vibrate. It was then I was smitten with – what?.

Resignation, I suppose.

How simple it was, how uncomplicated, all I had to do was lie there and wait for it to happen. Wait for what, I didn't know. The dog lifted its big forepaw, hung it limply by the wrist so its toenails teased my shirt collar and stayed poised in the hollow of my sternum, barely tickling the skin.

I closed my eyes.

Was this terror? I wondered.

Although I didn't feel afraid. Not at that moment. It was like an afterglow, one lover pulling close to another and whispering, I wouldn't mind dying right now. The Doberman pinscher was licking my face, kissing me, French kissing, even. Its gaze was steady, melancholy. It traveled the length of my body, then paused as if ashamed by the rip it had made in my pants. It kissed my knee and started chewing thoughtfully, like a student chewing a pencil. I couldn't move a muscle. I was still whispering, "Don't touch me. Don't touch me," but it was only reflexive, like the cough of a motor after it's been shut off. Then the cab driver poked his head out between the halves of the shower curtain and asked timidly if I was feeling okay.

The shower curtain was vinyl, orange and yellow plaid.

"I'm so happy I could die," I told him, weakly. He invited me in for some coffee, and when I didn't budge, came out into the yard carrying a glass of water in which were dissolving two Alka-Seltzer tablets. He pulled me up to a sitting position and held the glass under my nose. The carbonation hit my face. I drank, swallowed, thanked him, said goodbye, and kept sitting there. My pants were torn, one knee exposed and a little raw-looking, wet from the dog's saliva.

"You sure?" said the driver. "I could give you a ride."

He gestured toward his cab. It was a four door, but the doors on one side were fastened with a knotted extension cord, and there was a lawn mower doubled over on the back seat. Gail must have been the most beautiful, the most exciting thing that ever happened to him. After all, a cab driver in a town like this. . . maybe he mows lawns on the side. I looked again at his own lawn. There was a blue pile remnant I longed to lie down on, but instead I went home, limping, ignoring the rest of my mail.

Now, from the porch, I hear Daniel's near-whisper repeating after the doctor, *put her to bed, let her rest for a while, then wake her and ask her her name.*

Quietly I sneak past the swing and down the steps, then hurry next door to the redwood fence and shimmy through a gap into Nikki's backyard. Her yard smells sharply of citrus peel, the principle ingredient of her compost heap. Also, fresh cloves, which she sprinkles on top along with each new layer of vegetable peels, to mask the decay.

I pluck some cherry tomatoes off of the vine and eat them standing amid the neat, hoed rows, straight and furrowed as the cornrows in Nikki's hair. It's a postage-stamp yard, hardly bigger than the shed she tore down to make room for the garden, but very productive. A sprinkler is spinning. Against the back of the house are some tiered shelves for seedlings, while on her side of the fence are hung boxes of wax bean vines among flats of marigolds.

Next I go inside and start looking for Nikki's telephone. I've never seen it before but I know where it must be, buried under something sumptuous enough to muffle the sound when it rings. I go first to the couch, flip up the cushions, then upstairs to look under Nikki's pillow. No phone. In a minute I remember; off Nikki's clean kitchen is a laundry alcove, and on the floor in the alcove is always a basket of clothing – caftans, kimonos, flour sack trousers, saris, sarongs, and her big square head scarves – waiting to be ironed. I reach under the silks and soft cottons, pull the telephone out by the cord, sit cross-legged on the floor and dial my own number.

Daniel, just off the phone with the doctor, answers breathlessly.

"Don't worry about me," I tell him, my mouth still slushing cherry tomatoes. "I'm going out with Danka."

"But – " says Daniel before I hang up.

After that, I call Ben to ask after Stevie.

And next, I call Danka.

"Meet me at the old depot," I instruct her. "There's someone I want to spy on."

FOR A WHILE we lie on the grass, Danka and I, although it took us a while to get here. When she arrived at the depot, overdressed for a walk in the woods in her little black dress and stiletto heels, we had to hop in her car and drive back to her house for something more suitable. There, I saw the Soho Tree truck parked in her and William's driveway. One of their pines had grown top-heavy. They'd lose their homeowner's insurance if it wasn't cut down.

"Insurance companies make me want to pook," said Danka.

"Puke," I corrected. "I know. My neighbor chopped a spruce for the very same reason. The whole thing's absurd."

The workmen were having a break when we got there and were nowhere to be seen.

"Was the Tree Man with them?" I asked. "I haven't seen him in a while."

"The tree man?"

"The slender one. The one that looks like a bird. The one with the feathered hair. I haven't had a glimpse of him in days."

"Is he the one you want to spy on?"

"No. But I'm worried about him. He's delicate."

"Oh. I believe I saw him here. Yes."

She opened her door, slipped off her shoes, fished around in a pile of sandals, clogs, and boots in the hallway before settling on some dainty black sneakers. The hall smelled sour, from all of Danka's shoes, I thought.

"Where are William's shoes?" I asked.

"He's wearing them. He keeps his slippers near the couch, where he does his reading. He's shopping now. He loves it. It's a hobby. He drives all the way into the city for a bottle of wine... Last week he drove to the Amish country for cheeses. He orders suckling pigs by mail. Before we married, I knew about this shopping, I thought it was charming, like you. Only you don't look so charming today," she remarked. She'd put her hands on her hips and was staring me up and down. "You look – how shall I say? – excitable. Ordinarily you look so healthy. So contented. So – how shall I say? – quaint."

"I'm all right," I told her, cringing at the word. "I had a little run-in with a Doberman pinscher."

"Run-in?"

"It fell in love with me."

Danka chewed on a fingernail. "I think maybe we should not go out. A little something to drink... "

"I'm fine."

"I don't know."

"Danka, if you don't want to go, fine, but I'll go by myself.

That's all," I said. I held open the door while she tied the laces of her sneakers.

Now we lie side by side on our backs, the little fingers of our inside hands almost touching as if in careful mimicry of our bodies. Danka is worried about her husband, she tells me, for in his careful reading he has come closer to uncovering the identity of the City of Repose. For some time he seemed to have forgotten all about it, but just recently he came across another reference to its existence in ancient Palestine.

"What he still hasn't figured out is that its proper title is not the City of Repose but the City of Forests and sometimes the City of Refuge," says Danka. "I am thinking of sneaking some scissors into the library, if you know what I mean, so that he'll never come across it. I wander what the penalty would be. What do you think?"

"You might have to pay a fine," I say, shrugging. "What's so terrible about the City of Repose? That sounds beautiful. The City of Forests." I shut my eyes. "The City of Refuge. *Refuge.* What a beautiful word."

After a while, Danka says, "I was thinking you are the kind of person who will come into the library with me and stand guard at the end of the stack and keep watch while I snip. On the other hand, you can snip while I keep watch, if you prefer."

"Anything. Sure," I say dreamily.

"What kind of clouds are those?"

"Cirrocumulus. It's going to get windy."

"It's calm, now."

"I know," I say. So calm is the air that it blanketed us; upon seeing a flattened bed of tall grass we flopped down on it like Dorothy in the field of poppies. Around us, not even the petals of the daisies tremble.

"How hot is it now?" asks Danka.

"About eighty," I tell her, amused that she is asking me so many questions. It's clear she's impatient. Our roles are reversed; it is I who am leading this particular expedition although I've not yet told Danka on whom we are supposed to be spying.

"Imagine," I say to Danka. "Imagine a man who, when he runs into you in the middle of the woods, in the middle of nowhere, pulls his cap out of his pants and puts it on only so he can tip it."

"He ran into you?" says Danka.

"I mean, we *saw* each other." But that's not exactly it either, of course.

"Oh. So you're in love. Congratulations. I thought you had a wanderful marriage."

"I do. It's not love. I only want to know all about him. I don't want to *do* anything."

"Why not?" Danka asks.

I shrug, not knowing the answer, not knowing, suddenly, if what I said is true.

"I have a feeling he is what is known as *unsavory*," I say.

She perks up.

"Yes?"

"I ran into him once on one of my routes," I tell her. "It was a long time ago. He was calling his dog, who was standing behind him the whole time, nosing around his boots. He had on a Western-style denim shirt with embroidery on it, and I complimented him. He usually wears just T-shirts. I said, 'That's a nice shirt,' and he said something really strange. I mean, it struck me as strange at the time, although I haven't really thought about it since. But. . . "

"But what?" asks Danka, doing leg lifts. Her narrow black sneakers hover above, then slowly begin to descend.

"But now that I'm *curious* about him. . . . He told me where he got the shirt. You know where he told me he got it? At that shopping mall in New Jersey where that sniper shot some people a couple of years ago. That's exactly what he said: *At that shopping mall in Jersey where that sniper wasted a bunch of people.*"

The sneakers stop in mid-air. "So you think. . . "

"No."

"Why not?"

"It just never even occurred–"

Danka snorts. "But you find him interesting."

"Yes."

"Exciting."

"Well. . . ," I answer, suddenly smitten again. "It's not love. Just curiosity."

"Oh, yes. Curiosity. You mean you want to know what it feels like to sleep with a man whose wife kicked him out because he's an asocial slob who fucks like an ape."

"How do you know that about him?" I ask. "How do you know what you said?"

"Pardon?" says Danka.

"You heard me," I say.

"I've never spoken to him in my life," Danka says. "I've never so much as petted his dog, God forbid."

"What's the dog's name?" I ask testily.

"I don't know anything about him. Except he has a wanderful soft belly and his pants are slipping down always because he has no bottom."

"Christ," I say. And then, "I wouldn't think she kicked him out, exactly. I think she left him. I think she left him because he's unbalanced."

"Unbalanced," says Danka thoughtfully. "I suppose you think the rest of us are balanced? I suppose you think that unlike yourself I am perfectly matched with my perfectly balanced husband? I suppose you think William is perfectly balanced? Do you know what he's reading these days? My husband? He is reading the autobiography of a librarian. Does that make him balanced?"

"I think she needed some space," I go on. "I think she wanted to be alone."

"Me, too," says Danka.

"You want to be alone?"

"No way," says Danka. "I've had enough alone. I've had alone all my life. How many people do you think there are, that I will never see again? How many hugs and kisses that I can never return? I don't understand the past forty years of my life, Liz. I don't know what the point of it's been. It's been so untraumatic, so uneventful, so un-this, so un-that, but I don't trust it, you know? I think it's playing a game, and it's waiting till I figure out the rules. And now I've figured it out. All I need is a good long cry, forty days, forty nights, that kind of cry, and then I can kiss it goodbye, and then my life can start again. But I can't do it, you know? How can I cry about William, of all the ridiculous things. And that's what I like about *him,* you know? I could cry about *him* if he'd give me a reason to."

"About who?" I ask, although I know very well who she's talking about. It's Joe. It's got to be.

"Never mind," says Danka.

"Never mind what?" I ask. "Never mind how you know he's only half-civilized?"

"I never said he's not civilized. I said he's not circumcised."

"Very funny," I say. "What does he look like?"

Danka is quiet.

"He's ugly," I say, and feel keenly the fact of his ugliness as if struck in the eye by one of his slingshot missiles. "He has rotten teeth, right?"

Danka raises her eyebrows, and then we sigh in unison and watch the sky again. A plane soars past against the grain of a cloud, and when it's gone I believe I can hear the grass growing. How frenetically restful the close of the day seems to me, as if nearing its finish it slows to a halt just short of the first shadow. Is it possible to reach—as in *pitch of activity*—a pitch of restfulness?

I ask Danka what she thinks.

"Certainly," she answers. "When you feel so bored you could die."

I'm insulted. After all, this is *my* expedition.

"Not restlessness. Restfulness."

"Oh. Like death."

"Like absolute, quiet wakefulness," I argue, and, standing up, lead Danka along the trail away from the smell of daisies among some brambles to the train tracks. We are high up suddenly, on the plateau, dizzyingly close to the sky. This is the spot where I found the pole lamp and the doll, but now I'm looking only for a trail.

It's nowhere. We head up the tracks, glancing right, glancing left, because I can't remember just exactly where Joe was when he disappeared.

Perhaps, anyway, the trail was west of the depot, not east.

But here are the same raspberry bushes, still heavily laden, the same spiders still crouching, the same mosquitoes still humming, the same dogs still barking on the tract house lawns. Recalling how I'd felt so lost in the bushes, having pushed my way through them while picking berries, I shut my eyes and ask Danka to spin me around.

We do this, like children. Then I plunge here, plunge there. Still no trail. Maybe it only looked like a trail, with him standing on it. Maybe you need a dog to find it. Maybe if I simply set off. . . . So I do, but there's a fallen log, and having reached it I don't know whether to scale or follow it. I sit down on it. Danka asks me again how hot the day is, and announces that William, probably home by now from shopping, must be worried sick about her.

"He never worries about you when we're on one of *your* missions," I say indignantly.

"True. But I do not leave so suddenly, usually. Usually I do not forget a pot of soup boiling on my stove."

"Don't worry about it, Danka."

"But it will boil over."

"William will shut off the burner."

"But he's shopping."

"But you said–"

Danka sniffs.

"It was very difficult for me to have made this soup," she says.

A pot of soup, I am thinking. How can a grown woman get worked up about such a thing?

And then I realize it's not the soup, really. It's Danka's old, familiar trouble, come to rescue her again from having too much fun. It must have followed us here. If only we hadn't returned for her little black sneakers–but even so, it would have found us, sniffing out our peace of mind until it spotted us below. Now it swoops down to fetch us, now it leads us to her car. She insists that I come home with her and eat a bowl of her soup. She puts her hands on her hips again.

"Soup will make you feel much better," she says.

I tell her I'm feeling fine. In the car I ask, "What kind of soup?"

Danka doesn't answer, and remains petulant all the way home. The back of her house is all one long window. There is window in the bedroom, window in the living room, window in the dining room, window in the kitchen. The kitchen proper is William's domain, I've been led to understand, but Danka takes me right up to the stove and hands me a wooden spoon.

"Stir," she says. "I can't bring myself to do it. Tell me how you think it smells."

I lift the lid off the pot. There's a geyser of steam. At once I smell again the sour odor of her pile of shoes, but it's not the shoes, after all, it's the soup, in a big tin pot although Danka–William, actually–owns much better: cast irons, enamels, crockpots, woks. There's a skylight overhead, and around its bottom edge a cast iron rod holds his prized kitchen tools. He has marble rolling pins, French eggbeaters, beaten copper ladles, spatulas, whisks, and graduated spoons.

Danka doesn't use any of these. Instead she squats down before a low cabinet and rummages around among cheese graters and flour sifters before withdrawing a plain ladle, the kind I keep in my own kitchen, stainless steel with a plastic grip. Her soup pot is dented, and when she stirs the soup, it wobbles on the burner.

"Well?" she asks.

"Well, what?"

"How do you think it smells?"

"It smells. . . ," I say searchingly. "It just plain smells."

"Good," says Danka. "Choose an apron if you want."

She pulls open a drawer and flips through the stiffened folds of her husband's colorful aprons.

"No thanks."

"Only joking," says Danka. "But keep an eye on the window and tell me if you see him coming."

"Okay," I say, and keep an eye open not for William but for the Tree Man. The tree surgeons are working late; we passed them on our way into the house just a few minutes ago. They were all standing around the big jaws of the truck, except for one who was up in the too-tall pine, wrapping and knotting rope around the limbs, and then, having sawed them, tossing them down. I supposed it was the Tree Man, but it turned out not to be. It was a teenager in overalls. The stiff leather of the holster fit him like a chastity belt. He was gangly and skinny. No feathers. No grace. Maybe the Tree Man quit. On the other hand, maybe he's sick. I envision a wounded bird lying quietly among dish-towels in a cardboard box, its round breast vibrating under dampened feathers. When he eats, I imagine, it is to suck nourishment from the tip of an eyedrop.

"Is he there?" asks Danka.

"No," I say, still thinking of my friend and not of William. How worried I am. Somehow I feel responsible for the Tree Man's well-being. After all, it was I who kicked him out of my house, and out of the bed he'd shared with Gail.

For a minute, I stir the soup again. Such odd soup. Slightly viscous, and yet there is so little substance. A few shavings of–what?–potato? Onion?

Danka edges up close, finds her cigarette alight in its saucer on the window sill, near some parsley William planted in a crock. Danka drags thoughtfully, blows the smoke onto her ladle while cooling the broth. We both watch the smoke as it mingles with the steam.

"That's an idea," says Danka, flicking the cigarette over the pot. A column of ash tumbles in in one piece.

She stirs it with the ladle.

"That smoky taste," she remarks, giving me a smile and the cigarette another flick.

I smile in return. They do this at chili cook-offs, too. Texans do. Sometimes they unroll an entire cigar and dump in the shredded tobacco.

Danka lifts the ladle, holds it to her lips, then drops it back into the pot.

"I'm not ready to taste it yet. I know this is silly. I have to prepare. I have to meditate about it," she says, and makes for the living room. The Great Room, is what Danka and William call it. It's a room with no past. It has a freshly laid parquet floor, and its high-beamed ceiling slants toward the plate-glass window. To one side sits a grand piano sheltered by a tall rice-paper screen decorated with clusters of feeding Ibises. The frame looks freshly painted in slick, black lacquer. The piano legs, too, look hot from the lathe. Having sunk down into the couch, Danka reaches behind her for one of William's executive toys, a wooden elephant on wheels, designed for back massage. She rolls it up and down her arm, shuts her eyes and just sits there. It takes me a minute to remember that we'd come into the Great Room in order to meditate about her soup. I shut my eyes, too, and try to oblige.

"What's in it?" I ask.

"Turnips," says Danka, her eyes still closed.

"Turnips," I repeat, and get up and look out the window at the disappearing pine. With all the lower boughs gone, the tree resembles a broken umbrella, its spokes snapped inside-out.

"Poor tree," I say, at which Danka jumps up and goes into the kitchen again. She comes back looking hungrier then ever—starved, really—an expression I recall having seen before only in photographs. How pinched she looks, how hollowed-out, how desperate, even, as if she might die.

"What's the problem?" I ask.

"The soup," says Danka, and stops the elephant mid-thigh, and looks imploringly at me until I know what it's about. Turnips, I'm thinking, and cigarette ash. That smoky taste, she'd said earlier, as if to mimic what she'd described in the snack bar so many years ago. What was the scene? The barracks, the smokestacks, the bare earth cracked and frozen, the suddenly spilled soup, the stripe-clad skeletons lapping it up.

Just as, now, there's her own sudden, drawn, beseeching hunger.

"Try some," she instructs, when, full of dread, I follow her back to the stove. She sets a half-full bowl on the counter in front of me. The bowl is chipped. I study it, like looking for worms in a rain puddle. What's in it? A few leaves, a few twigs, muddy water.

Also the ashes, their soft, pale flecks drifting into solution.

I dip my spoon into the bowl, scoop out a few peels of turnip, prepare to blow off the steam.

Except there isn't any steam. On her earlier foray into the kitchen, Danka must have shut off the burner. The soup is lukewarm with an edge of cold.

I put the spoon back in the bowl, feeling nauseated.

Danka slurps enthusiastically.

Soon she ladles out more, makes a face, reaches into the spice cabinet, unscrews a bottle and drops in a pinch of onion powder. "It's still not quite right," she is saying. "There was a flavor, a hint of sweetness I can't get, what's that word–pootrid."

"Putrid," I say.

"Yes," says Danka. She eats. I lift the spoon to my lips, slide my tongue into the soup, let it sit there a while. Nothing. Just the sharp metal taste of the spoon. I slide my tongue further into the broth this time, actually nudging a turnip peel. Again, practically nothing, just salt, hot water, and smoke again. I remember a drink that my sister used to make, when she was in college. Hot Lemon Water, she called it, fine for sore throats and when you'd run out of tea. I open my mouth wide.

"Here's William!" shouts Danka.

Having climbed from his car, he is chatting with the workers. Danka grabs my bowl, dumps it out, rinses it fast in the sink, cradles it in hers and sticks both wet bowls far back into the depths of the low cupboard before tossing both dripping spoons into the garbage. In the meantime I tilt the big pot above the sink and switch on the disposal along with the tap. By the time William comes in, carrying shopping bags full of bottles, we are seated primly at the table reading gourmet cooking magazines.

"What's that smell?" William asks, wrinkling his nose, but then he sets to work putting the bottles away. He's purchased four of French wine, two of Californian, several brandies, several six-packs of coolers, a sherry, some rums, some bitters, some saki, some plum wine, several liqueurs, and five ornamental bottles of vinegar all of subtle pinks and ambers. These he sets in a row on the counter to admire. In each has been suspended a bouquet of herbs. Danka rolls her eyes, flips the pages of her magazine, and carefully rips out a page containing a recipe for oyster stew. She has told me in the past that she secretly rips out whatever she doesn't want William to make. When William comes back in, I am standing up to go, and for a minute he looks carefully at me before saying, "My goodness. What ever happened? You don't look well."

"I feel a little nauseated," I tell him.

"Let me offer you a ride home," says William, unloading from the shopping bag a corkscrew, some coasters, and some high-tech-looking bottle stoppers.

"That's okay," I tell him, but he's already found his car keys. When Danka rises to accompany us to the door, the soup ladle she's been sitting on falls on the floor with a clunk and a splatter of wet turnip peel.

"Don't forget your soup ladle," Danka says quickly, and gives me a meaningful look.

When William fastens my seatbelt, I feel like a school girl being driven home to supper by a playmate's rich father. How self-conscious I am; perhaps he believes that I carry a soup ladle with me everywhere I go. If only he would ask me what I'm doing with one in my lap, I might think of a suitable lie.

Instead he only starts the engine, and the tape deck clicks on.

"Renata Tarraga playing *Tres Pavanos*," says William grandly.

My Spanish is rusty.

Three peacocks, I suppose, and slide the ladle out of sight between my knees.

But the music turns out to be lovely. It distracts me. William, too. A tendon twitches in his neck in time with the melody, and he never does ask me why I'm carrying a ladle.

DANIEL AND STEVIE are waiting for me on the porch, where night seems absolutely to have fallen; they are rocking in pitch blackness. Stevie holds a box of Band-Aids, Daniel, a blanket and a tiny, lipped beaker of–what?–Sambuca of all things, a drink I haven't thought of in years. He drops a coffee bean in it and lights it with a match; the liqueur flares indigo, then subsides. Only now do I remember the Doberman pinscher; the way it straddled me, the way I lay there patiently, patiently, and then, afterwards, my surreptitious exit during Daniel's whispered call to the doctor.

When they lead me upstairs to the bedroom, I see that the sheet has already been folded back and the heating pad, plugged in and turned to a low setting, spread open on the pillow.

I lie down on the bed, arranging the heating pad dutifully under the curve of my neck.

"Sorry about that," I say apologetically to Daniel. "I didn't want to go to sleep earlier. Nothing hurts. I'm only numb. I don't need these things. You're teaching him to worry."

I gesture toward Stevie and take one of his proffered Band-Aids, a butterfly. Having unwrapped it, I press its narrow wings over the bridge of my nose, then wrinkle the nose at Stevie.

Daniel gives me one of his level gazes. I am hoping he is going to ask me why I'm carrying a ladle.

Instead he asks, "How do you feel? And what do you mean you're only numb? What part of your body is numb?"

"Danka made soup," is my answer, as I swallow the syrupy, licorice drink. "And not numb, really. Just sleepy, I guess. At rest. In peace. But don't touch me, please."

I say this last without thinking, and then there's a silence during which I could rescue us, take it back, un-say it, somehow. Instead I hear myself repeating it, softly, over and over the way I whispered to the dog. My fingertips are sticky from the drink, and tacky when I try to push Daniel away. "Get your paws off me," I finally say.

"Great," says Daniel. "And what did you say was your name?"

Stevie begins to cry.

STILL THE SUMMER goes on, in its strange, slow, spellbound way. On Morgan Street close to the creek, the fruit trees hold fast to their blossoms, first wilted, now flaccid and brown. Our own cherry tree is belatedly making its fruit, and when occasionally there is a breeze, the myriad pink globes tick faintly upon it while overhead our big evergreens creak and sigh. Cats fight late at night in the trees. When a dog barks, it does so thoughtfully as if waiting for reply. Several people around town claim to have heard coyotes howling. The air temperature, having climbed past ninety degrees to ninety-four, then ninety-eight, then ninety-nine, now drops to ninety-five. There has been thunder as well, along with a few sonic booms, and of course Nikki's music, which somehow registers so acutely the vicissitudes of weather as to predict the slightest changes in barometric pressure, the way arthritics feel such fluctuations in their ankles and wrists. Her music these days is a somewhat frenetic hum, mildly electric, purple-sounding, phosphorescent. Like neon lights. Nikki must know this, must accordingly plan her atmosphere, her studio lighted only through a half-open door by the indirect glare of the fluorescent bulb above her kitchen sink. I often watch her through the window. I'll be sitting on the hood of our still-defunct car in our driveway, as I've taken to doing while Daniel weighs his sugars, mixes his nectars. If it's raining I'll climb inside and turn the windshield wipers on, and sometimes the headlights, and once in a while, the radio. Tonight, with Stevie sitting in my lap, I unroll a ribbon of licorice and lean back against the windshield from where we have a view of Nikki and her apparatus, her digital sampler, her keyboard, her fingers darting from knob to button, button to knob – and of her pained-looking face. I've told her I do this. She doesn't mind. Every so often, while realigning some wires, or adjusting her foot pedals and earphones, she'll look at us and flash us a thumbs-up or down. Stevie waves. To him, each nightly performance is like a new, interactive video game. After he waves, Nikki comes to the window, raises the mike to her lips and mouths an invitation for us to come in. Still I can't shake the new, uncomfortable suspicion of Nikki getting ready for bed at night; unwrapping her sarong, draping it over a chair, then slipping a bracelet off her ankle before removing her teeth from her mouth and dropping them into a glass. When – toothless – she climbs into bed, it must be like a retreat; she wraps silence around her along with the sheets. I can't tell her this, of course, so instead I comment on her music, how it sounds like a downed live wire. How pleased Nikki seems by the simile; she bids me sit down and plays it again, the same hum, the same buzz, the same potent force lying untouched on a sidewalk while around it mingle all the small noises of a summer night.

One day there's a fight in the post office. Everyone is mystified about the man who started it. They call him a live wire, a loaded gun because he had no cause to go off the way he did, all of a sudden, kicking Gail's ex-lover George in the shins then punching the eyeglasses off George's face and down George's shirt collar into his shirt. Even though the local bookstore has formally closed, George still works there, packing and shipping remainders. He has taken to wearing man-tailored shirts, in pastels and pinstripes, but his eyeglasses are the same thick-lensed wire-framed ones he used to keep wearing even while screwing Gail's rival, the one with the antique dresses. When he fished the eyeglasses from inside his shirt, only one earpiece was bent, but by then his attacker had disappeared, screaming, after George bit his finger "down to the marrow." The fight took place in the lobby, which stays open so people can get to their boxes or to the stamp machine after the service windows have been shuttered closed. Behind them where we work – filing change-of-address cards, sorting, stamping, weighing, bundling – two big fans whir deafeningly. So no one even heard the screams, or George's yelling. He had to bang on the shutters, and when we got to him he blamed us for everything. His nose was running, some envelopes lay scattered on the floor, and one pane of glass was broken in the door. We all rushed outside to have a look and see who we could see, but there was nothing, only heat, and some blood on the wide pressed-stone stairway, a trail of drops that, still glistening, led down to the street.

"A live wire," someone murmured. "A loaded gun."

Someone else said, "It's gonna be a long, hot couple of months," while someone else asked George what he thought he might have done to deserve it. That was a joke; everybody knows George is a pain in the neck. George was bent over massaging first one shin and then the other, and when he straightened back up there was blood on his lip but we didn't ask whose; his or the other guy's. He said, "I didn't even see him, that's what I did to deserve it."

But the street was the scariest thing of all, how empty it was, nothing but heat waves and flecks of mica and no cars anywhere as if the man had made his getaway in every single one of them.

THEN COMES the Fourth of July, the anniversary of the day I first met Daniel eleven years ago in St. Louis. Every year I put on my commemorative costume, a variation on the clothes I was wearing when he set eyes on me. I was four-feet, eight-inches tall, dressed in an over-sized T-shirt, no jeans, no hose, no socks, just clogs and alligator earrings. Daniel told me later he didn't know I was a grown person until he looked into my eyes and what he saw there – "your womanliness," he called it – shocked him into falling in love with me. For tonight I've painted my toenails glow-in-the-dark blue, but my earrings are filigreed roses no bigger than split peas. I've put on a little eye make-up, too, because the Fourth of July is serious business – even Emily might be there. The festivities take place at the reservoir close to our house, but still we go early to reserve our box seat, a hunk of concrete that juts out over the water. Arriving just after seven with our pillows and blankets, we spread our traditional French breads with strawberry butter. From here we'll have a view of the crowd gathering on the field below, and of the launching pad, and of the fireworks reflected on the surface of the water. There's a rusty pipe embedded in the concrete that makes a fine bucket for wine; we drop some ice cubes in and slide the bottle in after. After that we light a citronella candle, lean back on our hands and watch the water for bullfrog rings. Stevie stacks plastic wine cups and knocks them over. A Frisbee game starts on the sunken field as Simon and Ben, awaiting the show on a blanket on the slope, raise the hand-held zoom at the sky and peer into it hopefully. More and more picnickers limp by on the footpath. Still, there are fewer than usual, because so many people have moved away. Just last week the public library shut it's doors, although the books are still shelved in the glass-floored stacks, the newspaper open on the rack in the reading room. "Tax base," the librarian whispered hoarsely to me, "not to mention insurance." Next year, I can't help thinking, if this keeps up, there won't be a Fourth of July at all.

Not until just before nine, when darkness has started to fall, do I notice my new friend, Emily, in her own box seat precisely across the reservoir from ours, sharing a loaf of identical French bread with her boyfriend. Standing up, I wave my loaf in figure eights until Emily jumps up too and waves hers in response, our very first communication since the day of the lawn party when we introduced ourselves. Now we try a little pantomime, our two figures gesticulating over the gleam of the water, but our messages are fuzzy in the dusk. I try to tell her with my bread that after the fireworks I'll meet her midway on the footpath, and that we'll sit together on the bench where we talked about our mothers. Emily's bread nods *fine* and points in the direction of the launching pad. The first of the fireworks is a dud, and after that a few nosedive and pop in the water, but still we stare at the blue black bowl of sky, wait patiently and are rewarded by explosions of color that in the galvanized air are peculiarly muffled.

The finale is purple chrysanthemums, and when they've dropped all their petals I can't remember on which side of the reservoir I'd told Emily I'd meet her.

I send Daniel and Stevie home to the porch, then stand unmoving in the current of the crowd which is thinner even than I had thought, just a smattering of clusters of people all limping toward the street, but no Emily.

No Emily anywhere.

If only I still had my loaf of French bread it would lead me straight to her, like a divining rod. But Daniel ate the last of it. Probably she's forgotten me, anyway, and right now is strolling home through the old arboretum, gathering azaleas and sticking them into her boyfriend's buttonholes.

Back on the porch, Daniel only nods sympathetically, as if he's known all along how foolish I was to think that Emily would meet me. Finally he says, "I bet you forgot the wine."

He's right. I left the half-full bottle in its ice bucket; by now it will be thoroughly chilled.

"So what?" I say.

"So it's up to you."

So I go back for it. The crowd has dispersed but trucks are cruising on the road and making U-turns, then drifting past the reservoir as if to catch sight of a few, residual sparks. One looks like the pick-up that chased me and Danka that night in Bloomingham, but tonight it's filled with teenage girls, not boys, while two big dogs crouch in the back. They watch over me as I walk along. In the reservoir driveway a car is parked, hazards blinking, no driver in sight, while on the other side of the water some people smash bottles one after another, popping them under their boot soles and kicking the glass around. Early in the day there was a fair in town, with a dunking booth, several games, and an old car that for a dollar could be whacked three times with a sledge hammer. The people smashing bottles are the same ones who kept paying for the privilege of wrecking the car, leaving only, once the hulk was towed, a layer of shattered windshield like ice-blue hailstones.

Our concrete slab is frosted with starlight; it looks alone as an iceberg, the water not lapping but only trembling with each pop of a bottle, each belated, distant firecracker. Emily isn't sitting on it; when something sways it is only a cattail. The city of algae is thinning out, its clumps of fluid skyscrapers dissolving into luminous threads where once, whole neighborhoods blossomed and clung.

At once I sit, and caress with my fingers the chilled, wet lip of the wine bottle. For days, since the Doberman Affair, Daniel and I haven't touched each other. Not even sitting on this iceberg did our hands make contact tearing chunks from our shared loaves of bread. Stevie sat between us with his stacked wine glasses, eating chunks of peeled apple and the last of our supply of walnut meats. How indulgent we are of our son between us; no sooner do I lay my hand on one of Stevie's shoulders than Daniel lays his on the other, and if I stroke Stevie's bare neck for even a second, Daniel will claim it when I let go. But we never so much as breathe on each other.

Emily would understand.

That is, she would ask the right questions, and at the end we would both understand.

Since when have you not been touching? she might ask, were she sitting with me on the iceberg.

Since the night of the day of the Doberman pinscher, I'd tell her. And then, *We were in bed, and I had told him not to touch me, but it didn't work out, I mean we started to do things anyway, and he was rolling my nipples the way he does, the way I like. He was lying on his back, and soon I was lying on mine arched over his belly. Ordinarily. . . . So I took his fingers—grabbed them, really, and shoved them up inside where they seemed to dissolve. To disintegrate. To not be there. I couldn't feel anything. We put his penis in me instead. After a minute I started to cry, I couldn't feel anything at all, only desire, only terrible, unfulfillable desire. I climbed off, I was sobbing, I took him into my mouth. I could taste my insides, my thighs were flooding the mattress, but there was nothing he could do for me.*

Nothing. I sucked and licked, but Daniel had lost his energy. Later on he asked, "Just what did you want, anyway?" and I said something really mean, I said, "You should talk, Daniel."

Then Emily might suggest, shaking her head in puzzlement. "*I think you ought to try and–*" but beyond that, the statement fades out. I know it would be simple, useful, obvious. I know it would help, but how? What I really want to know is – Have I fallen out of love? Except it doesn't feel like falling. It feels as if the love itself were lifted away. And what I really want to know is – What lifted it? And will it come back down?

So I sit on the iceberg and wonder. They are still popping bottles across the water, although the intermittent firecrackers seem to have come to an end. Someone slams the car door in the reservoir driveway, flicks off the hazards, drives to the end with no headlights at all, then does a U-turn too fast. Burnt rubber. Were Emily sitting here we would have finished the wine by now, having passed the chilled bottle back and forth. Alone, I haven't had a sip. I lift the bottle from the pipe, put its lip to my lips and tilt it.

No wine at all.

But something else is in the bottle; a tightly coiled ribbon of paper that when I flip the bottle upside-down and shake it, won't fall out. I try reaching in with a finger, to no avail.

So I carry the bottle home and stare into it under the porch light. Even from here, we can hear the glass breaking at the reservoir, the popping and the hooting.

"Emily left a message in our wine bottle," I say to Daniel in wonder, "printed on – get this – a roll of caps."

"Caps?" asked Daniel.

"You know. Gunpowder. You hit it with a rock and it discharges."

I point out to him the red coil of paper with Emily's neat, risky message printed along its length. We take the bottle into the kitchen, wrap it up in a dishtowel, slide Daniel's microscope out of harm's way and tap the towel several times with a hammer. When we pull back the towel, the bottle's still whole, intact. We wrap it up again and hit it more bravely. From over my shoulder, Daniel reads Emily's message aloud.

WEDNESDAY EVENING UNDER THE ELM, he reads.

That's it.

"What's *evening?*" I ask exasperatedly. It gets dark around here around nine. Is evening six o'clock, seven o'clock, or eight o'clock?

"And which elm?" Daniel asks.

"The one behind the slatted bench at the reservoir," I tell him, suddenly confident. It makes a lacy, spreading shade that will flicker on Emily's perfect hair. Her hair is blonde satin, all of a piece, and she'll have dotted a little perfume under the tresses that I'll smell when she shakes them in puzzlement.

I think you ought to try and – let's see – tell me how you got together in the first place. You and Daniel. Was it passionate?

It was like breathing, I will answer. *We didn't even fall in love. We were already in love when we met each other, like brother and sister, like two halves of one soul. We never looked at each other objectively, after the first hour or so. I felt as comfortable with Daniel's body as I felt with my own.*

Just be patient for a while, Emily will say, with a shake of her head, a faint whiff of jasmine. *I think you need –*

Need what? I wonder later, in bed with an understanding Daniel. He's in push-up position, his weight on his palms and toes, straddling me, just looking, not touching at all, a little worried around the eyes. The bedsheet, draped over his shoulders and haunches, makes a soft white tent that trembles with our breathing. We are breathing in counterpoint, my *in* to his *out,* my belly to his breast, my pudenda to his belly, not touching but hovering.

"Just be patient for a while," I whisper to Daniel, when he's made his careful way to the opposite side of the bed. "I think I need. . . I think I need a little. . . "

"Listen," says Daniel, because it's raining outside, and he knows I like the sound. He falls asleep as I listen, so I get up to go outside, barefoot and dressed in his cast off T-shirt. Down the front steps I go, across the lawn to the car, and not until I'm on the hood do I notice that the bottoms of my feet are still dry, and that my bare arms are dry, and that the car itself is dry, and that no rain is falling at all. I still hear it, however, in fact it's picking up speed. I hear it sliding in the gutters, gushing from the down-spout, sliding down glass.

I lift my palms into the air – nothing – and no smell of rain, either. Soon the sound of it slows. Plunk, plunk. Plunk. Plunk. Like drops in a bucket, and then I know that what I'm hearing is not rain at all, just Nikki, trying to tell us it's going to rain. I swivel round on the car hood to look in her window; she's there at the sampler, pulling a disk from the drive. When she sees me she raises her eyebrows, beckons me close, comes up to the window and mouths something I can't make out.

"What?" I say, so that she'll talk a little louder. She doesn't, though. She goes around to her door, sticks her head out a minute, and tells me, in nearly a whisper, "Just remembered. Some man who look like a bird been round here lookin' for you."

WEDNESDAY MORNING, Daniel and I give Stevie a bath, and that's the closest we come to touching each other. Daniel holds the washcloth to Stevie's eyes, I pour water from the cup onto Stevie's hair. I find the baby shampoo, Daniel squeezes a dollop into his hand. Daniel scrubs, I distract Stevie with toys. His favorite bath toy is a laboratory glove of thin plastic, to be filled at the tap, finger by finger until it explodes. When the bath is done I dress him in a sunsuit for daycare and set him down on Daniel's lap before combing his hair. I comb for nearly half an hour, enjoying such routine, thoughtless proximity. Even breakfast is more complicated, now that the supermarket's closed. No ordinary toast, and no cereal at all. I buy eggs at a farm stand I can get to by bike, and, from the Epicurean, some breadsticks, a jar of honey, and some apples so fancy they each come with their own little apple-shaped stickers. Now and then I think of borrowing a car, driving sixteen miles to the open foodstore, stocking up, but this is a small town, and the longer I stay comfortably inside it, the more sixteen miles seems like too much of an adventure. And in the end the thought of leaving town is as scarey as the thought of stepping free of gravity.

Daniel and I spend the day in a thicket of new-flowering jewelweed in damp woods at the edge of the old Boy Scout camp, near Bloomingham. Daniel had been puzzled to find jewelweed so early this year. The flowers of the jewelweed are a tawny, speckled orange and look like small snapdragons. By clasping, between thumb and forefinger, the two larger enfolding petals, we are able to expose the sexual parts. With a tweezer we pluck off an anther, then move the required distance away to pollinate the stigma of a neighboring flower and mark it with coded embroidery thread. At once we wrap the impregnated flower in gauze so that no bee, carrying offerings from yet other donors, will sully the union.

Daniel keeps a notebook clipped to his belt, along with a tape measure, a magnifying glass, his stopwatch and counter, and a zip-lock bag of cotton swabs. He is meticulous, dexterous, exacting as always, so I wonder if he knows what we are doing or if it has escaped him that in the absence of touch between ourselves we are engaged in this other procreative act, flower to flower, folding back the twin, moist, delicate petals.

Still, I bumble. I drop my tweezers, tear the petals off the flowers, knock off the small heads of anthers, and think of Emily. Today is Wednesday, I am thinking, today is Wednesday, Wednesday, Wednesday. This evening I am going to meet Emily at the bench under the elm. To distract myself, I try to recall the purpose of this particular experiment as explained by Daniel earlier. "To calculate optimal outcrossing distance," he said. "To see if it's better to mate with those nearest to you or those furthest away."

Now I'm all tangled up in a jewelweed bush. When I'm high-stepping out of it, stumbling, trying to keep my balance, I tear a whole clump out of the ground.

"I'm going to ruin your hypothesis for sure," I say to Daniel, and wave in his direction with the uprooted tendrils. Daniel barely blinks an eye. He is as steady as if peering into a microscope.

"You can't ruin an hypothesis," he says after a minute. "An hypothesis is only a supposition."

"Then I'll ruin your experiment," I say, and think of Wednesday, and think of Emily, and drop my tweezers yet again.

Daniel unites another few flowers, then pauses to concentrate on a bee. The bee alights on a fold of petals, tunnels her way inside, stays several seconds, then flies out and hovers for a moment near a flower bagged in gauze, before buzzing away from the patch.

Daniel smiles at me.

"The only thing that can ruin this experiment is rain," he says, and pulls a treat from his backpack; some gourmet chocolate serrated dessert cups meant to be creme- or cherry-filled, but we eat ours empty, straight from the box.

IT RAINS.

Not a drizzle so much as a crackle. At five, when we get home, is when it begins.

Daniel isn't bothered, but I stand at the window disconsolately.

"It's only one day of field work," he says from behind me, not quite putting his hand on my shoulder. "This kind of thing happens, you know. That day the deer ate half the flowers, that day the jeep drove through the meadow, that summer the gypsy moths came. You just go out there again, start over, there's nothing you can do about it, it's natural, it doesn't matter, etc. Okay?"

"Okay, etc." I say.

But still I worry. I frown. Not about our wasted morning, our wasted afternoon. No, it's the evening for which I am pining. Very likely if the rain continues, Emily will not meet me under the elm. I entertain a vision of the naked, slatted bench, rain dripping through the cracks, then myself sitting on it, getting itchy, lonely, soaked.

I sigh.

"Want me to tell you a terrible story?" asks Daniel.

"Please."

He tells a story about a pig. A male. This male pig, property of some geneticists at a university in Illinois, represents over twenty years of breeding. Having reached maturity, he is to sire a litter of piglets whose genotypes will answer myriads of pivotal questions about heredity. But on the evening before the mating is to occur, some teenagers break into the barn, lead the pig out of his stall, load him into a pick-up, drive him to a pit and roast him for dinner.

"Oh, no," I say.

And start to cry. Inching yet a little closer behind me, Daniel spreads his arms around and lets his fingertips rest on the desk top. Still, no parts of our bodies are touching. His posture mimics our push-up position in bed except that now I can't look at his face. Out the window in the pine tree, the blue jay is sheltered by needles. She looks cozy and dry, not in the least put-out. In the distance there is lazy, rolling thunder but no lightning at all. When it's over, I know, the air will be heavy again with the weight of the atmosphere, newly humid, shot through with lovely, bright prisms. All at once, all the petals will fall from the fruit trees, in one moment that no one will see, and then the sidewalks will be covered with the pink, steaming masses.

Daniel grunts, readjusts, rests his weight on his fingers, then on his palms. He must be standing on his toes. Still the front of his chest isn't grazing my back, and no breath even tickles the skin of my neck. For how long can this continue? I look up at the clock; it is past five-thirty. Evening? I wonder.

"Why don't you call her," he says after a while.

"Who?" I ask.

"You're impossible," says Daniel. He taps the window pane. The blue jay squawks. The rain comes down harder.

AT SEVEN-THIRTY I walk to the reservoir in the slight, descending mist that has taken the place of the rain. I wear a man's hat over big hoop earrings. My legs are bare but the thongs of my sandals lace up past my ankles. I feel light on my feet, hopeful, and romantic. Should I have brought along a bottle of wine? Maybe Emily has. If she has, she has probably brought goblets, too, which will turn out to be the twins of my own "quaint" ceramic ones.

From the road I see the splayed top of the elm rising over the roof of a house, shaking a little although the tops of all the other trees are motionless. How nervous I am. It occurs to me we don't know each other yet, Emily and I. But I have brought along a photograph of my mother and father, so that Emily, having examined it, will exclaim that my parents resemble her own and that even the house in front of which they are posing resembles the one in which she was raised.

Just be patient for a while, she'll say after a minute, with a shake of her cheerleader head, a whiff of jasmine. She'll take a bite of my ribbon of licorice and chew on it thoughtfully. *I think you need to take stock.*

Of what? I'll ask.

Of your body. It changes after so many–how old are you now?

Thirty.

And how old when you met Daniel?

Nineteen.

Bodies change in eleven years.

Mine hasn't, I'll say, with a glance at my T-shirt, at my bare, tawny legs in the criss-crossing thongs. *My body hasn't changed since I was about twelve.*

A little laughter. More exuberant, invisible pom-poms. Another whiff of perfume, and then Emily will say, *Then maybe that's the problem. Maybe you need to get away from it for a while. Maybe getting away from Daniel is like getting away from your own body. You know, like dying, floating up, looking down at yourself. For a while you float there, no body, all soul. The other day I saw a bed that had been loaded into a moving van. The back of the van was open. The bed was on castors. It was neatly made, the pillows plumped, the pillowcases smoothed, one corner of the blanket folded back. I lay down on it. I needed to. I didn't have a choice.*

Then what? I'll ask. Had she fallen asleep? Had they driven away with her?

But the bench is empty after all, and Emily is nowhere. The elm shakes again and showers the bare slats with rain water. I sit down on it glumly. If I wait for her, if I believe utterly that she will come – in her letter sweater, her hightops, her hair like yellow satin flashing good cheer – then maybe she will.

But it isn't Emily who appears on the path at that minute. It's those two fishing boys with their pail and rods, their skinny father making himself comfortable on the concrete slab, already lighting a cigarette. They walk the other way. They don't notice me. They position themselves on the bank and aim their lines into the reservoir conscientiously as if it were a bull's eye. Something bites. They reel it in, examine it, toss it back into the water. Above me the elm shivers again and splatters rain on my hat. I take the hat off, shake it, and am ready to put it back on when the tree reaches down and takes it out of my hand, ever so gently. I scream. It's the Soho Tree Man. None other than. He dangles, swings, then drops down lightly beside me on the bench.

He has left my hat up in the tree.

"It *is* you," he says. "I didn't recognize you in that hat. I thought you weren't coming. You don't look so glad to see me. What's the problem?"

"Nothing, really."

"Where is she?"

"That's just it," I say. "I thought she would be here."

"Here? She's in town?"

"Oh," I say. "Wait a minute. We're not talking about the same woman."

"I'm talking about Gail," he says.

"I'm talking about Emily."

"I'm talking about Gail," he says again, insistently. "The lady hasn't written to me."

"I know."

"I haven't heard from her."

"I know."

"Not a word," he says. "I say she found another man. No one as hot as me. But the lady forgets. She forgets."

"She'll come back, eventually," I say, realizing finally what he wants from me. Not advice, but simple consolation.

"Oh sure. She'll come back. To me, and to everyone else. Forget it, okay? I'm wavin' goodbye. This is it for me, you know? This is a first. No lady ever did me this way before."

"You're shaking," I say to him tenderly.

"Don't mention it," he says.

He sits there a minute and shakes, and sighs. He wears an open suit vest over a thin, naked chest, blue jeans, and a necklace of russet feathers that blend with his hair where it touches his shoulders. The haircut, well-executed, seems designed as if to augment actual flight. Wings, then barbs, then down.

"Why don't you fly around looking for her?" I almost ask, but instead say, "We should be better acquainted then we are already. I've been worried about you. I don't even know your name."

"Arnie," he says, and then, "I've been worried about me, too." He flips the hair out of his face with a backwards tilt of his head and shakes it to and fro.

"Tell me about yourself, Arnie," I say.

He tells me he quit his job.

"I already figured that out," I say.

He tells me he lives in a garage behind his parents' house on Edgemeer Place, one of the ritzier streets in town. The garage is fixed up like a studio, with carpet, double bed, skylight. There isn't a bathroom, so Arnie has to use the one at his parents'. His parents' house is empty since last spring, when they moved to Arizona.

"Then why not stay in the house yourself?" I ask.

"Gail made the curtains in the garage. Plus, me and Arnie Junior are comfortable. He doesn't need to stay in his cage, in there. In my parents' house, he'd have to."

"Arnie Junior?"

"My toucan."

"I thought maybe he was your child."

"More or less." Arnie gets melancholy after that. It occurs to me that unlike a lot of men his age – mid-twenties – he wants an actual baby, and that that's why he's stuck on Gail. Gail always tells her partners how fertile she is, as if she thinks they'll be happy to father abortions. She's had several since I've known her. Challengingly, I once asked her how many abortions she planned to have, but she answered in earnest. "It's hard to say," Gail said thoughtfully. "I hope no more than four or five, ideally, but that only leaves me with one more. Christ. I don't think I could get by with just one more. What would I do?" Maybe Arnie wants to save her. Maybe he thinks he can settle her down. Who knows? Maybe he can. I think of her postcards, the ones she sends to the men around town. How the postcards make her out to be cool and contained. All her fashion shows and exhibits, and how much her stuff brings in at auctions, and who commissioned her for what, and how much money she's making and how many interviews she's doing on the radio. That kind of thing – how independent she is – is all she ever talks about except sex.

"The lady's in love with herself," Arnie says reverentially, as if reading my mind. "She let me watch her when she was. . . you know. . . she could go on forever. . . and then just when she was about to come she'd stop and look at me but I wasn't supposed to do anything except watch it lubricate. She had the pinkest, wettest, most tantalizing. . . "

"Let's take a walk around the reservoir," I interrupt.

"vulva that I have ever seen, believe me. I can't get that out of my mind. I'm hypnotized." He rolls his eyes. For several minutes he won't look at me but sits with both hands clasped behind his neck, after which we start our walk in silence. He seems edgy about the night although the sky isn't yet black, just gray and rain-dimmed, and I can tell without his saying that he doesn't want to go too close to the woods, so we keep to the path on the edge of the water.

A minute later I ask him about it.

"Why don't you want to go into the woods?"

"You've got to be kidding," he says, and lifts the flap of the suit vest to show me. Some welts, I see, when I get up close. On the pale, thin skin are several raised, purple bruises that throw into relief what I hadn't seen before; how malnourished he looks, how unhealthy, and suddenly frazzled and limp, like a bird that flew into a window.

"Jesus," I say. "What's that?"

"I was mistaken for a deer," says Arnie. "Or maybe a coyote. Somehow I always wish he would mistake me for who I am but he won't give me that pleasure. Never. He gets this way. He doesn't like to be bothered. He likes to practice his German, if you know what I mean. Anyway, don't ask."

I don't ask. I want to, but I don't, and anyway I already know the answer.

Meanwhile Arnie sighs, takes hold of my hand, squeezes it tight, then lets go. The two boys and their father are gone. I keep expecting Arnie simply to vanish, and in the end that's what he does. We have reached the bench again, and before I know what's happening, he's gone. I am standing there alone when the elm reaches down and gives me my hat. He is perched in the spot where the trunk diverges, his bare chest sweating a silver sheen. Already he looks more composed, less a wreck than he did just a minute ago.

"Has Gail sent any of her famous postcards to anyone else around town?" he asks suddenly.

"What do you think?" and then, seeing how wounded he is, I add gently, "You and I are just about the only people in town who haven't heard from her. That must mean something, Arnie."

A breeze rustles the flaps of his suit vest. Above him, among the upraised limbs of the elm, the sky fades.

"I don't know what to think," he says, flustered. And then, "I just know she has the smoothest, slickest, most muscular, most responsive, most insatiable –"

I put on my hat.

"mind in the world. The thought of all of this time – whole years – if I don't see her again I'll kill myself."

"No, you won't," I tell him.

"Yes, I will," he says. He stamps his naked foot on air.

INTERVAL TWO

WHEN AT LAST Ben does receive a letter, on gilt-edged tissue printed with the message "An all night with you would be all right with me," it isn't from Leah at all but from Gail, signed with a G and her customary flourish of fraying lace. The fabric itself is provocatively open-meshed, cream-colored, with – yes – a pubic hair caught in the tendril of an orchid.

So of course I hesitate before showing it to Ben, out of Daniel's earshot and out of sight, even, of Simon, who is too young to have to witness his father's discomfort. Not that Ben has anything to feel uncomfortable about; Gail sends these letters to every man she ever meets, sooner or later, her way of keeping in touch, I suppose. We are sitting in my driveway, Ben and I, just lazing around on the hood of the car. Across the street on the curb lawn are six ladder-back chairs, abandoned by movers, lined up as if for a show. Already they've been sitting there a week and no one's made off with them.

"I have a letter for you that isn't from Leah," is my careful beginning.

"So what," says Ben unhappily.

"It's from somebody else."

"Wow," he says. "Imagine that."

"It's from Gail."

"I don't know any Gails."

"She might not have mentioned her name."

"Let me see that," says Ben. He takes the envelope out of my hand, opens it up, then flicks at the lace with a fingernail.

"That flooze," he says after a minute. "I know who she is. She never even got close."

"She's not a flooze, actually," I defend. "She's–"

"At that party last spring I had to play Toss the Nacho in the Cleavage in order to get her to pick on somebody else."

"She doesn't actually have a cleavage," I argue. "She–"

"Jesus. What if Leah comes back right this second and sees me holding this thing."

We glance at the sidewalk, in both directions, and Ben peers through the zoom at the ladder-back chairs. One has been white-washed. The others, mahogany, look waxy and bare.

Ben has tossed the letter to the ground, a gesture muted by humidity. The dampness holds the paper aloft so it balances on top of a stiff blade of grass. When he has left in search of Daniel and the boys, I slide off the car hood, pick the letter up and drop it back into the pocket of my mailbag thinking I'll give the lace to Arnie, who keeps a shoeboxful of snippets of Gail. Once, when I rescued a whole pair of briefs, Arnie was so happy he nearly fell out of his tree. We meet sometimes at the reservoir and talk about what he wants from life: Gail, and Gail's kids, and a house to be shared with Gail, and Gail's sandals in the closet next to his along with Gail's scarves and hosiery and Gail's locket with the photo of Gail inside. Sometimes I forget that I am talking to a man, when I'm talking to Arnie, although I never quite imagine I am talking to a woman, either. Usually I sit on the bench, and Arnie sits up in the crotch of the elm, so if I don't feel like craning my neck it's as if I'm talking to air.

I want this and that and this, the air always begins. *I want*

Gail and Gail and Gail, breathing eddies on the surface of the reservoir. The water spins around, and cattails sigh against the rocks on the sloping banks.

I say, "Hang on. I'll do what I can."

IN THE SAME POCKET of my mailbag is a second letter I need to deal with. It's not the usual forget-me-not, the usual *Come see me* with no address or phone number, no map, no way to get there. This one was postmarked in Erie like the others, but inside, there's a clue. It's for someone named Deets, and it begins all at once with the crazy message:

> Please please don't say say that you won't won't forgive us, that would break our hearts harder than we ever ever broke yours. Really, we mean it. And really, we didn't know we would want you as much as we do. Our missing you fills up our mouths whenever we open them, Deets. Why haven't you followed? Every morning we stand in the doorway and wait, and water the flowers, and chop tomatoes for gazpacho hoping you'll be here to eat it with us. Your arms and legs are everywhere we look; today beneath the dogwood we saw you lounging with some books, and yesterday on the porch steps, and tonight we'll hear you singing in the shower. Edwards is gone now, we've said our farewell. Not that we didn't find Edwards lovable but that Edwards proved no substitute for you. For example Edwards when cooking Indian chicken used cashews as the recipe dictates instead of peanuts as we all prefer. With Edwards we always felt we were missing somethings. Now the house is empty even of men's trousers which every time we looked at we saw only that you weren't in them, anyway. Why haven't you followed? Is it only that you don't know where to go? Really Deets, do you think we would leave you like that, forever? No way, but we thought you would figure things out. All you need to do is this: Pack your bags, shut the lights, and walk out

> the doors. Make up your mind that you're coming to us, and you'll find what you need to show you the way. Just think, and remember, and follow your noses, and it will be like the first times all over again, meeting each other, and falling in love. We mean to do it again and again, Deets, with you, Deets, and you, Deets–with you. Our missing you fills up our arms even when we hold each other, and it fills up our glasses of wine. Every night we drink to you, to your headlights on the road, to the screech of your four bald tires. Is that how you will come? If so, drive fast, and strap the kayak to the top, we can't imagine you without it, and bring your baseball mitts too so we can put them on the tables and fill them with fruit just as we are accustomed; the grapes here are beautiful, seedless, purple and round with gold flames on the insides. You don't have to bring us anything else, just your smells, your gestures, your footprints on the wood floor after showering along with your habits, the bad ones too, because we miss your torn socks on the stairways, we miss your fingernail clippings, your frayed bits of dental floss clogging the drains in the bathrooms. We have three bathrooms here, believe it or not, and in each is a supply of your Head & Shoulders although you know very well we don't need it ourselves, we need all of you, that's all, please hurry and fill up our tumblers, as Edwards would say. Edwards did say nice things, every once in a while, but not nearly so nice as you. Here's a kiss for the roads, our tongues on your sweet testicles we swear if you don't get here any minutes we'll scream.

On page two is a little drawing of a house in the doorway of which stand two stick figures, elaborately breasted, stick-hands on stick-hips, cockeyed and waiting for Deets. Dear Deets, says the letter, above the love note and under the date. The date was sometime last week. The surname, Deets, is not listed in the phone book or with the operator or in a single one of the extinct directories I've managed to dig up here and there, and no one I know knows a person with Deets for a nickname. On the envelope beneath the word Deets is the address 19 Oak Street, which seemed simple enough when I tried to deliver it because Oak Street is just off Cedar not three blocks from where Morgan meets the reservoir. It's a proper street more reserved-looking than most; green shutters, white-washed chimneys, not a flower pot out of place and the sprinklers timed even on the lawns of the houses of the people who have moved. The porches are tastefully numbered, in brass or wrought iron, from ONE to EIGHTEEN and then TWENTY, TWENTY-ONE, TWENTY-TWO. No number nineteen at all. I checked the side and back doors for student apartments, but found only a woman in kerchief and pedal-pushers, picking cones off a pine tree and dropping them into a basket. She held the basket by its handle in the crook of her arm. From the backs of her sneakers popped two cotton balls.

At my approach she stood still as a frightened deer, actually on tiptoe. Only after I spoke did she let herself down. Her accent was Irish.

"Deets?" she repeated. "Can't say I've noticed."

And she couldn't think of where the number nineteen might be unless her neighbors to the left kept a tenant upstairs.

They didn't, I already knew.

The thing was, there was a spot where a nineteen would likely have been if there had been a house to nail it on. But there was only a barbecue grill whose hollow belly made a bath for finches and jays. Some kitchen tongs still hung from the handle of the grill, while between its slender legs spread a moist patch of mint. Standing there, looking, was when I unsealed the letter for the very first time, hesitating just a minute before reading it through. It seemed a shame not to do this in light of the circumstances, that is, I'd have to send it back to Erie, and then they'd send it back to me, and then I'd send it back to them, and on and on forever like a word not spoken, that kind of thing. I plucked a mint leaf for nibbling while walking home reading of Deets, whoever he is.

Or was.

The two stick-women, it occurs to me today, might share not just one man but two – Deet and Deet – and in that case share twice the misdemeanor having left both Deets at once just to move to wherever. Still I see no proper course but to mail the letter back to Erie this minute. Stevie likes to mail letters, as all children do, so I put him in the stroller, let him hold it in his lap, and set out for the mailbox at the corner of our road. Being a TLC, I should have known it had been dismantled. Taken away, really. There's a storage alcove in the basement of the post office, strewn about with moldy mail sacks and heavy-duty staplers, but no postal boxes. Perhaps they sell them at auction along with the jeeps. Meanwhile in my chest beats that sensation peculiar to the delivery of a letter – generosity, purpose, impatience – but the mailbox is gone. In its place is the cement pillar upon which it had stood, all covered with moss. It must have been there all along in the shelter of the box, home for brittle-shelled snails no larger than droplets of water. How *eternal* it looks, like a few other objects I've noticed of late around town. They look like ruins, as if they'll be here forever, after everything else is gone. There's the water fountain with the dandelion growing out of the drain, and the electric sockets fitted to some trees in the quadrant of the square where, before the fiscal cutbacks, festivals had taken place. The best is a sign – one of those standard, institutional signs designating the names and functions of campus buildings – only this has only an arrow stenciled on it. No name. No function. The arrow points along a paved path running between some low brick dormitories, and that's where Stevie wants to go, when our search for a mailbox proves unsuccessful. The one on Professor and Forest is gone, and so is the one on Elm.

IF WALKING, as an anthropologist once said to me, is really nothing more than controlled falling, then Stevie's halfway there. I try telling him this but it makes him more frustated then he was before. He knows what's in store, and he knows what it will bring him – independence, adventure, a body that can think with its legs and not only with its mind – but his feet won't listen yet, they stumble, they trip, they won't hold him up, they fail him. Lately, he sits forward in the stroller straining like a coachman at the reigns of a carriage, trying to make me take him where he wants us to go. Several hundred yards along the path he points eagerly into the grass, so we veer off the sidewalk and loll around under a shade tree. I pop a licorice lozenge and suck on it carefully so as not to dispel the abandoned, cooling quiet of the clustered dormitories. Near the stoops are some flowerbeds piled with woodchips adorned with small, round, feathery plants. I lay Stevie's palm on top of one; it's soft as the head of a beer. The dorms are all locked, and in the few rooms whose drapes are not thoroughly closed there are nothing but stripped beds and dressers. I recall having been in this courtyard before, just once, pre-Stevie at some kind of all-staff picnic where Frisbees buzzed over the tops of the food-laden tables. It was August and the dorms had been opened for airing; small children played in the polished hallways, and we sat on the steps drinking Strohs and feeling the heat. The restrooms were co-ed, and at the door to one was where we first met Mike, of Mike-and-Angela, our friends who have since moved away to Chicago. Mike would not let us in. That is, he would open the door for me but not for Daniel, because his wife was inside.

"But these restrooms are co-ed," I explained.

"We know," said Mike.

"I just finished three bottles of beer," said Daniel.

"How long is she going to be in there?" I asked, feeling affection, suddenly, for both of them: for Daniel, who needed to go to the bathroom, who bounced clownishly on the balls of his feet, and for this strange, new chivalrous husband inappropriately dressed in a long-sleeved, button-down shirt.

Then the door swung inward and Angela walked out, blushing when she saw us.

That blush is still vivid, pink as can be, sudden and sharp as my first, surprise bite of the licorice lozenge. Our friendship went like this: they introduced us to their dogs, who'd spent that evening in a pen. The dogs were knee-high. Three sides of the pen were of fencing, but the fourth was a side of the house. The dogs had been eating the shingles; tearing them, chewing them, spitting them out. Even so, Mike fed them hamburger brought home from the picnic, then led them inside where from the couch they witnessed our first midnight game of Monopoly. Our tokens were makeshift and personal; Angela always used one of my earrings. All things considered, their leave-taking was ordinary as leave-takings go; they knew they were moving, and we knew it too, and so did the dogs, who ate the handles off the camp trunks along with a pile of packed kitchen towels. They stopped by our house as they drove out of town, Angela at the wheel, Mike passing milkbones back to the dogs so they wouldn't bite the top off the gear shift knob. The tape deck was whirring – Books on Tape – and the motor was on, so we stood in the road and leaned in through the windows for kisses and hugs. Then we stayed there and watched as the car drove away. But around the block it went and came back for more goodbyes.

This happened once, twice, over and over.

The woman on the tape said, "Keep the pressure gentle, working the fingers in circles."

And then, "by kneading the flesh of either buttock exactly as if you were preparing bread for –"

And then, "from the genitals, between the buttocks, up the spine and onto the back of the neck."

The dog biscuits were gone, but the dogs were only drooling, their spit making pools on the chewed seat covers.

"We'll miss you," I said, sixth or seventh time round.

"We already miss you," said Mike. He spread his fingers on Angela's knee. When he gave it a squeeze she put her foot on the gas, and that time they didn't come back. We retreated to the porch swing and cried, a little.

I cried, anyway. Daniel never does. He gets logical, solemn, and cool.

"If they had never lived here, then we never would have gotten to know them," he said, or something like that, and fished our car keys from my pocket and gave them to Stevie. Stevie was an infant. He touched the keys to his tongue, then dropped them through the porch slats onto the dirt. Neither one of us moved to retrieve them. Two years later the feeling is different; it's not like missing Leah and seeing her negative shape, and longing for it to be filled. In fact I don't miss them at all, I realize with sadness. I only miss missing them. When did this happen? Two years from now I'll miss missing Leah, and I'll miss missing missing Mike and Angela.

SUDDENLY it's nearly dusk, and the sky has a tornado look about it: buff-colored, distant, still. We get back on the path and follow it resolutely, cutting past some more dorms before the pavement abuts at a curb. No arrow at this end, but Stevie points across the road at a mailbox. Not until I've got the chute open do I realize Deets' letter is no longer in Stevie's hand, and that it's not in my pocket or wedged in the seat of the stroller. So we bang the chute shut and cross the road again, looking everywhere into the fast-falling darkness, even into the rooms with the half-drawn drapes, at the bare, striped ticking of the mattress covers.

Now the wind has picked up, a bit here, a bit there, whipping the pale, frothy tops of the plants. *Poor Deets* says the wind, *Poor stick-figured women,* until we reach our street and find Daniel seated on one of the card chairs, quiet as anything, eating an apple. He won't look at me but he takes Stevie in his arms and holds him close to his chest. He looks shocked, like Ben; at once I know he thought we'd disappeared.

"Tell Daddy we were mailing a letter," I whisper into Stevie's curls. "Tell him we've been on our way home."

"Fine," Daniel says.

He pats the chair next to his so we sit side by side and stare into the curtain of sky. He must have figured it out, I am thinking, but only to an extent. He knows the women leave first, but not that they mostly leave children behind, with lovers, with husbands, with grandparents, with friends. I almost tell him, *Don't worry, I won't take him from you,* but of course I can't say that; it's too awful a thought. If I had been by myself, and if I hadn't lost the letter, and if the mailbox hadn't been there I might have kept right on walking, not following the road but the vast playing fields on the opposite side, that end overlooking a highway.

If, I am thinking. *If, If, If.*

And then, *What if?*

P A R T   T H R E E

Stewing

ONLY WHEN I am seeing my doctor do I realize for the first time how tired I've been; a relentless fatigue like the fatigue of pregnancy, the limbs wrapped in near-palpable, cottony substance to be pushed aside with every minor gesture, every flicker of the eyelids, every turn of the head. At first I blame it on my walking but very soon I know that I've got it mixed up; it's not the walking that is causing the fatigue but the fatigue that is making me walk even further than I need to, because I don't want it to suck me under.

"It's like an excess of gravity," I say to my doctor. "It must be the weather, the humidity."

When I was pregnant I blamed the weather, too, before I knew. It was summer, hot and damp, and each afternoon I napped helplessly on our low bed before the whirring, ticking fan, dreaming of jungles. At dinnertime I rose, found Daniel, and together we sauntered downtown for an ice cream to be eaten on a bench on the square. When friends passed on the road we waved our ice cream sticks in greeting, talked, hung out, then dispersed, went home, and barbecued chicken or burgers. By ten o'clock I was sleeping again, my body dissolved in a pool of heat in which it lay as though limbless, and when at midnight Daniel climbed ever so gently into bed it was as if a tree had fallen on top of me.

"You all right?" he would whisper.

I'd be slick with sweat, but inside, thirsty as a rock.

"Turn the fan on," I'd tell him, kicking the sheets to the floor.

"It's on."

"Bring me some water."

He did, always, and when I sat up and drank, water spilled in two streams from the flacid edges of my mouth and over the secretive shape of my belly. My ankles felt tangled in air, which to me felt no cooler than the record-breaking June of our arrival in town six years earlier. Then, we'd driven in from St. Louis at midnight, pulling a U-haul, car windows rolled down to let in the seared smell of lightning. There was neither moon nor stars. And no street lamps, either. Just a few scattered porch lights up and down the town, and then a sheet of white lightning that gave us a glimpse of the square. How stark and flat it looked, but studded with trees, like a forest with no undergrowth. We drove several times around it before finding the street on which we were supposed to be living, and each time around there was lightning and a glimpse of the negative spaces flashing among the trees. Our apartment was the second story of a house whose first floor was already occupied; in the stairwell was a desk with a gooseneck lamp, some papers and books, an ashtray, a smell of cigarettes. On our door was a note, folded and taped, whose message – Call if you need help or food, or anything – irked me, so that my first thought upon opening the door was, Why do these people think we'll need help? Why do they think we won't have enough food? Why do they think we'll need anything, even? and my first thought upon stepping into the room was, Oh. Here's why.

Because it was so horrible. Unpainted, with filthy windows, and the light bulbs bare on the cracked ceiling.

"Oh, Daniel," I said, but he was carrying up our sleeping bags. We were to sleep in a room with two curtainless windows, so with every flash of lighting I saw the dirt on the panes. All night was like that – the heat, the humidity, the dry inside of my mouth at the sight of that filmy glass.

"Bring me some water," I said to Daniel, just to talk, but Daniel said our cups were still packed in the trunk of the car.

So I went into the kitchen, naked, barefoot on corroded linoleum. I can't live in this town, I thought as I switched on the light. Which blew out with the start of another big round of lightning by which I found the cupboard and the single, plastic cup. I turned on the hot water and rinsed that cup for maybe five minutes before I dared drink from it, and then I carried it into the bedroom and sat, and drank, and gazed at the black space made by the empty closet, and listened for mice, and wondered how Daniel could sleep.

"How can you sleep?" I said to him.

"I can't. Not with you asking me questions."

"How can we live in this town?"

"I don't know," he said, and turned over and slept. There was another round of lightning and I noticed some blinds on the windows. I pulled them down.

In the morning I remembered the note on our door. We need breakfast, I thought. We need light bulbs, curtains, sponges, buckets, mops, brooms and anything else you can give us.

But we had no telephone. No toilet paper, even. Mouse droppings lined the drawers of the built-in cupboards.

We dressed, went out, found a perfectly normal-seeming hot summer morning in which the tree-studded square, so eerie the night before, looked green and nearly cool. That day we unpacked, got a telephone, called a window washer. Played house for a while, was what it felt like. Not until the week had passed did we phone the people who had written us the note, to thank them.

"Is this Ben and Leah?" said Daniel, to the woman who answered the phone.

She invited us for drinks. In the kitchen was a shelf stacked with mugs of all colors and sizes. There was beer, wine, tea, tomato juice, orange juice, lemonade or gin and tonic, said Ben and Leah.

Gin and tonic, said Daniel.

Tea, I said.

"Please," said Ben

We looked at him.

"Say please," said Ben.

My tea was iced, in a mug. The mug was wet with condensation. When Leah handed it over, the ghosts of her fingers were still apparent. We sat outside under a weeping willow, sharing two recliners and a blanket. Daniel and Ben had one recliner to themselves. Straddling it, face to face, they were talking about comics; about which strips the local paper carried, and which they thought were funny, and which they thought weren't. I said to Leah, "That's how men get to know each other, by talking about *things.* It's like they're haying a game of catch."

"I know," said Leah. "It's cute, isn't it."

We looked at them indulgently and smiled and then just sat, quietly, happily, as if in imitation of our friendship to come, a friendship bound by its beginning, a day under a willow watching the sporty volley of our men's conversation. Leah and I have never had that much to say to each other simply because there is little that needs to be said. We are like women sharing a room in the maternity ward of a hospital, who, having had their babies, proceed to nurse, diaper, receive visitors in unison then pass each other going to or from the bathroom, adjusting sanitary pads on the way and then in privacy applying squirts of Betadine to their identical stitches, their identical, burning crotches. In fact Leah and I, when we finally had Simon and Stevie, shared not a room but a stick of cocoa butter for massaging onto sore nipples. Leah's were cracked; I know because I heard Ben telling Daniel about it one day on another of our shared picnics. Leah heard him, too, so she knew that I knew, and that was what was important. Our two families, over time, formed a bond like the corners of a cardboard box; simple but necessary, as if the comfortable shape of our friendship existed solely because the box was there to contain it. Even the children came to know what to expect of each other; when Simon threw himself on Stevie, pummeled him and knocked him to the ground, not even Stevie was surprised. He pulled himself up, stuck out his lower lip and attached himself to another of Simon's toys while Leah and I sat and watched and listened and sipped our tea.

"Weird tea," said Daniel, that very first day when I gave him a sip.

"The stuff's wicked," said Ben. "How do these women drink it?"

"Don't ask me."

"Don't ask us, either," said Leah, and they didn't, and we went on sipping, sipping. Which is how we were, together. If Daniel and Ben went out to play pool, Leah and I stayed home, apart in our separate houses but together in our welcome solitude. At midnight sometimes, we'd phone each other.

"Must have gone out for a drink."

"Yep."

"Night, Leah."

"Night, Liz." Then back to our books, our thinking, our dishes, our tea, our letters, our showers, and when we were pregnant, our fierce, shared exhaustion.

"When Leah climbs steps, her hands cramp up," we heard Ben say to Daniel.

"Liz fell asleep at the post office," said Daniel. "She has a special cot there to lie down on in the safe."

"In the safe?"

"In the safe."

"With the 'Cash On Deliveries,'" I'd tell Leah, and that would be all, because the rest she would already know. How the tiredness felt, like wine in the veins, so that lying there I floated in the mildew-scented safe inert as the CODs.

As I did again today, three years later. The cot had mail sacks on it that I had to move out of the way, and when I lay down I felt like one of them, so lumpy and insensate that the news circulating out in the mailroom failed to excite me; there'd been another "attack," people were saying, like the one on George in the post office lobby, only this one had been in the bank, but just as brutal, just as sudden and pointless and desperate and quick as lightning so there were no witnesses, only the victim who had a broken rib, who said the guy had "kicked him out of nowhere" and then run off. When it was over, the street was empty like before.

"Makes me tired just to hear about it," I thought, and lay looking at the shelves of the safe and sniffing the mildew. I dug around in my pocket, pulled out a licorice toffee, then fell asleep chewing it.

When I woke I said to no one, "Bring me some water."

And rose, and went into the mailroom where it was closing time, where the shutters were drawn, the fan just ticking to a stop. Someone banged shut the door of the safe, and I knew that had I not wakened I would have been locked inside.

"SO THAT'S what's happening," I explain, yawning, to my doctor. "It's the weather, I think."

Dr. Kirshner says, "Maybe it is. Maybe it isn't."

"The humidity," I add.

"Could be." She seems more preoccupied than usual, a bit tense, actually. I don't blame her. While sitting in the waiting room I heard her on the phone at the receptionist's desk. The waiting room was empty except for myself, and the receptionists were gone, and the files hung stiff and untouched in their racks. The doctor was booking a night flight to London, although midway she started asking about Paris as well. Then, London again. Her lover, a tax consultant, lives not far from us in a house whose lower half he has converted into an office. I picture him up in his bedroom, changing pinstriped sheets, unaware of the fact that his lover has booked herself a one-way ticket to London. I wonder, Why London? of all places on earth.

"Do you have anything you want to talk about?" I almost ask, but don't, realizing that she is my doctor, that I am her patient, that the question would go answered, anyway.

"Why am I so bloody bushed?" I ask instead in my best Londonese, but get no clue in return, no spark, no lift of the eyebrows, just her skilled, gloved fingers probing my vagina at which task she is appropriately, tactfully silent. Male doctors always start small-talking the second they make the plunge, as if, were they not asking me what movies I'd seen lately I might think they were putting a move on me. Doctor Kirshner squints, cocks her head as if listening to the scrape of the swab on my cervix, then withdraws the instrument, performs a few palpations on belly, breasts, underarms. "Hold your breath," she instructs, and I'm reminded of the Doberman's sloppy attention, and then of Daniel in his by-now familiar push-up posture, our bodies not touching, his worried eyes traveling the naked planes of my torso. Planes, not curves, but a torso undeniably female in the way it has learned to accommodate itself to this particular choreography. Every woman's life is graced by this same pas de deux, her healthy body supine under the scrutiny of another living being. As a rule, men don't undergo this, unless they are sick. Daniel, as far as I know, has never lain belly-up under the gaze of a doctor, practically naked, having to answer questions about feature-length films. I told the last gynecologist who asked me my favorite, "An autopsy flick for pre-meds at the college. A little slow, and the guy was deadpan but convincing."

It was then I switched to Dr. Kirshner, who to her credit has never mentioned that my uterus is tilted. Dr. Kirshner has a crease between her eyebrows, blonde hair cut in mild, abbreviated spikes, and a stethoscope with glow-in-the-dark ear pieces. We've joked that her examining gloves should be phosphorescent, too, but it's a joke that the doctor doesn't take seriously; her sense of good fun goes only so far. Today she maintains an introspective air, as if her finger in my rectum might be grazed, unpredictably, by one of life's sharp truths. I wonder how impatient she is for whatever awaits her in London, and think sadly that this might be the last chance we have to examine each other. Already, I miss her, although we've never once spoken outside of the office. It seems to me I can't look at another woman without wanting to be her friend; otherwise, when she's gone, I might forget all about her and she about me, and then, what will have been the point? The point of what? I think. Of anything, of all our hearts and souls, and reaching down I wrap my fingers around the wrist of her still-gloved, still-exploring hand.

"Sorry," she says, "Did I hurt you?"

"No. I mean yes. A little."

"You're fine," she says, and removes the glove and drops it into the wastebasket. The basket is empty except for that glove. The parking lot, too, was empty, as were the slots in the appointment book open on the desk.

"I'm tired," I say. "I didn't menstruate last month."

"You might be a little depressed now and then, without even really knowing that you are. That happens sometimes," says Dr. Kirshner.

"I don't think so," I say. I'm wishing we'd get to the point. Part of me wants to, part of me doesn't. A urine test, I'm thinking, but the doctor is still distractedly talking.

"You might not be drinking enough water," she is saying. "Fatigue is commonly associated with thirst."

"I drink tons of ice tea," I tell her.

"Tea is a diuretic."

"I drink licorice tea."

At this the doctor perks up; the very spikes of her hair begin trembling eagerly.

"Licorice tea. Hang on. Back in a jiff," and then she smiles and walks out the door leaving me to contemplate the British lilt of her "Back in a jiff" along with the notion that if it is possible to be thirsty without knowing it, and if it's possible to be depressed without knowing it, then it must be possible to be *anything* without knowing it. Well, almost anything, I think, pulling on my clothing in the curtained enclave, then pausing, finding a paper towel, wiping myself dry of petroleum jelly, of sweat, of–yes–desire. Is it possible to be desirous all the time without knowing it? I think of asking the doctor, when she bolts back in waving a sheaf of papers.

"You say you've been tired?" she asks.

I nod.

"Amenorrhoea?"

"Excuse me?"

The doctor sighs impatiently.

"Skipped periods," she answers.

"Yes. Well, one."

"Bloating? Achey limbs?"

"I haven't noticed," I say.

She looks disappointed.

"A little headache now and then, recently," I realize.

"Right," says Dr. Kirshner, scanning her papers. "How much do you eat?"

"Varies. Depending on what we can track down. Lots of zucchini, lately, and croissants, pates, imported marmalades, and–"

"No. I mean licorice. How much in a day?"

"A lot."

"A lot."

"Yes."

"Cut it out," says the doctor.

"Cut what out?"

"Cut the licorice out of your diet. At once. You are suffering its effects."

"What effects?"

"Mineralocorticoid," says the doctor resolutely. "Low potassium, high salt. Do your eyes hurt, yet?"

"No."

"Are you repelled by light?"

"Never," I say. "Are you sure you think you're on the right track? Do you think maybe I could be–"

"That's fine. Very good. Throw the licorice away. You could end up in hospital."

In hospital, I think. Daniel won't believe this.

THE FOOTPATH that was gone, the time I looked for it with Danka, is here the very second I arrive at the plateau, with Stevie in the backpack, pointing the way. It opens just on the opposite side of the tracks, like a doorway that somehow was closed on that earlier afternoon and now stands hospitably open. At the spot where Joe turned to me and tipped his cap, I pause to examine the plunge of the trail. It drops at an angle of around sixty degrees over hard-packed earth, stone, and tree root, winding this way and that among straight trunks and half-embedded boulders awash in blue shadow. There are no footprints.

At the base of the slope, the trail swings left into a broad open stretch that I recognize at once as part of the college's long-abandoned arboretum. A formal array of Asiatic magnolias, planted opposite one another along what was once a gravel footpath, makes a passageway from near to far. At the end the trail detours the dense pokeroot border that I once explored with Daniel. There we found the ruins of a medicinal garden left to time and weather, its triangulated pathways nearly lost beneath an overgrowth of grass, periwinkle, and catnip. The pokeroot must have made the border, with the yarrow just inside, and with the triangles, Daniel supposed, planted according to use and property: one for gout, one for bites, burns and poisons, one for digestion.

"And one for sleep aids," I guessed.

"And childbirth," said Daniel.

"And aphrodisiacs," I said, and plucked a stalk of sweet cicely and made love to him with it so that when we were done he smelled faintly of–what?–I can't remember, and today there's none growing. Instead I pause for a look at the pokeroot flowers –the slender, tapered clusters–before continuing on through the arboretum past a row of water spigots among lichen-covered rocks. Stevie, squealing, points up a slope into some woods again. It's not steep, just a gradual slide, and the forest thins out as it reaches the crest. Just ahead under a hedge apple tree stands a little greenhouse no larger than the bed of a pick-up.

At once I know that this is where Joe is living, so I walk straight up to it, casually and eagerly as if I know no such thing at all, as if I'm thinking it's only a potting shed and feel like looking at the pots.

Of which there are quite a few all of varying sizes, all terra cotta, in stacks on either side of the door. The top half of the structure is glass, including the levered roof. Along the east-facing wall have been tacked strips of burlap of indeterminate color, all faded and water-stained.

Cute, I am thinking. Joe doesn't want the dawn to wake him up. He likes to sleep late – sleep good – he would say, fondling himself, curled up in his Cro-Magnon nakedness on his bedroll of coarse army blankets, a sack of wood chips for a pillow.

He must get splinters in his ear. He must get splinters in his skull unless he sleeps with his cap on.

He must keep a kerosene lantern.

He does.

And a camp stove.

Yes.

And a pallet for Eva the dog.

Yes.

And a sink, a washcloth, a roll of toilet paper, a shelf of books, and underneath, a pink laundry basket piled with clothes.

Cute, I'm thinking. And what does he eat?

No evidence of that. I'm glad, anyway, remembering the slingshot. No pelts, no bones, no paws, no stink.

Maybe Eva buries the remains.

No can opener, even. Just a knife, a plate, and a box of kitchen matches.

And a bottle of Red Devil Louisiana Hot Sauce.

No salt, no fork, and a citrus crate for a table.

On the table, a placemat from Disneyworld.

Cute, I think. Just what I would have guessed from a man like

Joe. He grunts, he sees, he wants, he takes, but he doesn't want much, just enough to get by. Just enough to survive. Just enough, I am thinking, looking at the bedroll and the woodchip pillow – to share.

WHEN DANIEL asks where we've been I tell him there seems to be somebody camped out in the greenhouse behind the old arb.

"You mean to tell me you seem to have been snooping around," says Daniel.

"I mean to tell you it seems to be public property," I say. "I mean to tell you it seems to be made of glass. I mean to tell you I let Stevie point the way. I mean to tell you it seemed pretty interesting."

"I'm sure it did," says Daniel.

I tell him there were books, that the books were big and frayed, and that hanging from a nail is one of those chains carved out of a single block of wood. I describe the rust stains in the sink, the algae on the windows, the dampness of the floor. Deliberating, I tell him also about the caps – one painter's, one trucker's – that sat on top of the laundry basket.

I don't tell him that I recognized both caps, or that the books were printed in German. They appeared to be war diaries, their spines ribbed and threadbare, their pulpy frontispieces adorned with tinted photographs of bearded and uniformed men.

Nor can I bring myself to tell Daniel about the strange vase of flowers, which I would have missed had it not been for Stevie, for it was Stevie who saw it as we walked out the door, and squealed until he got my attention. Daniel probably would think nothing of it, would go on doing what he's doing and forget what I'd told him by the time I had finished; he is in any case thoroughly engrossed in the project at hand, an examination of female floral parts under the gaze of the dissecting microscope. I am reminded of me and my doctor. Having sliced open a style he examines it for evidence of successful matings – the grains of pollen having sprouted, the slender tubules gaining access to the ovaries. This particular female appears to have been unyielding; Daniel grunts, nudges the slide with the tip of the dissecting needle, moves on in search of more receptive tissue.

He takes it personally, I know. We collected these flowers together. In the field recently we've developed a rhythm like the rhythm of sex – a slow, measured descent into the damp part of the woods where the jewelweed proliferates, a careful inspection of the site while we check to see if any blossoms have been eaten, trampled, or otherwise trespassed or violated, and then again to see what wilted, what dropped, collapsed, withered. After that, more hurriedly, we assume our positions, Daniel here, myself there, and begin impatiently the act itself as if after foreplay, plucking and peeling, then touching blossom to blossom over and over in a rhythm reminiscent of Daniel's kisses in the hollow of my neck. Afterwards, we are damp, thirsty, sticky, tired, and climbing up from the patch, wordless.

"There were some wildflowers in the greenhouse, too," is all I finally tell him.

"What kind," he asks. Hunched over the UV light, his face has a worried, lavender cast.

"Some umbel. I don't know."

Grunt, grunt. Nudge, nudge.

"In a really weird vase," I continue weakly.

Daniel glances up at me, gives a little nod, lowers his pursed lips closer to the specimen.

Instead, I'll tell Nikki about the vase.

But carefully, in keeping with the newly enforced silence about her house; when she shuts the door after me, it is with such cunning that the hardware never clicks, and then she leads the way on stockinged feet into the living room where she perches on the edge of the coffee table.

When she crosses her legs, the sheer, nylon layers of her sari whisper around her ankles.

I sit on the beanbag chair, which farts magnificently even under my scant weight. Nikki raises her eyebrows and offers me a handful of the miniature marshmallows her brother brings over. Coming in, I glanced into the kitchen and noticed on the counter the preparations for her lunch; a little platter of tofu, sliced egg, and dressing. Not a thing that makes a sound when it is chewed. No wonder her garden has been so full. Nikki has lost some weight, I see now as I look her full in the face; the tilt of her cheekbones more pronounced, the fine shape of her skull more delicate, somehow, beneath the heavily beaded tug of the braids. She eats only one of the candies, solemnly chewing while I tell her about the greenhouse.

"There was this really weird vase," I begin. "I don't know if I told you about the day Stevie and I went raspberry picking. We were up near the tracks, on that high plateau, and we were picking berries but we had nothing to put them in except – Have you ever been out to the old arboretum?" I ask.

A shake of the head.

"Did you know it was there?"

Another shake of the head, a shrug.

"So we went back there today, me and Stevie. I'd been out there before with Daniel but not in years, and this time I found that greenhouse and I –"

Nikki's still shaking her head, and when I've paused I can hear that she's saying something under her breath. "That bastard," she's saying. "That bastard, that bastard."

Her brother's name is Dewey, I know.

"You doing all right, Nikki?"

A smile, and after that she asks "Want to hear something?"

"Sure."

She takes her place at the keyboard, switches a switch, flicks back the loose sleeves of her sari, slides a disk in the slot and having readied her hands at the keys, starts playing. The beaded braids sway just a little, but her eyelids never flutter, they just stay half-closed, and there's that same, pained expression on her face. From what, I can only guess. Not music, I hope, because there isn't a sound coming out of her speakers. Not a note, not a trill, not even the whir of the technology.

"I don't know a thing about music," I say nervously when she's done, and Nikki grins in my face before leading me to the tv and showing me what happens when we turn it on – nothing.

Same with the lights.

Same with the washing machine, the clothes dryer, the hair dryer in her bathroom. She holds it up, I press the button, nothing happens, no air, no buzz, no whir.

"Oh," I say, "I thought maybe you were losing your – "

Her what? Her mind?

"I thought maybe you were losing your hearing," I say.

"I wish," Nikki says.

So I don't tell Nikki about the flowers, either, but maybe that's just as well. After all it was only what anyone would put flowers in when they didn't have a vase. It was the body of the doll, with the drying purple flowers pin-wheeling out of the headless neck. Joe had been careful to pour in water, but the water had seeped from the hole in the doll's crotch and made a puddle between her feet. I imagine Joe returning to the greenhouse to find the wilted flowers, then, puzzled, holding the neck to the rusty tap. Even balancing the doll attentively on her chewed toes he doesn't notice the puddle growing before his eyes but instead settles down to the preparation of his dinner as just at this moment Daniel and I settle down to the preparation of our own. We're having stewed zucchini from Nikki's garden, and more croissants from the Epicurean. Also, a jar of tiny marinated onions. The croissants are filled with almond paste, presenting a dilemma: dinner, or dessert? Perhaps I should have told Dr. Kirshner more about this new, imposed diet: smoked oysters, guava jelly, creamy spreadable cheeses and canned patés, chutneys, even a jar of lemon paste that I don't know what to do with, eat it with a spoon, maybe, or spread it on toast although we don't have toast, just Carr's Water Biscuits. We get fruit only every so often, when the wild berries ripen or when the Washington Apple basket in the Epicurean is restocked, and these days we're eyeing our cherry tree, shooing birds from contemplation of the hard pink sour spheres although I have no sugar to cook them in. All the markets have closed for eighteen miles around, and even Danka's finicky William had trouble recently finding bottles of tonic water. I told him they might have some at the Epicurean. They have licorice, at least; yesterday I bought Dutch, in leathery black guilders, which turn out to be chalky, not sweet, but licorice just the same, the black mineral flavor like sucking a lozenge of coal. I've got a five-guilder coin in my mouth this minute – a secret from Daniel – as I scrub some of Nikki's zucchinis. Daniel slices them up, dropping bite-sized strips into Stevie's mouth. Stevie eats even onions, and whole green beans, but never those yellow embryonic peppers we discover now and then inside the hollows of the big green ones, like curled-up Easter chicks.

"What do you think about fish," I ask Daniel, who doesn't understand me with the guilder in my cheek.

"What do you think about fishing?" I repeat. "People do it, you know, at the reservoir."

"At the woolywoo?"

"At the reservoir." I slide the licorice under my tongue. Captured like that, the burnt flavor swells like a sponge.

"Blue gills?" says Daniel. "Sorry. I like my fish to fight back when I reel them in. I'd rather buy a new car."

"You would?"

"Well. . . " he says, and meets my eye, because he knows I know how much he likes the romance of living like this, with only a bike and a backpack to scavenge for food. Our legs are sinewy, our shoulders solidly reassuring, our son a blonde cupid pink-lipped from wild raspberries. Only our bellies show the jars of Macadamia nuts, the cartons of Haagen Daz.

"Anyway a car is too much of a pain in the neck," says Daniel. "Besides, what about those clippings?"

"What clippings?"

"Excuse me?"

"What clippings?"

"Those *clippings.*"

"Oh." I remember I showed him my stash, a paperclipful of order forms from Harry and David, Hormel, Hartwell's Gourmet Gifts, Omaha Steaks. If the Epicurean folds, and when Nikki's garden gives out, we can order whole banquets from here and there provided there's somebody left to deliver. Sides of beef, whole smoked salmon, cartons of tangelos, of kumquats, of coconut paste. I wonder, what do you do with coconut paste? The same thing you do with lemon paste? And what about tea?

"What about tea?" I ask Daniel.

"Harry and David have tea, I bet."

"Maybe."

"Probably," says Daniel.

"Possibly."

"Excuse me?" says Daniel.

"POSSIBLY POSSIBLY POSSIBLY" I yell, spitting licorice juice like chewing tobacco all over Daniel's julienne strips of zucchini.

Silence.

Daniel sweeps the zucchini into a colander and showers it with tap water.

Then he sets the colander on the cutting board, and puts his hands not-quite-on-my-shoulders. Just about, but not quite.

He's about to be diplomatic.

"I have a feeling it might be worthwhile to remind you that your doctor pointed out to you that this sweet tooth of yours seems to be interfering with your health," he suggests.

"I have a feeling it might be worthwhile to point out to you that Dutch licorice is chalky, not sweet. Besides, I seem to have a craving for it, Daniel."

Besides, I have to stop myself from saying, I can live with aches and pains, with thirst and fatigue, but if I can't have licorice to fill me up, I'll be hungry for something else instead. For something more elemental. For something primitive, Daniel. For the thing that makes me hungry in the first place, Daniel. You don't want to know, you'd be appalled, I could say. *I* should be appalled, but still I can't stop thinking of it. Of him. I'd do his ears, first, then his bald head, then every inch of his backbone straight down to his combat pants. I'd chew on the camouflage, then crawl under the sink and swallow him whole while he skins and trusses our dinner.

Our squirrel.

Joe would be careful to skin it over the sink, then lay it flat on its pelt to drain it, behead it, de-paw it, de-muck it. He'd feed the globules of fat along with the innards to Eva, but outside, in the spoon-shaped cleft in the flat rock to the left of the hedge apple tree. Then he'd slide in a skewer from anus to neck, and hold the animal over the fire pit while rolling the skewer evenly between the palms of his callused hands.

We'd eat it sitting outside; a single plate, no napkins, and the bottle of Red Devil Louisiana Hot Sauce. Later, in bed, we'd be all grease, all pepper, all soot, all thirst.

Through the gaps in the windows we'd hear Eva at her spoon-shaped trough in the rock under the hedge apples, munching bones. Her approach would be practiced and delicate; having split a bone in half she'd lure the marrow onto the tip of her tongue, the bone upright between her paws, her tail rigid with concentration. She would have eaten the head in similar fashion, the soft tissues licked out of the skull while close by on our blanket of scratchy wool we mimicked her sighs and sucks, her groans, thumps, and pauses. Every so often she'd stop what she was doing and listen warily for noises from the woods and the trails, for the snap of a branch, the rustle of dry grass, but there would be nothing – no coyote, no fox, no feral dog – only the peculiar silence of all three of us listening, lying in wait. Joe would keep his pocketknife close at his side, and at these intervals he'd stroke it. But then the ritual would come to a close; Eva returning to her bones, Joe turning to me with meaty tongue; soon he'd flip on his back, lift me up on the palms of his hands, lower my body precisely onto his own.

Later, in sleep, he'd insist on the dead weight of me lying across his chest, and would not allow me to turn on my back to look at the moon through the algae-streaked glass of the greenhouse roof. Instead I'd watch the glint of moonlight on my earrings swinging from the chewed fingers of his flower vase, the very thought of which fills me with anguish so persuasive that

Daniel's fistful of chopped vegetables stops mid-air over the sizzle of the wok as he turns to me and asks what's the matter.

Stevie, who on the floor fills his own pot with invisible zucchinis, pauses too in imitation and looks at me.

"Nothing. Just hungry," I say, and think of Joe at this instant unfolding his pocketknife while between the legs of the doll the little puddle spreads incrementally. Still he doesn't notice that it's there, so absorbed is he in the scraping of his knife blade across the pelt of a squirrel, in the snugness of the cap upon his head, in the view through the glass of the bunches of hedge apples bobbing on the limbs of the tree. So intent is he on the solitariness of the moment, so contented with his reclusive, far-fetched abode that when he's thirsty it's never beer he wants or even water but just the feel of the tin camper's cup against his lips. It's the cup that he ordered from a hunting magazine. When he reaches for it, that's when he first sees the puddle, and then the doll's damp legs and the hole in her crotch. How appalled he is – how embarrassed – by this fact of the doll's anatomy; how could he not have noticed, how could he have overlooked, and now, what to do with her? Throw her out the window? Banish her? But in the end he only stuffs up the hole with a thread pulled from the splitting seam of his combat pants, refills her with water, rearranges the flowers, and restores himself with another glance at the mute, misshapen hedge apples, enough to assure him that he is still alone, unbothered, unmated, isolated as he intends to be.

"Actually, since you asked, I'm bummed out because Nikki shut off her electricity and I won't be able to hear when she's playing her music," I lie to my husband, and pour a beakerful of strictly rationed soy sauce into the wok as he drops in the last of the zucchini.

"Why'd she do a thing like that?" he asks.

"Privacy," I tell him. I pick Stevie up and rock him.

SEVERAL NIGHTS LATER I come home from a late night meeting at the post office (we're discussing shrinking routes, depleted staff, depleted need, depleted inventory, and we always hold our meetings late at night because even though our supervisor left town, she was a night owl and we all got used to it) and since I'm not quite ready to go to sleep, myself, I go out to the cherry tree to find the fruits – so late to begin with – already soft between my fingers as I pick. No music from Nikki's studio, of course, but the crickets are humming and now and then someone slams shut the door of a moving van and starts up the engine. Past three a.m. I go inside, rinse the cherries in the colander, set them to drain, have a glass of water, then head for the guest room, stripping in the hallway as I go. No need to wake Daniel upstairs, I'm thinking, as I open the door and just climb into bed. And there's somebody in there, naturally.

Under the sheets in the darkness.

NOT ARNIE, although at first I think that's who it must be, a man asleep on his belly, his hands hidden under the pillow and just the top of his head exposed by the flipped-back sheet. I see a mass of hair, but not Arnie's, not feathery, not tremulous enough to be his.

Not Joe, either, then.

Not bald.

Curly.

Maybe Ben.

Maybe lonely in the house without Leah, Ben made his way over here with little Simon murmuring in a blanket in his arms, and laid Simon asleep in the crib next to Stevie, and talked to Daniel after that – about me, probably, about Daniel's husbandly worries. Just recently, and briefly, Ben hooked up with a group of men whose wives and lovers had, like Leah, disappeared, but the meeting, which took place in a church basement, was unsuccessful according to Ben. "All they did was talk semantics," he said. "Like whether she left *me*, or whether she just *left*, but not whether she might come back." In any case he didn't go to the next of the meetings, but came to Daniel instead and talked about it with him, the two men all the while poking around with the microscope or mixing dyes to be applied to some pollen grains. They work happily together, Ben and Daniel, like boys hunched over a toy, their bodies colliding every so often while reaching simultaneously for a focusing knob.

Leah and I used to spy on them, our arms folded over our chests. They talked about David Letterman, Doonesbury, baseball. Then one would knock a slide off the edge of the counter and the other would catch it before it hit the floor.

For a moment I wish I hadn't missed the sight of their happy camaraderie or of their foreheads banging together over the ocular.

"Cute," I would have said.

And Leah would have answered, "Isn't it."

So it is best I wasn't there, my very posture making visible the fact of Leah's invisibility. Leah's absence is a blind spot in the corners of our eyes, these days. Ben sometimes breaks down and weeps, but momentarily, because he doesn't want Simon to see. When we visit their house, they are always in the backroom playing basketball – the ball is foam rubber, and the basket has a suction cup that holds it to the inside of the door – or else they're on the porch with the scooters and trykes. The rest of the house has an unlived-in look, because the mess doesn't change: same toys, same magazines, same books, same couch cushions knocked off in the same places. Occasionally the television has been left turned-on, or there's a red light blinking on the stereo. Ben doesn't water the plants, and he doesn't clean the toilets, but he's determined to feed himself and Simon well; he cooks lentils from the jars Leah stocked in their kitchen: red lentils, blonde lentils, green. All the while Leah's absence stands tall and narrow in the doorway, relieved that he's getting by.

Ben has a bull neck, but when, carefully, I've peeled back the sheet from the pillow next to mine, I find a neck so smooth and so well-made that for a minute I just lie there admiring it, and trace with my eyes its ascent behind the ear where the flesh is untouched, hairless and tender, until in contemplation I nearly place my finger on that ear and slide it down past the lobe to that vulnerable spot. But then he wakes and flips over, half-sitting up, and I can see how the pony tail was wrapped under his shoulder and I can see how shocked he is to find my hand so close to touching him, no more than an inch from his face.

He smells of croissants. How could I not have noticed?

For a second we lie there like that, and then he lies back on the pillow and blinks up at me.

"Sorry," he says finally, just a little sarcastic. "I know what you're thinking. I didn't do this on purpose, you know."

At once I believe him, because Daniel never lies.

"Guess who's up there," he says, and points in the direction of our bedroom.

"Who?"

"Gail. She's wired; you probably shouldn't go up there till morning."

With that he gazes at me for some time while reaching slowly for one of my earrings: concentric hoops of brass, bronze, silver, and copper. He plays with the four hoops gently until I'm aware of our bodies. His own is taut beneath the sheets, poised mid-signal. Mine just seems to be dissolving. Daniel purses moist lips, then opens them just inches from one of my nipples til I reach out a hand, like a mime's hand designating a wall between us..

Daniel stops.

I think you need to take stock of your body, I remember Emily saying the last time I didn't see her, on that evening we didn't sit together on the bench. There was a little laughter, an exuberant shake of her cheerleader head, a whiff of perfume. What scent was that? I can hardly remember, it's been so long since I haven't smelled it.

Jasmine.

Emily said, *The other day I saw a bed that had been loaded into a moving van. The back of the van was open. The bed was on castors. It was neatly made, the pillows plumped, the pillowcases smoothed, one corner of the blanket folded back. I lay down on it. I needed to. I didn't have a choice.*

Then what, I asked.

Then I waited. says Emily now, tonight.

For what?

I didn't know, says Emily. *That was the point. It was the waiting that was necessary. The anticipation that I needed more than anything. The desire for something to happen, more than the thing itself. So I lay in the van until–*

Daniel sighs, hovering.

Until what? I ask Emily, but there's no answer and besides, as usual she has made her point perfectly well, and my body is in perfect sympathy. In sympathy it balances on the apex of desire not wanting to be fulfilled, like someone standing on the ledge of a building, unable to jump or to climb back in.

"Don't touch me," I whisper to Daniel, so at last he retreats and lies back on the pillow, closing his eyes.

"Seems like I wouldn't mind knowing what seems to be going on," he offers.

His way of asking, Do you love me, or not?

If I could, I would answer, but how can I know? What is the litmus test? What experiment could prove that I do, or don't? And how irrelevant the question, I suddenly decide, knowing Daniel and me. We're two halves of one soul, remember? Asking me if I love him is like asking, Do you love yourself? What does it matter? We live with ourselves. We make do with ourselves. We celebrate ourselves. But love? What kind of problem is that? Who needs to know?

I do, I think.

IN THE MORNING I go upstairs to get us both some clothes. It is just eight o'clock, and Gail is curled under the sheets so I can't see a bit of her. She's got the pillows in there, too, along with a bathtowel whose corner has flopped to the floor. In the bathroom I find a small Japanese print of an erotic nature, hung on the wall under glass, so I suppose that means Gail plans to stick around for a while.

At nine, the bed looks exactly the same, but at ten, one leg has uncovered itself, the foot just teasing the edge of the mattress, the sheet twisted underneath it.

By eleven, that leg has resubmerged, but one arm has pulled free of the wings of the sheet; the whole thing reminds me of Leda and the Swan.

"Her nape is still caught in his bill," I say to Daniel when I've tiptoed back down, and then I tell him what I've seen, the most amazing thing, a man's signet ring that literally slipped off her finger while I watched, centimeter by centimeter.

"I caught it before it hit the floor," I tell him proudly, and then, showing it to him, I see that it's not a signet but a scarab carved from amber. Inside, trapped bubbles. "Finders keepers," I say, so Daniel hunts for a roll of masking tape, wraps a few inches around the band and, with impossible delicacy, so that our hands don't quite touch, slides it onto my middle finger.

At noon I can make out a pillow and Gail's familiar soft afro, the same limp, corkscrew tendrils, but with a faint, ashy rinse to complement the tint of her eyeglasses, which lie open on the windowsill above. By now the whole room smells strongly of sleep, and walking into it I feel my eyes begin to close. When I've steadied myself on the doorjamb to yawn, I'm surprised to hear an answer from the folds of the sheets—another yawn, more protracted, far more murmurous than mine.

"Dazzy sucka ma below," says the yawn, concluding with a pleasurable sigh.

"Gail?" I say, but there is only a crazy flopping under the sheets and then stillness.

At one o'clock, after lunch, all the sheets have been tossed to the floor and Gail lies on her belly in restless sleep, in a nightgown concocted of bridal veils. How like a mermaid she looks, but very nearly out of water, the whole length of her body twitching and flopping as if trying to fall back in.

By the time I leave for work, her frantic breathing has subsided and the smell of sleep has drifted downstairs into the hallway.

I call Daniel from the post office before beginning my route. "Out like a light," he says. And a bit later from a pay phone along the way. "Still nothing," he says. "What's new in the rest of the world?"

"All of King Street is gone," I tell him.

"King Street?" Daniel doesn't have a good ear for names.

"That little court off College Street. You know, four houses, where Mike and Angela used to live except that now their house is moving, too."

"Meaning what?"

"Meaning, they're digging it up. They're moving it."

"Who is?"

"I don't know."

"Where to?"

"I don't know. Daniel, stop being such a scientist. Bring Stevie down to watch. They've got half the foundation uncovered already. I didn't know they still did these things these days. There's a backhoe, and a couple of people standing around with pickaxes. Tell Stevie to bring his shovel."

"Where is it?" says Daniel.

"On King Street, I said."

"No. The shovel."

"Upstairs."

"I'd hate to wake her," says Daniel, but he pedals past my route just a short while later, with Stevie strapped in the bike seat waving his purple shovel, looking innocent and glad. At once I begin to regret; suppose the idea of a moving house is too strange for the grasp of a toddler. Or worse, suppose it seems normal? Suppose he begins to expect it? And suppose, already, that the sight of two people carrying a couch, a table, a bed, across a lawn from house to van is no more surprising to Stevie than, say, the sight, to me at his age, of someone carting bags of groceries up from the car? Suppose *that*. Suppose he's used to it already. Suppose the sight, so familiar, of someone dismantling their home, is actually a comfort to him, a sign of the ordinariness of domestic life?

But still there's the mail to deliver, and today it's quite wonderful, really, a box of perishables for someone on Hollywood Street. Hollywood Street, like King, turns out to be no longer there. Gone absolutely except for the sidewalks and a few curved front walkways leading into stubble. In the box are some Toll House cookies and a loaf of banana bread, a little stale, but Stevie will love it.

Walking home, later, I am eager to give it to him, and then to sit down and talk to Gail. I plan to ask about her sex life, and after that we'll just talk, about her sex life, probably, and after that I'll cook dinner and she'll tell me about some of the men she's been fucking.

Inside the house the smell of sleep has dissipated, and the moist summer air has drifted in to replace it. Upstairs there's no Gail, no eyeglasses open on the windowsill, no overnight bag, and no Japanese print, even, under glass in the bathroom.

It is six o'clock.

The bed has been made just as Daniel would have made it, meticulously, the shape of each pillow distinct beneath the sharp folds of the spread. The bedroom curtains have been drawn the way we like them.

My heart is beating very fast as I walk downstairs.

But she is not in the guest room, either.

Not even her diaphragm, which she'd left behind on her last visit and which I'd stored in a canister of cornstarch on a shelf in the downstairs bathroom, is where I'd left it; there is only the faintest sprinkling of cornstarch on the floor.

Stevie and Daniel, back from their King Street excursion, are in the yard digging plastic Monopoly houses out of the sandbox, then loading them onto the rig of a Tonka. They're shirtless, and they've discovered the banana bread where I'd left it in the kitchen. The cookies, too. Stevie eats his with milk from a 50 ml beaker, drop by drop.

A puff of cornstarch, I think, *That's what's left of her,* and go outside to tell Daniel, and nearly trip over Gail's long legs. She is sitting on the porch swing, not swinging, her suitcase wedged under her heels.

"Hey Liz," she says.

"Hi Gail. Where's the Japanese print?"

"In my suitcase. I can't hang around. Bad Vibes. Bad Vibes." She is wearing the tinted eyeglasses, so I can't tell if underneath them her eyes are still green. She wears a paisley mini-skirt and a skin-tone top with a mock turtleneck and no sleeves. Her hair is a halo, backlit by new dusk. It's getting later much earlier than usual, I note, and then think how well-rested she looks after the quintessential beauty sleep. Even her suitcase, carelessly closed, a fold of bunched satin showing at the clasp, appears rested. Bad vibes? What is she talking about? Her missing amber ring? Embarrassed, not wanting to give it up just yet, I slide my hand into my pocket. Still, I can't stand the thought of her leaving, now, before we've had a chance to talk. I want to hear about the penises again: the big ones, the small ones, the middle-aged ones, the Moroccan ones, the French ones, the good ones, even the bad ones. I want to hear how they climb all over her the second she takes off her sunglasses. I want all the details. I want to know how she knows, when she meets them, which one she's going to end up with, first, and how long does she like to anticipate, and where does she take them to do it, and what are the complications, and what are the delights, and are there some she remembers and others she forgets, and do some of them talk in the middle of it and what kinds of things do they say? I want to know if it's usually morning or evening and if they eat breakfast or dinner before or after, and what are their names, their jobs, their physical descriptions, aspirations, failures, flaws, and shoe styles?

"I've always liked to think I could tell whether a man was comfortable with himself or generally uptight by looking at the kinds of shoes he wears," I suggest.

"No way," says Gail, leaning back on the swing, pushing off a little with her feet. "You know," she continues, "your teeth are black. What have you been doing? Chewing tobacco?"

"No," I say. "It's licorice. What kind of bad vibes?"

"Like insomnia," Gail says. "Like, no sandman. Can't relax."

I break into a grin. "That's funny, Gail."

She frowns. "It really screws up my system not getting any rest. I planned to do the whole number, you know? I needed it."

The whole number, I reflect. Tossing, turning, swooning, the whole bit. It occurs to me she's skipped a day, that's all. She thinks it's morning.

"What time is it, Gail?"

"Breakfast time. I want some OJ, please."

"Gail. It's evening. Dinnertime. You've been sleeping all day. Upstairs. You slept the day away."

She looks shocked. "With who?"

"With nobody, as far as I could tell."

"Shit."

She really does take off her sunglasses now, and with her thumb and ring finger squeezes the bridge of her nose. Then she shakes her whole head, wet dog style. I can't believe how beautiful her arms are. Shapely as legs, and I'm still thinking this when Daniel, with Stevie on his shoulders, walks past and gives me one of his "I know you" looks. Which is more than the usual "I know you" look coming from the usual person. From Daniel it's rare, he gives it only to me, and it means, *So, more licorice, but I'm still glad I know you the way I do. If I wasn't married to you I'd have no one to talk about. Later on, can you help me with this paper I'm writing?* and only lately, a sort of addendum, *I don't know why you don't want to touch me, but I'd like you to know how incredibly patient I'm being.*

"I know how patient you're being," I say out loud as the kitchen door bangs. And how careful, I think tenderly.

"Patient about what?" asks Gail.

"Never mind."

Gail shrugs, then pulls her bare knees up to her chin and sets the heels of her sandals against the slats of the swing. Her lace panties are of a feathery, leafy design like the pattern made by frost on a window pane. The sight of it – the ferny delicacy of the fabric pulled smooth above the shadows of her body – remind me at once of Arnie.

At once I feel guilty for not having thought of him all this time.

The other day he saw me on my route and called down to me from the branches of a sycamore.

"Oh, Mailma'm!" he called.

I looked up and saw a streamer of peeled bark spiraling toward me.

"How *are* you?" I asked, when I'd caught it, and got a glimpse of him hiding behind the silvery green of the tree trunk.

"I'm dying," he said.

I looked harder among the flat, mitten shapes of the leaves.

"How are you really?" I asked.

"Really?" said Arnie. "Wasting away," and he was as serious as he was playful, I knew, because I saw how his suit vest flapped above his ribs where the hands of the sycamore leaves reached in. *I want this and that and this,* they tapped out on his chest. *I want Gail and Gail and Gail.*

"I think there's someone I should take you to see," I tell Gail. "Someone in love with you.

"I doubt that," says Gail, who is absently kissing her own knees, her moist lips opening and closing as they travel the clefts and rises. "Anyway I think it's better when they have a chance to think about it."

"He's thought about it," I say. How frail Arnie looked the other day in the tree, so that I thought of a sparrow again, wrapped in a dishtowel in a cardboard box, its heart trembling under ratty feathers, a drop of liquid clinging to the point of its beak, unswallowed.

"Then you agree?" asks Gail.

"With what?"

"That it's better when they have a chance to think about it, and especially if they've noticed you with somebody else, or if you happen to have been with one of their friends. . . The thing is, if they get too into thinking about it beforehand it can backfire, if you know what I mean, sort of a mess all over the place. Every so often you get someone who can't bring himself to admit that's what happened, or they get so embarrassed–"

"Gail–" I interrupt.

"which puts me on edge, because it makes me feel maternal. I don't like to feel maternal when I'm – "

"Gail – "

"What?"

"Gail, I think we should talk about Arnie. I think we should pay him a call. He really misses you, you know. He's in love with you. It hurts him, Gail, that you left so suddenly, and that you haven't written him, and that you haven't come to see him."

"I haven't written him? Who?"

"Arnie. You know, the Tree Man. The one you stayed with in my guest room last time around. The one with the feathery hair."

"What about him?" she asks, testing again. It's clear she's not accustomed to things like this – some man missing her, hurting, wanting her to come back. She needs to hear it again, so I tell her. Now she's kissing her arms. I have to lift her by the elbow to get her to stop, and after poking my head in the kitchen to tell Daniel I'll be back in a while, we climb down the steps to the sidewalk. Across the road, still grouped on the curb lawn, is that same row of ladder-back chairs, a suitable audience for Gail's happy confusion. Their dumb applause fills the air as I lead her up the street.

THE HOUSES on Edgemeer are bigger, their side lawns wider, their fancy lawn chairs set in clusters around wheeled tea tables. Grackles perch on the arms of the chairs, and on the limbs of the pruned fruit trees, but there is only the sound of Gail's disheveled suitcase bumping against her hip. It gives her walk an extra sway. How at home she appears with this notion of travel, scouting the too-empty streets. My route rarely takes me to Edgemeer, so I don't know which of these fancy, abandoned houses belongs to Arnie's parents. Quite a few of them have studio garages, and one has a true carriage house, white with red trim and its own little forlorn garden.

Gail can't remember which house is Arnie's either, so we are looking for the curtains she made for its windows. We find chintz, madras, gauze, and several American flags.

"Not his," says Gail.

Several garages have no curtains at all, and inside, these are bare, with not even a shelf of gardening tools.

"Not Arnie's," Gail says, and shifts her suitcase to her other shoulder while bending to pull a grass stem from the strap of her sandal. It's a long straight stem, and she slides it between her teeth.

"Something's familiar," she says, and leads the way along a drive to another garage, set back further then the others near a rusted jungle gym under the shade of a tree. This one has lace curtains, and from the cracked-open door comes the sound of a radio. I stand back near the driveway while Gail bends to peer under the door. Then it opens and she steps in, and before it closes again there's a rushing, flapping noise while something flies straight past me from inside the garage, then circles and lands with a crash on the jungle gym.

"Arnie Junior," I say.

The toucan steadies himself on the bar. Held daintily in his beak is a toy telephone, and as I walk up closer he gives it a shake. It rings.

I N T E R V A L   T H R E E

TURNS OUT there's a third reservoir we never knew about. Ironically, it's the working reservoir, the one that provides our water, and that we've managed never once to suspect its existence is a source of, for Daniel, both mirth and chagrin. Daniel the scientist. Daniel who can not brush his teeth without charting the direction of the swirl of the water as it goes down the drain. Daniel the conservationist who, when I am brushing *my* teeth, sneaks up behind me and closes the faucet. Not easy these days, when even my elbow is off-limits to the merest caress of his T-shirt, but Daniel manages. Daniel manages also to appropriate Gail's tinted eyeglasses whenever Gail is in bed with Arnie in the back room. They come here for variety, Gail says, and to try out their new magic act on Stevie. They're putting together some kind of show. Stevie's eye is discerning, and they figure if he catches on to their tricks, then the tricks are no good. Besides, he is duly enthusiastic, and healthier because of it. Healthier, because every time he claps his hands they throw him a kumquat, fresh from Arnie's parents in Arizona. Arnie Junior, outside on his perch on our cherry tree, gnaws on the rinds. Also, he eats the stubs of Gail's candles, that flicker all night on the sills of our guest room windows. After Arnie and Gail have gone, the house smells pungently of cloves and sandalwood and of Gail's three-baths-a-night. A bath for each lovemaking session, I guess. Arnie is grateful to me. Already he looks fit as an eagle, in his top hat and cloak. Today, finding the top hat upended on our kitchen table, I reach in and pull out countless shoestrings of licorice.

Daniel doesn't notice. He's at the computer, with Stevie on his lap, Stevie's small fingers hovering over the keyboard.

"W," Daniel instructs.

Stevie pushes the W.

"H."

Stevie pushes the H.

Together we gaze at our son. Well, not really. We gaze at each other gazing at our son, just as, in lieu of touching each other, we touch our son's curls, our son's fingers, the wings of our son's shirt collars. Daniel looks fine wearing Gail's eyeglasses, although the stylish big frames give him a kinky appearance out of touch with the rest of him. He wears them in order to emphasize the fact that from behind the tinted lenses he is staring at me. Constantly. Not imploringly. But penetratingly. Meaningfully. *Scientifically.* He is trying to figure me out.

He forms hypotheses concerning my behavior, then disguises his experiments with innocent queries.

"How long are you going to be out today?" he asks.

"I didn't know I was going to be out," I say, knowing full well the minute I say it that of course I'm going out. I go out fairly often these days after work, still in uniform, my mailbag still slung on my shoulder. "Going out" means I take a walk somewhere before eventually making my way back home. It's safe with my uniform on, somehow: I can't imagine leaving town in my oxfords and too-long shorts.

"The usual," I answer.

Meaning: about half an hour, or maybe less now that by asking he's made me feel guilty about going at all. Or, maybe more. The crux of this experiment: if I feel guilty, will I come home to him earlier or later? I don't know, although Daniel, behind the ashy lenses, already has his suspicions.

"I'm just going for a walk, Daniel."

A raise of the eyebrows.

"If I don't walk," I tell him, "I'll fall asleep."

Another nod, another lift of the eyebrows. It's the licorice that's making me sleepy. This morning I could barely get out of bed. I feel bloated all the time and my ankles are swollen, but even now I am planning my next taste of candy. In the pocket of my mailbag are the shiny black shoestrings I pulled out of the top hat, the ends of which I've knotted together for convenience while chewing. The knots are the best part, anyway, sinewy and resistant, and if on my route I run into Daniel I can always bite the knot off, slide it under my tongue and slip the rest of the shoestring back in the bag before he catches sight of it.

"I might head for the new reservoir," I tell Daniel.

Another nod.

"Daniel?"

Another nod.

"Stevie's still pressing Ws, Daniel."

THE THIRD RESERVOIR, off a road leading out of town to the southeast, sits on a hill even steeper than that of the second reservoir adjacent to the golf course. There you climb a slope of loose, sliding gravel amid clouds of yellow dust; here, at the third reservoir, is a stairway so steep that if halfway up you turn to look down at the sign in the parking lot, you get dizzy all at once in the knees. The sign designates a picnic area at the base of the slope, where on a plot of tended grass are several tables and a drinking fountain. We never realized our town had a true, picnic spot. Anyway, nobody ever comes here to eat. There's no shade except what's thrown by the outhouse, and the place has a middle-of-nowhere feeling, surrounded by sorghum fields. Crops spread to the east and south; densely planted, broad-leaved, newly tasseled. In comparison the picnic spot looks naked, its grills spotless, its single trash can empty but for one orange juice carton, the tops of the redwood tables bare even of bird droppings.

I am a mile, a mile and a half, maybe, from home.

From the top of the steps, the third reservoir looks like water in a sink; its surface unmarred, its shape uniform, with a collar of poured concrete. No algae at all, and no floating, drifting branches. Across the way can be seen the very tops of some trees and some power lines.

Circling the water is a little paved trail, someone's idea of a joke, I remarked, when Ben first led us to it. Poor Ben was searching for Marnie and Chevy and Red. Marnie and Chevy are females. Chevy left babies still in the burrow, and Marnie left tracks in some mud at the edge of the meadow, heading southeast. Red left nothing. Red is Ben's favorite woodchuck, a rangy male affectionate with the younger animals who like to have their faces stroked by Red's red paws. It was Red who greeted Ben whenever Ben arrived at the study site, a greeting with a sound like a bell ringing under water. Several days ago upon Ben's lunchtime visit, Red stood yipping for longer than usual, clasped his front paws together and shivered excitedly, then ran in a sloppy figure eight among the burrows of the colony; it was that day that Chevy first failed to appear. Ben thought nothing of it, however. Chevy was probably inside with her newborns, he speculated. She was healthy and starting to put on weight, and her molt had been clean and efficient.

On the second day, Red performed the figure eights again, and on the third day, Red himself was gone. Ben crept closer, then closer, to look. His woodchucks, he once told us proudly, sweep their tunnels once a week and leave the mounds of fresh dirt at the entranceways. Chevy's dirt looked stale, and Ben could hear the mewing of her babies from behind. Marnie's burrow had no mound of dirt at all. That afternoon, Ben phoned us and asked if we'd accompany him to the third reservoir in hopes that we'd find some trace of his woodchucks. From the high asphalt ridge, we scanned the furrows of the sorghum fields, sharing the hand-held zoom among us. Strapped to Ben's head was his newest devise, a Bionic Ear, which identifies the origin of sounds, he explained. But there were no sounds except for those made by our children – no bells underwater, no mewing, not so much as a rustle in the stand of trees. How dejected Ben looked, dragging his feet in their untied sneakers, the Bionic Ear alert on the crown of his head.

"The only thing I can think of is that they're dead," he began, "but if they were, we would smell them. And if they were living, we'd smell them, too. I don't smell a damn thing anywhere, do you?"

I sniffed, and Stevie sniffed in the backpack behind me, and Simon stopped on the trail and wiggled his nose. I smelled water, that's all. Daniel, who wanted to make Ben laugh, held the zoom to his nose. Ben scowled. He flicked a switch on his Ear, then bade us sit still at the edge of the water. We held the children in our laps, and gave them some candy to suck on. Stevie and I sat facing in, while the men faced out. The water was utterly still. No dragonflies, even. No frogs, no turtles, just the vast, metallic surface. I caught Daniel's eye. We both knew what the other was thinking. It wasn't woodchucks Ben was so worried about. Daniel sighed. Ben gave him a nudge to keep quiet. For what seemed like forever we sat there, then switched positions, so I faced out and the men faced in.

"Woodchucks sometimes climb trees, believe it or not," said Ben when the children couldn't keep quiet.

I looked to my left at the tops of the trees. Leaves flashed in the sun. Craning my neck, I could just see the base of the stand of trees where it shaded the first few rows of crops. I caught a glimpse – just a glimpse – of her, standing there.

I did not say a word.

It was Eva, Joe's dog, wearing a lilac bandanna.

JOE'S CAR is navy blue with scattered rust stains like parched continents on a map of oceans. One windshield wiper is missing, and so is the side-view mirror. Joe doesn't drive much, anyway, at least not any more, and when he did, in the days when I hadn't quite noticed him but noticed only his car, it seemed engaged in a game of cat and mouse, a sort of musical parking lot. I rarely saw Joe's car on the road, but in a parking space behind the public library, or along the southern – always the southern – perimeter of the square, or on one of the side streets – Prospect, Hollywood – where no one would take any notice. This was several years ago when the supermarket was still open so if he parked in the supermarket lot it was only late at night when everyone else had gone home. Then he slept in the car, I suppose. He kept a striped wool blanket always folded on the ledge under the rear window except late at night when you couldn't see it, when he must have rolled himself in it on the back seat, and the dog always sat in the front passenger seat with just the tip of her nose out the window. I was always with Daniel when I noticed these things; we'd be strolling home from the movies or from visiting some friends, and Joe's secretive car would be part of the scenery. At the time I was not yet a TLC. I worked nine to five in a place that sold frozen yogurt, that no longer exists. I used to take the shortcut home from work: out the service entrance into the parking lot, then in through the service entrance of the Five and Ten and through the Five and Ten to where the main door faced the square. Then I'd walk across the square and across the church parking lot from where I could see our apartment building and whether Daniel was already seated on the fire escape landing, waiting for me. If he wasn't, I'd sit there and wait for him. There was a big lawn, and beyond that another parking lot, and beyond that the road that Daniel would be coming home on. Occassionally Joe walked by on that road as I sat watching for Daniel, and sometimes Joe's path crossed mine in the middle of the square, but I wasn't so interested in Joe, those days. I was more interested in Eva, Joe's dog, who trotted a few feet ahead of him, sniffing the air, looking cool, independent, and loyal. She's a shepherd with a light, easy gait, but somehow she managed never to precede Joe by more than the length of a leash.

Somehow I knew even from a distance and without consciously thinking about it that Eva was female; she had a fierce canine femininity, like a wolf's. It was admirable. In retrospect I wonder if it was Eva's femininity I was noticing, or if what I was picking up on was the way Eva contrasted with Joe, who followed Eva with his slow, even, masculine rhythm. Perhaps it was the gait that most caught my attention, although I didn't know it, at the time. It was as if he had all the time in the world. As if there were no place he needed in particular to get to; he just needed to *be*. He was a presence, like part of the weather – big, far-off, and electric.

But he's not here now, in the clearing in the woods at the base of the slope of the third reservoir, and neither is Eva, thank goodness, so, having circled the paved trail and climbed down the slope, I can sit on the log near his car and contemplate. He must come to this spot for his drinking water. In the shade under the car are two five-gallon water containers of durable plastic that he must fill in the reservoir, then shove under the car to keep cool. I imagine he makes his way from the potting shed once a day, maybe more, to fill a canteen. The car looks dug-in, as if it hasn't moved in weeks: no tire tracks at all, and no leftover odor of gasoline. Still I have the feeling if I sat down in it, it would take me somewhere, ultimately. Joe would show up, thirsty, dusty, and there I'd be sitting, looking casually through the contents of his glove compartment or through one of his too-heavy books, my thighs parting under the weight of the spine.

Suddenly there's a rustling in the trees, and with no second thought I've made a leap for Joe's car and am sitting inside it with my mailbag on my lap before I look up and see – what? – not Eva, not Joe, but two woodchucks, big bellied, low to the ground, who make their way neither up toward the water nor into the sorghum field but along the base of the slope before disappearing around the other curve of it. Male or female, I don't know, but I must tell Ben, except I can't get out of the car. Something's hooked through my belt loop, holding me down. It's a hand, I know, although I can't quite see it, but the striped wool blanket is spread out on the back seat with someone curled underneath and just a hand sticking out to grab hold of me.

"Joe," I say, at which he sits up fast, and drops the blanket from his face, except it's not Joe's face at all.

It's Danka's.

Scowling at me. Mean women are meaner than mean men, I remember. If I didn't know her, I'd be scared. But I stay where I am, and so does she. It's my body that wants him, my legs that won't budge, my butt that won't lift itself out of the seat. It's hot in the car, so I crank open a window. We might sit here all night, breathing in and out the close air of our new rivalry. I want to tell her, *He's mine, he asked Pebbles if I was married, he sticks his flowers in the body of my doll.*

"Let's just both force ourselves to get out at the count of three," I suggest after a while.

"One two three," says Danka, and then when we're both still sitting there, she tells me Joe's the one who beat up Gail's old boyfriend, George, in the post office that day.

"He's the one who beat up someone in the bank lobby, too," she goes on reverentially. "I know because his car backfires when he drives away. Like a gun going off, a little salute, and when it's over he's forgotten what he did, but I won't let him forget what he does to me, and I won't let him drive away from me until I am ready, and then I will kick him goodbye. Remember the other night we were talking on the phone and my soup pot boiled over?"

I nod, remembering that I still have her ladle although I don't use it, of course. From over the phone I could practically taste the most recent concoction – potato peel, ash, turnip broth – as it splattered then stuck to the burner on William's stove. Danka was thrilled when the soup boiled over, because the smell, she exclaimed, the very terrible, scorched, fragrant odor, was the smell she'd been after, the one she'd been trying to duplicate. But now she is quiet about it, so I assume it didn't work, it didn't free her the way she had hoped, gulp after gulp and she still couldn't make herself cry.

Now she lights up one of her cigarettes. Feeling sorry for her, thinking I should give her what she wants, I'm climbing out of the car when I hear another rustle. Footsteps this time. I make a leap for the trees and have hidden myself by the time Joe steps into the clearing. Slingshot in hand. No Eva in sight. He stands still for a moment, listening, actually sniffing the air, before taking a step toward the base of the slope. I step hard on a twig in my oxfords, it cracks underfoot, Joe whips around, missile poised, stands there a minute with his eyes glittering. Then he gives a low whistle, for Eva I suppose, stands a few seconds longer before dropping the missile back into its leather pouch. He slides the sling shot into his pocket, then reaches down into his pants and scratches himself. When he reaches the car he doesn't get in, just squats, pulling the two water containers out from under the fender. One of them is empty, the other nearly so. But he doesn't climb the hill toward the reservoir. He takes the path that the woodchucks took, so close to my tree I have to hug my arms to keep them from grabbing him when he walks by. No sooner is he gone than Eva trots into the clearing, still wearing her lilac bandanna, and growls at the doors of the car. At this, Danka climbs out, nervous but trying not to show it; smoothing her hair, taking off one of her pumps, spitting on it, and wiping it on the hem of her little black dress.

"Eva," I say cordially, "This is Danka. Danka, Eva."

Pleased to know you, says Eva with a lift of her nose before walking a few steps away from us both, squatting, and urinating.

Danka snorts.

I tug a shoestring from the pocket of my mailbag and stick the end in my mouth. Danka blows a smoke ring. We are both looking at it when we hear Joe's whistle. Eva takes off around the curve of the slope, toward the water fountain. I take off into the sorghum field, close to the trees, and Danka follows. About a quarter of a mile away, we pause at the edge of the road for breath, and for Danka to put on her shoes.

"Sometimes I wander about you," I joke, but Danka just scowls and sticks out her thumb. No sooner does she do this then

Joe's car appears. It slows nearly to a stop, but there's room for neither one of us. On the back seat are both big containers of water and in the passenger seat sits Eva, one elbow propped daintily on the armrest, her eyelashes fluttering.

"Sorry," says Joe, and smiles his crooked smile before stepping on the gas.

PART FOUR

The Top Hat in the Kitchen

"EMILY CALLED," shouts Daniel as I walk in the door.

The two words – their soft syllables – have the intonation of a song, so for a moment I think he is playing a game with Stevie. But Stevie's by himself in the study, on the floor before the computer, gazing dreamily at the blank and luminous screen. When I ask what he's doing he pulls himself up, presses the space bar and sits back down. What a silly question, this gesture seems to say. *What do you mean, what am I doing? I'm contemplating.*

I find my husband in the kitchen hunched over the balance, shirtless, his hair shiny moist from the shower. Even from the doorway he smells mintily of soap, and I can see the wet sheen on his back and arms. He has velvety skin and a flawless, comforting shape, untouched by me since the Doberman pinscher affair. Thirty-one days. I wouldn't know offhand how much time has elapsed except that Daniel, in his way, has been keeping me informed, marking each passing day on our wall calendar with a tiny, careful drawing of a hand. It is my hand, I know, because on its middle finger is the ring that fell off Gail's finger, and he knows that I know it. He tested me. On Thursday last week, the drawing was missing.

"Where's my hand?" I inquired at dinner.

Daniel squinted at my forearms, pointed with his fork, went back to his escargot. We'd found them packaged with their shells at the Epicurean, and sautéed them in garlic and butter. Dessert was a tinned fruitcake, the closest we could come to what we both really craved–Sara Lee.

"Where is it?" I insisted.

No reply, and I knew that he was after an admission of sorts.

"Where's the picture of my hand," I asked carefully, "that you draw on the calendar every day?"

No answer.

"Where's the picture of my hand that you draw on the calendar every day that we don't touch each other?"

Still nothing.

"Where's the picture of my hand that you draw on the calendar every day that I don't touch you?" I tried.

Daniel sucked at his snail, grimaced, nibbled a fleck of garlic.

"Where's the picture of my hand that you draw on the calendar every day that I don't touch you and that I don't let you touch me?" I asked at last.

"I forgot," said Daniel. He slid the half-eaten snail back into its shell, got up, sketched a drawing of the hand on the calendar, added Gail's ring, and sat back down.

Tonight I very nearly do it. Touch him, I mean. My hand reaches for his hip, but at the last second steers itself through the opening of his pocket and pulls out a couple of jewelweed fruits. Each is marked with a colored embroidery thread, like a gift-wrapped, miniature pea pod. He collected these himself. It's been a while since I've gone with him into the field although we still talk about my going, with a tone reminiscent of the way we used to anticipate sex–flirtatiously, at once jokingly, seriously, gratefully. I pick a jewelweed fruit open with my thumbnail, peel the two halves apart, gaze at the nestled seeds. One seed is plump, but the others are shriveled.

"What out-crossing distance was this?" I ask.

Daniel glances at the thread.

"Third nearest neighbor," he answers. "They don't seem to be selfing, so far, and the best yet is first nearest neighbor."

He says this with emphasis, happily convinced of its absolute rightness. Daniel hates plants that self, that is, plants that mate with themselves, but he is happiest with flowers that mate close to home. He finds them reassuring. Tenderly he slits open a fruit, removes a seed with a tweezer, places it onto the scale. He always loves what he's doing, no matter what it is, even weighing jewelweed seeds. He likes modest pursuits, incremental gains, so long as each small quantity of new understanding further bridges the gap between humans and flowers, humans and bees, humans and natural law. Still, he takes umbrage at Ben for having gone so far as to name his woodchucks. Yesterday, Marnie and Chevy came back, both limping, both bruised, both caked here and there with patches of blood, but Red is still gone. "From the face of the earth," Ben said to Daniel, gloomily, while feeding Marnie and Chevy spoonfuls of rat chow. Then he fitted them with collars, part of his new radio tracking system. Each collar had been threaded with a transmitter and with a slender, concealed antenna.

"So, what do you think?" I ask Daniel.

Meaning, is Ben going too far? Is Ben all right? Lately, every night when Ben comes over for dinner, he brings a handful of photographs of trips he has taken with Leah; to the Maine seacoast, to New Mexico, to a bog where they once hiked in West Virginia where cranberries grew. We pass the photos around as we eat, then lay them in a fan on the center of the table, to be studied and admired. There is always one of Leah by herself, on a sand dune, in a crater, at the prow of a boat, squinting casually into Ben's camera.

"I think he's keeping himself sane," Daniel says resolutely, switching off the balance and going into the hallway to check on Stevie. From the study he calls out again, "Emily called," and this time I hear it exactly.

Emily called.

Calmly I walk to the telephone, stand in the half moon curve of the desk, and dial her number.

Nothing happens. The phone is dead.

I pull the cord from the jack, slip it back in, do the same thing again with the bedroom phone and fall asleep holding the silent receiver.

NOT UNTIL NOON the next day at the post office do I learn that the local phone system has been entirely shut down. Two days later the radio station closes as well, and on the fourth day the local newspaper publisher holds a party in the middle of the square, a gala farewell with big kegs of iced tea, trays of homebaked cookies and a couple of untalented, limping clowns who must have slashed their feet swimming in the reservoir. One wears striped, one-piece swim trunks but the other wears a bodice of pearl-studded lace with a satin applique of a butterfly. Each butterfly wing very nearly conceals a breast. It's Gail, in white face with exaggerated eyelashes and brows. Gail's suitcase, wide open in an oblong of sunlight, is crammed with clown make-up and props and Gail's diaphragm case where everyone can look at it. Gail hasn't noticed me, yet. She is juggling pieces of fruit, just two, an apple and an orange, and not very well, and when the second clown throws her a banana, it hits her in the stomach and thuds on the ground. I make a lunge for the banana, thinking how much I'd like to have it, not for me and not for Daniel, but for Stevie, who hasn't had a taste of potassium in months, but just as I reach it, Arnie Junior swoops out of the tree, squawks, scoops the banana into his beak and flies it over to a crook in the tree where with great flourish he drops it into the upturned top hat. Then he lifts the top hat by the rim and carries it to Gail, who with equal flourish reaches in and pulls out – what? – the same banana. The crowd titters. Gail throws the banana to me, and, undeterred, beckons a third clown out of the tree. It's Arnie, of course, in sequined tails and his usual naked feet. He tweaks the wing of Gail's butterfly and then his own rubber nose. A stream of water squirts out, missing Gail's face by an inch or two. The crowd titters again but gets quiet when Arnie pulls a handkerchief as if out of nowhere and lets it drop gently over his fist. With his free hand, he recites an incantation, then holds the cloaked fist toward Gail who whips the handkerchief away. Underneath is Arnie's fist, the same as before. Even when he opens it, spreading his fingers, nothing falls out. Gail sighs while the third clown, the one in the swimsuit, kicks at the edge of the suitcase.

"I thought you practiced," I whisper to Gail, who has picked up the apple and is juggling again. She takes a bite of the apple and mugs for the tiny crowd.

"Who says we didn't?" says Gail under her breath, still grinning. "Who says this isn't how it was supposed to turn out?"

Then she kisses the apple and tosses it over my head. In white face, with her lower lashes painted halfway down her cheeks, she looks fundamentally changed. She looks happy, her giant eyes glittering. She makes a gesture toward Arnie, then slides a hand down the front of his pants and pulls out a purple balloon.

THIS MORNING I had a dream about Danka and Joe.

They were rolling around in the potting shed, having trouble with the zipper of Danka's little black dress. They had trouble as well with her brassiere and garters, and Joe never took off his cap, which in the end slid off his head onto Danka's closed eyes. Afterwards, Danka made one of her soups, with turnips, potato peels, cigarette ash, and whatever was left of Ben's favorite woodchuck, Red. From the bottom of the pot, from underneath the steam and simmer, Red's shrill peeps rose and floated free of the pot, but Danka didn't notice, she was too busy looking at Joe, thinking of how when he got sick of having her around, he'd tie her to one of the Asiatic magnolias in the old arboretum and walk away from her forever.

For most of the dream, I was sleeping, for some of it, I was awake. Anxiously I tugged on the sheets, until Daniel woke and asked what I was doing.

"Dream," I said.

"About what?"

"About Emily," I lied, for no reason at all that I could think of. On my tongue I tasted Danka's cigarette ash, bitter and dry.

"What about Emily?"

I didn't answer. I went back to sleep. But after breakfast, Danial said, "Why don't you go visit her, talk for a while, tell her how you're feeling?"

"I might."

"You might what?"

"Go over there," I answered.

"You won't," said Daniel.

Reverse psychology is one of Daniel's specialties. It works every time. He pulled himself to his elbows and gave me a challenging look. I met it by walking out of the house, past the row of empty card chairs and down Forest Street, toward Emily's.

NOT UNTIL I've reached the corner do I realize what I've done.

How naked I feel, walking alone in my blue jeans, T-shirt and sandals. No oxfords, no regulation pleated shorts and button-down blouse, no mailbag, no mail, no backpack, no stroller.

No Stevie.

How empty-handed. How *free.*

This could be it, I am thinking. I could be leaving, going away, not coming back.

For a moment I pause, and consider turning around. If I just turned my head I would make out the side of our house in the distance, the porch in the sunlight, the porch swing motionlessly hanging.

But I don't turn my head. Instead I give it a shake to feel the comfortable swing of my earrings, and then I start walking again, one foot in front of the other, filled with nervous embarrassment and a palpitating dread. I'm just taking a walk, I say to myself as if I were talking to Daniel. Don't worry, I'd say. Don't get so worked up. It's nothing. Just a visit to Emily's. Emily will counsel me. Emily will tell me what to do. Emily will tell me how to come home.

Emily lives in one of those sections of town that for some reason my mail routes only rarely intersect and that I never end up visiting otherwise, these days. Off the state road on the opposite side of campus, on Hazelnut Street, her house is not far from the building that Daniel and I first lived in when we came into town, in a neighborhood of ill-cared-for college rental apartments. On that edge of town the perfume is not nearly so dense as it is near the reservoirs in this unusual August, when the blossoms at last have vanished but the crab apples hang rotting and sweet in the trees. Every night now it pours, but by morning just several more pulps have been knocked from the branches. By dusk, they've been tunneled by ants. Near where Emily lives, there is only the sharp smell of soil, and no wonder, because so many of the houses have been demolished, their dug-out foundations filled up with dirt. It's the college, saving money on their useless properties. We know all about it, of course, but still I'm surprised by the sight of our own first apartment building so absolutely vanished; not a sliver of filthy windowpane remaining and the dirt-walled cellar not yet refilled with soil, its steep drop-off guarded by posts tied with flagging. At the bottom, some weeds have already shot up, and there's a clump of pigeon feathers. How pitiful it looks, not ghostly at all but just a hole in the ground; I feel a twinge in my throat just to think of our old, naked light bulbs. For a while I stand around and kick here and there in the grass until my toe hits something–a piece of roofing shingle that I pick up and slide around in the palm of my hand before dropping it dispiritedly several blocks past. It could be someone else's roof, it could be Emily's roof. What if Emily's house has been demolished, too? At the corner of Hazelnut Street is a U-Haul, so I make a dash for it not wanting it to take off before I have a chance to say goodbye. We need to finish our conversation, Emily and I. Where were we? A moving van, I recall, and she was lying on a bed inside of it, waiting for something to happen.

For what? I asked.

That was irrelevant, Emily insisted. She said the waiting was the point. *The desire for something to happen,* she said to me, *more than the thing itself. So I lay in the van until–*

Until what? I demanded, and demand again while standing uncertainly, at the rear of the open U-Haul, looking in. No bed to lie down on in this one, and no chair to sit in. Just some stacks of cardboard boxes and a potted acacia tree. The acacia is sickly and so fragile that one sneeze might strip it completely. Even the thorns appear insecure; when I poke one with a finger, it crumples accordion-style.

Until I'd had enough, says Emily. *Until I felt bloated with waiting. Until I was only desire. Only. Nothing but. I hadn't reached a peak. I was the peak itself.*

I nod, confused, looking her over. She doesn't look like the peak of desire. She looks like fulfillment. She looks like Emily. She's all color coordinated: white socks, lavender sneakers, white T-shirt, purple earrings, white shorts with purple suspenders. On the T-shirt has been silkscreened, in black, a bold Chinese character.

And then what? I ask.

No answer.

No Emily, of course, because the U-Haul isn't hers. Her acacia, if she owned one, would be sturdy, not dying, and the packing tape fastening her crates would be more neatly–more symmetrically–applied.

Emily's house is farther down the block on the opposite corner. Approaching it, I know I've been in it before. It's Gail's old house from Gail's Underground Railroad days, pale green with dark gingerbreading and that maze of subterranean hallways, abrupt stairways, and door after door after door.

Except that now it is painted not pale green, but white, and the trim a ripe plum, as if to better match Emily's shorts and suspenders.

On the floor in the front hall lies all sorts of inexplicably, never-delivered mail–flyers, circulars, even ordinary letters–originally destined for places all over town. There's the same row of mailboxes except for one new one that is Emily's, shiny brass among a row of old tin, and there's the same scuffed carpeting in the hallways and at each door except for Emily's, which has a fresh welcome mat. I wipe my feet on it and knock, and am surprised to see it opened so quickly. Not by Emily, however, but by a man I recognize as her boyfriend, who in white jeans and a letter jacket is just the picture of a man who would fall in love with Emily. He looks like a jock. Behind him on tv is a tape of football bloopers.

"I'm Emily's friend, Liz," I tell him. "We haven't met."

"Liz!" he exclaims, and claps his hands on my shoulders and squeezes, hard, before saying, "But Emily just left. She went to *your* house to see *you*."

"My house? You're kidding."

"Near the reservoir, right?"

"Walking or driving?"

"Roller-skating," he tells me, frowning, not taking his hands from my shoulders. "Why don't you sit down and wait?"

"She might be sitting down and waiting at my house," I say.

"She might," he agrees. "But I doubt it. New skates. She might be on her way home. You'll pass on the road. Or she might take a spin around campus, first. She likes to skate around the track a couple times. You know Emily."

He grins, his hands still at rest on my shoulders. On tv the crowd is cheering. For a minute we stand there like that, huddle-style, in silent agreement about Emily. Emily gliding through space. Emily's skate wheels whirring and roaring. Emily in purple. Emily in plum. Emily spinning, dipping, swaying, turning.

"Bye," I say.

"Bye," he says, and releasing my shoulders, still grinning, goes back to his show.

I follow the hall to where some wind chimes are chiming, then climb down some back steps to the floor where Gail stayed for a while, with its shared bath, shared kitchen, shared wall phone. After that I get lost in a stairwell, open a door, end up in a boiler room, set off down another hallway, make a few odd turns, descend some steps to a kitchen that is not the shared kitchen but a different one, turn back up the steps, take them too far, end up in an attic, push open a door and step into that sea of lost letters again, in the front hallway under the row of mailboxes.

How I happen to find it is a mystery to me although of course it's the simplest thing in the world, how I reach in and take hold of an envelope and hold it up to the window for scrutiny.

How wind-blown it looks, and how terribly, terribly worn.

When I open the flap, a caterpillar drops out amid a shower of fine, dark sand, and the paper feels of tissue, softer than before, velvety and damp. There are blots everywhere, and smeared muddy caterpillar smudges throughout, the ink bleeding to watery pink, the message abbreviated, obscured, surrendered as if not to weeks but to years.

Dear Deets, I read,

> Our missing you fills up our mouths whenever. . . haven't. . . stand in the doorway and wait, and water the flowers, and chop tomatoes for gazpacho hoping you'll be here to eat it with us. Your arms and. . . everywhere we look. . . Why haven't you followed? Is it only that you don't know where to. . . bag, shut the light, and walk out the door. . . think, and remember, and follow your noses, and it will be like the first times all over again, meeting each other, falling in. . . our missing you fills up. . . on the road, to the screech of your four. . . drive fast. . . and bring your baseball mitts too so. . . with. . . the grapes here are beautiful, seedless, purple and round with. . . else, just. . . your fingernail. . . frayed bits of dental. . . three bathrooms here, believe it or. . . please hurry and fill up our tumblers, as Edwards. . . a kiss for the roads, our tongues on your. . . we swear if you don't get here any minutes we'll. . .

Testicles, I remember, and *scream.*

Soon I turn to the sketch of the road and the house and the two, identical stick-figured women. No smudges here, but the picture is different, somehow, a bit grayer around the edges, while in the doorway the women, stick-hands on stick-hips, appear less jaunty somehow than they did before, less energetic, more resigned. They must have waited too long. They look close to collapse, as if had I opened the letter not today but tomorrow I might have found them on the threshold like a heap of pick-up sticks, their arms and legs akimbo, their hands and feet confused. Around them the page looks blank and pale, and as I fold it up I'm thinking how sad it all is, all those caterpillar-nibbled sentiments and crumbling postures, how sad to wait and wait and then, exhausted, fall to pieces. I think of Leah full of hope, missing Ben, wanting him to follow, then waiting, waiting, waiting, losing hope all at once, giving up, and forgetting.

How could I not have thought of this before?

Those few lines in the letter, now faded and smudged. Barely readable, but not gone, not quite.

Something about a clue. Something about packing your bag. Something about hurrying. Something about falling in love. . .

We mean to do it again and again, Deets, with you, Deets, and you, Deets–with you. . . Make up your mind that you're coming to us, and you'll find what you need to show you the way. . .

So, I set out to look for Ben.

But first I fold the letter on the crease, slide it back into its envelope and into the pocket of my jeans, along with a few other letters to be dropped at the post office on my way back through town. Crossing the square I catch sight of William, Danka's husband, looking elegant and distracted as the White Rabbit in the looking glass. I have to pause in my step so he won't knock me down, and as he passes I hear that he's whispering, over and over, "Cariatharim, Abu Gosh. Cariatharim, Abu Gosh. Cariatharim, Abu Gosh."

So, he's found the City of Repose.

So of course I must tell Danka, but no sooner than I must tell Ben about the letter and the clue, or perhaps I should tell Ben first and then Danka, or Danka first and then Ben, or perhaps I should tell both of them at once, somehow, somewhere.

I climb the steps to the post office two at a time and trade my overdue letters for a set of jeep keys. The jeeps are parked in the back, so I have to go out through the sorting room, nodding hellos and goodbyes to the other TLCs standing in a huddle near the fan. The fan is turned low. Apparently there is some sort of conference in progress of which rightfully I should be part.

"Liz!" someone calls, and they beckon me over, but I pretend not to know what they want. Instead I throw them a kiss and push open the door. Still, having glanced only once at their faces I know full well what's happening. I've been expecting it. Everyone has. We're being merged. In other words, we're closing. The windows will be shuttered. The fans will be still, the radio silent, the stamp rolls, stamp books and stamp sheets dispersed. We'll be expected to hand in our mailbags, but we'll all keep souvenirs; a strap, a buckle, a pocket, a patch. We'll be happy to give up our trousers and our faulty cans of Mace, along with our blouses and blue knee socks. We'll hang on to our visors and rain hats and wear them now and then, here and there, whereever we end up living. Behind the closed shutters, the door to the safe will be left ajar and my cot left inside with some old mail sacks on it, making odd, twisted shapes in the endless dark.

I won't miss it, though, I realize, as I head for the jeep. In the sunlight it beckons and glints, and as I slide inside I know it will take me somewhere, somewhere special, somewhere I need to go. I turn the key in the ignition, put my foot on the pedal and drive, just drive, and find that I've driven to the old depot. But I don't stop there. The jeep bumps from the pavement onto the grass and eases through a strip of woods to where the railroad ties start. The jeep straddles the tracks. The tall weeds whisper between the wheels before popping up behind them as straight as can be.

Maybe this is where I'll find Ben, I say to myself. Maybe he'll be looking for his woodchucks in the woods.

Or maybe this is where I'll find Danka. Maybe she'll be looking for Joe.

MY MAILBAG is of a comfortable, practical, sensible weight, evenly distributed, designed for equilibrium. Unless I am digging around inside of it or slipping letters into one of its pockets I don't notice that it's there; its very nearness and familiarity assure it of the status of, say, an article of clothing, so that more than once I've sat down at the dinner table still wearing it the way a shopkeeper might dine with a pencil still wedged behind one ear. Too, the mailbag seems as accustomed to me as I am to it; removed and slung over a chair, for instance, it holds in its creases echoes of the unshapely shape of my body; my "boyish" hips, my "boyishly" articulated shoulders and small, pointed breasts, along with what Daniel calls my "womanliness" – what he saw in my eyes that first day we met. When pressed for explanation, Daniel names a few qualities that change each time I ask: sometimes gravity and melancholy, sometimes mirth and impulsivity, sometimes dreaminess and meditation, or meditation and gravity, or dreaminess and mirth.

Even so I would never have imagined that without my mailbag in tow I would feel the way I do, stripped naked, bareboned. Not to mention the fact that with no backpack, no stroller, no Stevie, I feel fluid and limbless as water, helplessly flowing. There is a moment of panic, then a queer, contented calm as I walk through the tunnel of ancient magnolias to the hill where I can look at the hedge apple tree. In the limbs the gnarled fruits look bright and strange and heavy like all that is left of my body, whose very center is desire like a fist I'm sitting on, opening and painfully closing.

The greenhouse, when I've paused at the crest of the hill to look down on it, shows evidence of continued domesticity. On the stone slab under the hedge apple tree is a ramshackle, woven beach chair with no legs, the kind you sit on at the barest, frothiest edge of the surf, while just outside the door in a terra cotta pot is a totem pole with no faces carved on it, just text. Joe must have carved it himself; the letters, though crude, have a certain, primitive grace. I can't read it because it's in German, but I imagine it says either No Trespassing or Welcome, and not knowing which, I open the door and step over the threshold, and gaze down at the bedroll of burlap and woodchips on which I long to stay put for a moment at least, like water in an eddy, turbulent as ever, waiting for release.

On the edge of the sink stands the body of the doll, headless beneath her umbrella of Queen Anne's lace.

I pull the door shut behind me and take off my clothes, with just an instant of regret that I hadn't listened harder to Gail's advice long ago on that night she first appeared on my porch. She would have made me a loin cloth of wedding gown lace tied with ribbons of satin studded with pearls. I'd slide my hand underneath it, feel the smoothness without and the softness within. Above me the sun beats hard on the glass, and around me the greenhouse is pure, white heat. I lie still in the throb of it, arching my back, my legs parting to open, then faltering, slowing, stopping altogether.

There are footsteps outside, soft on the grass. I swear I can hear the flap of his boots, and Eva's deep, measured panting.

So this is where the postal jeep has brought me, I think: to Joe.

Except he doesn't come inside. When finally I sit up to look, pressing my face to the algae-streaked glass, it's not Joe I see but Daniel, and Stevie in the backpack, each of them carrying a radio. Stevie's is a toy that plays Jack and Jill, but Daniel's is for real.

IN RETROSPECT I know it's because I didn't want to see it. For how obvious it was, Daniel looking so busy, the strap of the radio slung over one shoulder, on his face an expression I'd grown accustomed to seeing on Ben's—worried and sad, with a hint of desperation just rising to the surface of the brow. He sat down on the beach chair and let Stevie turn the knob on the radio, then gazed at its secretive, squat, square shape as if it could tell him everything. He was deep in concentration, as he most often is.

At first I thought he was looking for Red, Ben's woodchuck.

When the radio beeped, Daniel swiveled the antenna. Swivel, beep beep, swivel swivel, beep beep. Stevie beeped in response, and Daniel put a finger to his lips while cocking his head and listening. For a moment he looked away, dropped his guard, sighed, rested his cheek on the palm of his hand. I had never seen him do this before. I had never seen him cry. He was just on the edge, just holding back because Stevie was there. He was wearing Gail's sunglasses, not on his face but clipped by the ear piece to the pocket of his T-shirt, blinking in the sunlight. I was thinking of the feel of the jeep keys tight in my fingers, and of the seat of the postal jeep breathing under my weight, and I only thought that Daniel's face was not appropriate for the face of someone looking for a woodchuck, even if the woodchuck was Ben's.

For a moment I supposed that Daniel was looking not for Red but for Leah herself, and crazily I wondered if Daniel was in love with Leah, had been in love with her all along or perhaps had just recently fallen in love with the memory of her as if it were an echo whose source he had to locate. When the radio hummed, he swiveled the antennae, and when it beeped – with a higher pitch, with more certainty, than it had before – he got out of the beach chair again and turned not toward the woods and not toward the railroad tracks but toward the little greenhouse at which I thought that maybe he too was looking for Joe. I didn't think about *why*. I only pulled on my clothes in a kind of a daze, still steeped in the hot, liquid wash of my body. I slid my feet into my sandals and then stood for a minute, too excited to move. Daniel leveled the antenna toward the totem pole, and squinted. The beeping was fierce when I walked out the door.

AND IN RETROSPECT I know I must have been thrown off balance by what Daniel had done, as if by doing it he had protected me from the knowledge of it. I was wearing my giant oval locket earrings containing photos of Daniel and Stevie, and riding home in the postal jeep they swung wildly to and fro but I thought nothing of it, I thought only of opening the earrings when I got home, and looking at the photos, and then looking at the real things, at Stevie and Daniel, and then looking at the photos again. I thought of doing this day after day, ritualistically.

Daniel was driving. I held Stevie in my lap and breathed as if nostalgically the scent of his curls.

We saw no people at all for the entire drive, and only one or two U-Hauls parked here and there at the curbs. The sidewalks were swept free of blossoms, the edges of the lawns neatly trimmed. There were clouds in the sky but their shadows hadn't fallen; they hung reluctantly above among the tops of the trees and threw a silvery gaze on the bright, clean streets. How abandoned looked the streets, with not a sound to be heard above the purr of the jeep on the smooth asphalt, but there was nothing new about it – that eerie pitch of peace and quiet, that breaking point that wouldn't break. We had seen it before, and we knew that it signaled a fresh exodus, and that when morning came we would see how the town had grown smaller again overnight. I told Daniel that the post office was closing, but he told me he already knew. Other than that we didn't talk until we nearly reached our house, when Stevie started snoring. Beneath the hiked-up hem of his T-shirt his pale belly quivered in dreams. When we'd parked, we heard our stereo playing from out in the street. Our speakers are in the living room. On the couch was a clown wig of purple yarn. Two giant, clown sneakers lay askew on the floor, pigeon toed. Daniel kicked a clown nose and followed me upstairs where I laid Stevie in his crib, then down into the kitchen, where Arnie sat cross-legged on top of the refrigerator, practicing tricks. He held a glass of clouded water that turned suddenly blue when he dipped a finger in. Applause broke out from the corner of the room, where Gail sat in a terry cloth bathrobe, carefully pinning a hemline in the fabric of my own wedding dress, or rather, what was left of it; a sort of mini dress, camisole style. The shoulder straps were strings of seed pearls. It was summery, simple, romantic, with lace insets in the sides.

"Hurray," said Gail, with a mouthful of pins, drops of shower water glistening in the tendrils of her hair.

Arnie grinned. He wore a suit jacket over his naked chest, and I could see his chest swelling with pride.

"Tincture of Iodine," said Daniel when the clapping had stopped. "And cornstarch on your finger."

"God damn it," said Arnie, deflating.

"Really?" said Gail, as Arnie hopped down to the floor, box of cornstarch in one hand, glass of blue water in the other. He dumped the blue tinted water in the sink, filled the glass at the tap, added a few drops of iodine from a bottle in the pocket of his jacket, moistened his finger and was just about to demonstrate when Gail said she'd better hurry or she wouldn't make her plane.

"What plane?" said Arnie casually, but I could see that he was scared. He raised the glass to his mouth as if for a sip, then made a face at the smell of the poison. He put the glass on the counter and gazed questioningly at Daniel, who shrugged and took a seat at the table, leaning back against the door frame so that he watched us from under half-closed lids. Watched me, I should say, and never in my life have I felt so much the subject of a person's concentration; I was like a single actor on a stage and Daniel the sole, huge audience or more specifically, Daniel the scientist and myself the cell throbbing under the microscope. For weeks I'd grown accustomed to Daniel's steady, endless gaze under which everything I did – the tying of a shoe, the scrubbing of a pot – seemed designed to emphasize that whatever I was doing was not what Daniel wanted me to do, for I was not touching him. I might be polishing an apple but I was not touching him. I might be sleeping but I was not touching him. I might be staring back at him, but not touching him, and all the while he'd be watching, or if not exactly watching – if he was in the other room, say, or even upstairs – then still he'd be aware of me and of what I was doing and of what I wasn't doing. Aware of me, yes, monitoring me, yes, but as a scientist might monitor the progress of an event. Not to change it, but simply to predict and understand it. How passive that gaze had come to feel, on my back, on my hands, on my feet, and now how eerie to begin – just now – to suspect that it had changed.

He had taken Gail's sunglasses out of his pocket and laid them on the table, and now sat quietly with the radio in his lap, his finger just hovering over the dial barely moving even when Gail said the dress was for me, and that I could wear it on the plane.

"I'm thinking St. Lucia, St. Kitts, or St. John," Gail went on. "I haven't decided yet. St. Lucia is volcanic, and there's the bay where they filmed *Doctor Doolittle.* I know a guy who cooks banana fritters in the cabin of a boat moored there. Pretty tasty, actually. I could go check it out. He might not remember me."

"He'll remember you," said Arnie, who put a hand on my shoulder, then let it drop to his side.

"St. Kitts is smaller, cleaner, and better kept-up," said Gail. "Black sand, I think. Seems to me there was someone – but maybe that was St. John. I have things there in several boutiques. Caftans. Sun hats. A sun hat would go really well with this dress. What do you think? Cream lace at the hem, or black? I wonder if it *was* St. John, come to think of it. That guy was pretty sweet. You know what it's like when you like someone from the beginning. That's what it was like."

She was stitching careful tucks in the bodice of the mini dress, forming small, breastlike hollows of the gently luminous cloth. I was touched by those tucks, because they did look like me – like my body, my breasts – but very suddenly I wanted Gail to leave, with Arnie if possible, but certainly not with me. I wanted our house to ourselves, to me and to Daniel and Stevie, and I wanted those clown shoes out of the living room even if it meant they had to walk out alone. I was impatient even with Arnie, with the way he tensed up when Gail bit off the thread. The thread was of silk, and her bright green eyes were fixed although not on the knot she was tying. She was gazing at my ring, the one that had slipped off her finger, the scarab I had taken for myself. The wad of masking tape, which Daniel had so meticulously wrapped around the band, was gluey at the edges but still secure. I'd grown fond of the ring, of its clumsy size, of the strange, foreign shape of the beetle. Still, it was Gail's. I pulled it off my finger, unwrapped the strip of masking tape, then with a fingernail scraped the residue of glue from the thick gold band. Just as I was handing it over, Gail stood up and went out to her suitcase on the porch, digging around for her pin cushion, I supposed. I gave the scarab to Arnie, who held the ring between thumb and forefinger while delivering it to Gail. He slipped out of his jacket, draped the jacket over the ring, waved his free hand around, and pulled the jacket away. The ring was still there, but Gail was nowhere in sight. Not even her suitcase was where it had been. The porch swing shivered, and something moved in the yard, low to the ground. It was Eva in her lilac bandanna, nose in the grass, rump in the air, tail swaying a little with every step. That's what I like about Eva, I thought; she's true to her nature, and so feminine. She is fueled by the spur of the moment. Now she slunk past Nikki's fence just as Arnie stepped into the yard. He'd been standing on the porch, looking here and there for Gail.

"She forgets," he was saying. "The lady forgets." For a moment he gazed at the ladder-back chairs, but soon he started down the road. He didn't walk on the sidewalk. He stayed on the curb lawn, and I kept my eye on him until he vanished among some trees. The leaves appeared to heave and then settle around him.

Meanwhile Eva reappeared in the yard, nibbling a green bean from Nikki's overgrown garden. Delicately, she spit the husk between her paws, then paused, cocked her head, and trotted back through the gap in Nikki's fence.

A second later, Joe followed, twanging his slingshot as he ducked behind the posts.

"HAVE SOME WATER," said Daniel then, when everything had grown still. He dumped out the glass of iodine, washed it, filled it, and gave it to me.

I closed my eyes as I swallowed, and was afraid to open them. What would I see? On the table lay Gail's ring in the folds of Arnie's jacket, while from the back of a chair slipped the unhemmed dress, little by little. In the yard lay Joe's painter's cap, upside down. Looking dignified and pleased, Eva trotted out alone from among the pine trees, mud on her nose. From her teeth hung a rope of small, hard red onions that swung to and fro. Soon she crouched on her forepaws to snack. She did so with great elegance, peeling with her teeth the onions' fragile, insubstantial coverings.

Daniel was staring at me. He set the radio upright and turned a few knobs. It beeped shrilly – frantically – until he turned the knob again. In the sudden peace and quiet I heard a faint humming. Rather, I felt it. It tickled. It vibrated, and my whole body seemed to vibrate with it. Horrified, I slid my hands into my pockets, then felt around my blouse and the buckles of my sandals. In retrospect I know I saved the earrings for last, certain all the while of what Daniel had done. He must have done it while I slept; opened an earring, slid the transmitter inside.

I closed my fingers on a locket. It had a pulse of its own, a faint humming vibration as familiar as the pulse of our marriage.

Daniel looked scared.

"You didn't give me a choice," he said. "I was scared to death you'd leave us."

"So was I," I said.

INTERVAL FOUR

ONLY LATER that night, after dinner and the rain, did I remember the letter to Deets. Still in my pocket, it must have played on my awareness just exactly the way, if the phones are in order, a ringing phone might haunt the edges of a deep slumber. How the ringing persists, its implications woven carelessly, influentially, into a dream.

Ben was in our kitchen helping Daniel with the dishes. Simon was asleep on the living room couch with Arnie's jacket for a blanket. I took hold of Ben's elbow and steered him toward the table where I spread open the fragmented letter and held it in place.

"Read this," I said.

Daniel stood at Ben's shoulder and read it, too.

"It's definately a letter," Daniel said when he was done.

"It's one letter from two loonies," said Ben. "That's all. What do you want me to do? Go live with them? Go eat their gazpacho? You don't want me to come here for dinner anymore, I won't, I promise."

"Listen," I instructed, and I recited the part about falling in love. "Leah said that to me once," I told him.

It was a lie but it felt right to say it. She could easily have said it. She felt it, I knew, because I've felt it myself.

"She wants to fall in love again, with you. She wants you to find her."

"Oh, great," said Ben.

"She wants you to *try,*" I went on. "See, it says right here, pack your bag, shut the light, walk out the. . . and then think, and remember, and follow your–"

"I can read," said Ben. "I've always had a feeling that's what I should do, but I felt too stupid to do it."

"Do it," I said.

"Do it, I guess," said Daniel. "You can always come back."

"No way I'll come back," said Ben. He lifted Simon from the couch and carried him out to his car. Half an hour later he was at our door again, to show us what he'd found in the inside pocket of Simon's miniature Ghostbuster suitcase. He'd found a bead, that's all, from one of Leah's necklaces. The necklace, of clay, had been made by an old friend of Leah's in Boston.

"That's a long shot," said Daniel, when Ben had driven off. "Boston's a mighty big place."

I nodded. I took off my earrings, undid the clasps of the lockets, slipped the transmitter out and laid it gently on the table. I put the earrings back on and finally let our eyes lock.

"Over the river in Boston. That's what he said. He'll find her," I said, and thought of fish and flower markets on sun-heated cobblestoned streets, and of a doorway with a potter's apron hanging on a hook. In the distance the river might stink of debris, but in the shop would be the sweet, penetrating odor of mud. The floor would be concrete splattered with slip, and on a shelf in the rear would be a row of jars of pigments amid packets of oxides and ores. From behind a low partition would come the whir of the potters wheel along with a voice from a radio. Ben, creeping closer, might see the top of her head bent over her work, her hair coming undone from a ponytail. Near her elbow would be a yogurt container filled with water and several paintbrushes and utensils and on the window behind her would be her sunglasses hung on the curtain rod. Still Ben won't say anything to get her attention; instead he's looking for signs of a lover, looking to see whether she's healthy and whether her clothing under the apron is the same sort of clothing she wore when she left him or whether she's changed her style. There might even be a photo of himself and of Simon, so of course Ben stares at it thinking that since it's on the wall behind her she only looks at it when she comes in in the morning and maybe when she stops for lunch and maybe when she goes home but not while she is working at the wheel. After that he examines the pots, to see if she's been productive, to see if she's feeling creative, to see if she's had luck with glazes and if the kiln is reliable. If Leah still hasn't noticed him he might lift a finished pot off a shelf and tap his fingernail lightly against it to test its construction. The more thin-walled the pot the better, Leah always claims, the very beauty of a piece of ceramics being that wedding of fragility and durability.

Then, when she still hasn't seen him, Ben, at a loss for words and action, leaves the studio and steps out into the hot street again where he sits on the edge of a wall and watches the doorway before circling around to the back to make sure there is no second exit. There is, naturally, leading out to a yard where the kiln sits, but there's a wooden fence around it with no gate. Ben will not have brought Simon, having left him in the care of some people he knows. Around noon he goes back into the shop where the air feels still moister and cooler than it did before, and where the radio is off and the potter's wheel silent. He has a moment of panic before seeing Leah's sunglasses still hanging on the curtain rod and then Leah herself at the sink preparing a sandwich. Bologna of all things. As far as Ben knows Leah never ate bologna while living with him, and the sight of it on slabs of her usual homemade, whole wheat bread weakens anew his resolve to speak to her, so he goes back into the street again. The air smells of dead fish. There he sits until the shop behind him closes its doors and there are no longer quite so many tourists on the sidewalk. The tourists have been following the Freedom Trail, a painted red stripe that on the sidewalk at Ben's feet has worn to a few red speckles. When he goes into the shop again, Leah is gone. Her sunglasses are gone from the curtain rod. The potter's wheel has been sponged and scraped clean; the utensils, freshly rinsed, lie drying on a paper towel next to the sink.

"Oh, no she doesn't," Ben says aloud. "No, she doesn't. No, she doesn't. No, she doesn't."

He pokes his head outside the door again and looks both ways on the Freedom Trail, which angles down toward the river and up to a place where the buildings are tall and narrow. He might call her out loud, his first utterance, but remembers too horribly the long silent seconds following his calls on the very night she disappeared, his head in the dark of the eaves just next to their bedroom. He makes his way through the studio to where the back door leads to the fenced-in yard. He opens it gently and steps just onto the threshold. The kiln yard is small, no more than twelve feet from the door to the fence, and the shapeless brick kiln takes up half of the space. The rest is ramshackle lawn adorned here and there with Leah's pots planted with flowering vines. Leah is stretched out in the middle of them on a chaise lounge, reading a book. She has taken off her smock, and Ben recognizes her khaki shorts as the ones she always wears on summer evenings, and he recognizes the blue halter top, and the strong, bony angles of her legs and arms, and even the book, or in any case its author of whom Leah has always been fond. Now that she is again no more than six feet away from him, Ben cannot make himself call out to her or even whisper her name, and he can not move himself through the door to approach her. He only stands and watches, wondering at her sheer inability to see him – she is sitting at an angle; it is not out of the question that she should catch sight of him from the corner of her eye. Experimentally, Ben tries a few gestures, first flexing his fingers, then lifting the whole hand, running the fingertips through his hair, and at the end a little wave in his wife's direction, but Leah only turns the page of her book and keeps on reading. She crosses her long legs, angles her face into the last of the warmth from the evening sun. She has not lost weight, as he has. She has not gained weight. What is different about her is only this queer, unsettling self-absorption that even the noise from the street can't penetrate. It seems to Ben that if he were to walk straight up to her, sit down on the edge of the chaise lounge, remove the book from her hand and lean forward to kiss her she still would be unaware of him. He needs to wait for an opening, a crack in the empowered glaze of her exterior. It might never happen, Ben tells himself.

Some time later, Leah rises, walks barefoot to the kiln, checks the fuel and the temperature and then, satisfied, returns to her book. Ben ducks inside the doorway as she crosses the yard. Her naked feet are painfully familiar. So is her habit of reading in dwindling light; Leah often reads in near darkness, in the bedroom late at night after Ben is in bed, with the glare from the hallway her only source of illumination. Next to her he'll lie awake and hear the comforting sound of her pages turning, reassuring as a heartbeat. Leah never falls asleep while reading. She marks her place in the book, closes it, lays it flatly on her night table and is asleep within minutes but never without first reaching for Ben, always with the identical gesture; her knuckles caressing the hairs on his chest, her fingertips stroking the expectant peaks of his nipples.

Now all at once the book tumbles to the grass. It lands on its spine. Its pages fan out and then flop back together. Leah's right hand slides from her belly as if in pursuit, her knuckles caressing the dry tops of the grass, her fingertips searching the hard topsoil – searching and searching. Ben feels in his nipples the familiar, upright tingling, and sees the yearning in her fingers, in their persistence and frustration and in the way they close finally on air only to open again and resume. This is the crack, the opening for which he has been waiting. Still he waits a minute longer just to be certain, and a minute after that. When he takes off his shirt, he believes he feels the heat from the kiln rolling toward him in waves across the narrow fenced yard.

ONLY AFTER I've convinced myself of the inevitability of Ben and Leah's first kiss on the chair in the heat of the kiln yard, do Daniel and I make contact. Touch, that is. We are lying in the guest room, on top of the covers, and we both catch sight of the same thing at once; what has happened to the wall. A blemish in the plaster, a faint haze of white dust with the moonlight slanting through from the other side of it. It is not a large hole, about the size of–well–about the size of one of Joe's slingshot missiles. And there's another where the wall meets the ceiling. Gazing at them, and at the night coming through them, our touching each other doesn't come as a shock. In fact several seconds pass before I realize that my open hand is resting on his. *In* his, actually, for he has closed his fingers over my palm. For the first several seconds our two skins feel like the usual no-man's-land, that half-inch of empty space to which we've grown so accustomed, and I think nothing of it. But then–how warm it becomes, my skin against his, his skin against mine, the skins of our two hands so distinct, for a minute, from the rests of our bodies that it's as if we are again touching anther to stigma, petal to petal, out in the woods together. This time of year, the woods have a damp, creeky smell, and there is always the sound of water dripping although the drops are not to be seen. Perhaps the sound is only sap popping out of the trees, for everywhere the leaves are spotted with dried sap which clings also to the stems and bark and makes a sticky mist over the leaves of the undergrowth and over us as well; on our hair and clothing. Its presence is subtle, cobwebby, easy to overlook, but its flavor on Daniel's lips is sharp and quite unusual so for a moment I can almost believe that I am only tasting, like someone sipping a glass of wine not from thirst but curiosity. Then all at once there is the flavor of his tongue, dense and familiar, and the scent of shampoo at the roots of his hair, and the sweet, urgent smell when he no longer holds himself back. I'd forgotten about that; Daniel, my scientist, letting himself let go. How naturally it happens, and how he welcomes his own astonishment–crying out, gasping, sweating, tears in his eyes–so for a minute I am like a person in the eye of a tornado. Around me spins a tunnel of breathless, purple air as if love itself were composed of one fierce spiral, and before morning it is that that sweeps me off my feet, not the plunging of Daniel's body but the height and duration of love as it hovers, then touches down. All along it must have waited in the wings for this moment, whirling and whirling, gathering intensity.

"I missed you," I say.

My last thought is of my fingers and of Daniel taking hold of them; how eager they were for the touch of his hand.

P A R T   F I V E

Hungry Love

FOR OVER A WEEK, rain falls. Noon brings intermittent thunder bursts followed by slow spells of increasing humidity; at night there is the plunk and trickle of water in the gutters, water on the roof, water threading through the needles of the pines outside our windows, and by morning a chilly mist blankets the sunken lawn next to the reservoir. The water has risen until no more than a corner remains visible of the concrete block on which the father of the two fishing boys used to sit while smoking his cigarettes, and even that is damp to the touch. When the sun comes out, once each mid-morning, it seems only to draw the moisture out of the ground, between the cracks of the sandstone sidewalks, in sparkling patches that dim as the clouds converge, and in pools spreading out on the meadow under the fruit trees.

None of which is unusual; it happens every year about this time – mid-August, late August, early September – and every year when the rain ends and the sky is free of clouds, that is the day when summer is understood to be over and autumn to have begun. That morning, we notice that the leaves on the tops of the trees have started to turn, and that day, the wind starts blowing in circles, and that evening, during our walk, the sun sinks before we've made it around the reservoir instead of waiting until we're home, and that night, lying in bed, we hear the college students partying on their way to the second reservoir to skinny dip, and we turn to each other and say, "They're back." But this year, when the weather clears sometime midway through the second week in September, it's not autumn at all but clearly, unabashedly summer again, and the students have not returned. The creek has risen a bit since the day the rains started, the path is muddier, the rocks and tree trunks mossier, and here and there are a few odd debris that must have made their way over from the center of town; a supermarket cart, a municipal trash can, the chained, sodden phone book from a public phone booth. In places the creek is motionless, and on our walk one night we lean over the bridge railing and count an army of mayflies skimming upstream from one motionless patch to another. We count over seventy of them, and when we're finished Daniel tells me, very calmly and matter-of-factly, with his arm around my shoulder and my arm around his waist, that the Latin name of the flower we've been pollinating all summer is *Impatiens* and that the common name, more common than jewelweed, is *Touch Me Not*, and that all summer long he has been unable to use either one of these names in my presence.

Now he takes his T-shirt off, draping it over one shoulder. I plant a long, wet kiss on the other shoulder and am embarrassed by what I see when I've pulled my mouth away; a smoky echo of the kiss, a licorice shadow. With the hem of his shirt I wipe the black kiss from his skin, not meeting his eyes. Only this morning, while showering together, he commented on my girth (increasing), my breasts (swelling), my eyelids (fatigue), my mornings (sickness). After the shower, Daniel held up my toothbrush (black). Dr. Kirshner would be appalled if she were not by now in London.

"I tried to quit," I told Daniel. "I tried throwing it away right after I bought it, after only two bites, but I couldn't find a trash can. I tried giving it away, but I couldn't find a person to offer it to. I tried offering it to you, if you remember."

"I don't. Besides, you know I hate licorice. I didn't see you offering it to Nikki."

"Nikki took out her teeth," I tell him. Terrible. But true. I've been saving this fact for a moment like this, when I want to distract him.

"Nikki took out her what?"

"They were false to begin with. Her teeth. Nikki's monkish. Maybe shy. She doesn't want to have to talk anymore. And there's always somebody she doesn't want to kiss, I think."

Her brother, I was thinking. But I'd save that for next time.

"That's grotesque," Daniel said.

"No, it isn't," I defended. "It's just the way she wants to be. Undesirable. Invisible. Nikki doesn't want to be sexual, ever," I told him, and remembered what she told me once while sweeping her steps. There were no dust balls, just a fine, misty cloud that fell past her braceleted ankles. 'I want to be like the tree in the forest,' she'd said. 'When I fall, no one will hear me.'

"Or social," I added. "She only wants to retreat. It's not the solitude itself that she's after. It's the act of retreating. Long. Drawn out. Like sitting backwards on a train. First she stops writing music. Then she stops recording. Then she shuts off the power. Then she stops talking. Then she takes out her teeth. Then–"

I stopped. I didn't know what came next. Her tongue? Or perhaps she'd stop opening the door, even to me. Perhaps she'd stop coming downstairs, even. Last time I saw her, her hair was undone. No corn rows, no clattering beads. Only a magnificent, silent afro, spongy, enormous, and dense, beneath which her ears were invisible.

"She likes to read," I said to Daniel. "She likes sweeping, too."

"Sleeping?"

"Sweeping. She likes cleanliness. She likes to know that everything's where it belongs."

"Like what. Her teeth?"

"Daniel. . . It's sad, okay? I know. I know. It's weird. But it's not grotesque."

"It is grotesque. And anyway what does Nikki have to do with what we were talking about?"

"What were we talking about?" I asked. I stepped out of the shower and covered myself with a towel, Nikki-style, a knotted rosette blooming over my sternum, and retreated to the bedroom where I lay on the bed to sleep. Daniel followed from the shower, placed a dripping wet hand on the secret, firm curve of my belly and shook his head in wonder.

"I can't believe you don't know what we're talking about," he said to me. "I *don't* believe it, actually."

"Believe it," I said.

STEVIE HAS STARTED to walk, penguin-style, but only inside the house, not out. If walking really is controlled falling, then there's proof in each one of his steps. How it catapults him forward, free of balance, slave to gravity, ahead of himself by as far as his eye will take him, before the next foot shoots out and sends him forward again. He shuns tables, chairs, hands, walls, anything that might redirect the impetus of his body and send it where it doesn't mean to go. He likes unimpeded trajectories, corner to corner, the longest straight path from here to there, provided *there* is far enough away. His favored route is hallway to kitchen, kitchen to living room, living room to study and then living room again. We wonder what will happen when he starts outside.

Outside, for now, retards him. He falls. Or else he's like a sail against a too-stiff wind, straining and straining, motionless.

Sometimes he spins a slow circle, looking carefully around. Other times he tilts skyward. Other times, he bows, forehead to the sidewalk, butt in the air. It's as if there is too much space, as if the space exerts a pressure, as if the pressure holds him still.

He looks with special admiration at the trees, as if they're waiting, like he is, for the purest, surest moment in which to take their first steps. As if they've waited all these years.

Outside, his favorite spot is the smallest of the three balancing posts at station three of the Fit Trail at the edge of the playing fields, on which he perches unaided once we've lifted him on top of it. There, if he wedges the toe of one sneaker into the instep of the other, he can stand on both feet, and once that pose is accomplished he shoos us away and extends both arms for balance for as long as he wants, admiring the vast acreage of the playing fields – the goal posts, track, and tennis courts, the bleachers, baseball diamond, and football field – while we stand and admire him. He could be the earth's axis, so seriously does he take his new position, so profoundly do we stare at his perfect balance. Daniel says that it's all inner ear, but I say it's all patience and watchfulness. Daniel says that in this town anybody who is watchful must also be patient. While I stand on one foot, Daniel straddles one-half of some parallel bars, and for a while we join Stevie in his reverie of space, which in this town and in this oddly prolonged summer becomes equally a reverie of time. We did this yesterday, too, and we'll do it tomorrow, although tomorrow we might do it at the third reservoir, where from the gravel path the soy fields still look green and steamy as if trapped in summer, and not a person in sight. Stevie is like a lighthouse keeper, scanning the damp, windswept radius for no company other than that of the landscape itself. How patient he is. How watchful. Is this from child- or adulthood? Daniel says it's from neither. Daniel says it merely comes from being so innocent in a town that is disappearing. Neither of us has actually put it so bluntly before – a town that is disappearing – and in the dense, thrilling silence we lift Stevie off the balancing post, hoist him onto Daniel's shoulders, and carry him to where the running trail veers off into the soaked, unmown grass of the cross-country route. The grass is waist-high on us, taller than Stevie. We push through it to the trees, then parallel the woods until we come to the spot from where the highway is just visible. State Route 139. Stevie likes waving at cars and trucks, and if we're lucky, we'll see one, although there aren't so many even on the highway, these days.

Today, as I'd been hoping, there *are* two cars, travelling

caravan-style, practically bumper to bumper. First comes William in his suburban wood panelled station wagon, then Danka just behind in her little black cat of an Audi.

"Wave to Thank You," says Daniel.

Stevie waves happily.

The Audi is crammed with Danka's suitcases of clothing and cosmetics. From the open windows of William's station wagon float the strains of Ranata Tarraga playing *Tres Pavanos.*

They are headed for the City of Repose.

William had found, in an atlas he had purchased from the library of the college museum on the day the museum officially folded, a reference to a biblical city corresponding to the City of Repose. On the map it lay north of Jerusalem, a speck in what appeared to be a mountain range composed chiefly of sand and eminent ruins. Cariatharim, Abu Gosh. William, looking closely with his magnifying glass, had decided that the speck was a drawing of a palm tree, and told Danka that night of a grove of such trees on a sand dune in the desert near the ruins of a castle. He had already packed their hammock, he said. The hammock had been a gift from William to Danka many years ago, and had been strung in their yard in the shade of a pine tree until this summer, when the tree was chopped down.

He'd bring anything she wanted, he told her, including her soup pots and little black shoes. He knew all about her soups, and her crazy midnight drives, and he knew she made fun of his aprons, and he knew that she thought him a fool. He knew she never read the books that he bought her, and that she hated the tapes he played. But he surmised that deep down, she needed them, and that deep down, she needed him, too. He actually said, "I can't imagine your life without me in it," and went on to describe the things that she needed the most. She needed to watch him fold his jockey shorts after the laundry. She needed his finickiness, his elegant manners, his chivalry, and the way, before dozing off to sleep, he pulled the afghan from its place on the arm of the couch and wrapped himself in it. She needed everything about him that she claimed she couldn't stand.

One day, sooner or later, she would realize this. But for now, she only had to believe him. He was going to the City of Repose, and he wanted her to come although he wasn't going to force her to do it, he said.

"Damn straight he's not forcing me to do it," said Danka. "He couldn't force me if he wanted. He couldn't force me with my hands behind my back."

"But are you going?" I asked.

"No way," Danka said.

I had found her just where I had thought she might be, on the grassy plateau near the railroad tracks where I first found the pole lamp and the head of the doll. First, I'd gone to her house, but found only William, up late, packing his books in a trunk. I wanted mainly to say goodbye, because I knew she'd be leaving one way or another. It was midnight when I found her, and the moon shed an eerie, silver light on the tracks. Because the ground was still moist, Danka sat on her suitcase, smoking a cigarette and trying not to look impatient. I knew just what she was doing; waiting for her trouble to roll down the tracks and rescue her. When I said hello, she didn't turn around. I was wearing my seashell earrings, two miniature windchimes that lately Daniel breathed against whenever we made love. Their faint chiming as I walked was like the murmer of arousal.

"Don't you seem relaxed," said Danka suspiciously when I had sat down beside her. "Don't you seem like your little Daniel is everything a woman ever wanted."

"It's been good," I conceded. "Wonderful, really. Better than I ever dreamed."

Danka blew an angry smoke ring into the night.

"But it isn't what you would expect," I went on. "Not that different from before. Not unfamiliar, at all. He does things basically the same, the way he always did, and I do the same things, too. No fancy new tricks. But there's something about it... Something about the way my skin is prepared for his touch, alert to it, but ready to be surprised. And his skin, too. Something electric, preceeding my touch, then following it–"

"I don't have to listen to this," said Danka.

"And then we sort of sink into each other–"

"God damn you," said Danka.

"until there's no hard edge between body and soul. We're falling in love, again, if you know what I mean."

"I don't know what you mean. To me it's all a bunch of hopscotch."

"Hogwash," I said. "but it isn't, you know. It's necessary, Danka, if not always entirely dependable. It takes you out of yourself. It gives you a context. It makes you see things more clearly. Think about it. It's adaptive." I was shocked. Not even my Daniel would say such a thing. "What's a kiss, Danka? It's a scent mark. So you know who's who, so you can find each other."

"I'll never know."

"Yes, you will."

"No, I won't."

"Yes, you will," I persisted..

There was a brief, careful silence, broken simultaneously by each of us telling the other what we knew about William and the City of Repose. I told her he'd been packing earlier that night, and she told me what he said about the way she needed him. Then she told me no way she was going to go.

At this she climbed off her suitcase, opened it, and started rummaging around. Half of William's mail-order drugstore was in there. Hand creams, bath oils, perfumes, depilatories, shampoos, douches, and soaps, all of the highest quality, the soaps packaged in fine wrapping, the perfumes in crystal, the hair brush and mirror tied with black velvet. Also a zippered cosmetics pouch, some mascaras, and several cartons of cigarettes.

"What's in the paper bag?" I asked, as Danka pulled out a bottle of nail polish remover along with some cotton balls. Her nails were flaking and chipped from her walk through the brambles. I reached for the paper bag and looked inside. Turnips. Bulky and misshapen, they put me in mind of Joe's fondness for the hedge apples plunking to the ground just next to the greenhouse, and then of his woodchuck stew. Joe would not have understood Danka's Skarzysko soup, I knew. He might have found it delectable, even when it had cooled. For a moment I regretted it wasn't Joe for whom Danka was cleaning her nails. This she did with unusual care, rubbling the cuticles clean. Soon she fished in her suitcase for a bottle of Cappucino polish, unscrewed it, and pulled the little brush daintily out. I wanted to tell her that William was right. In the City of Repose, I would tell her, he'll fan you with a palm leaf and bring you cool drinks on brass trays while you sway in the hammock scheming of mean men and nasty places. William knows how sad you are, Danka, and he knows you're not as tough as you think you are, but he'll never say a word. He's not boring, I'd say, only tactful and devoted.

Instead, I said, "Maybe you should spend the night here. Then, when you go home in the morning, William will already have left."

Danka spread her fingers to the breeze and held them wide open. The breeze whistled as it came down the tracks. In the woods at our backs, darkness rustled the tops of the trees, but no dogs barked in the tract house yards.

I wanted to say, This is the last night we'll see each other.

I wanted to say, Give me a piece of your sorrow, just enough to fill the ladle you forced on me.

Instead I said, "William was packing his aprons, every one of them. Imagine all the drawer space you'll have when he's gone."

"I can't believe he said what he said to me," said Danka. "Even William. Imagine saying that to a person. *I can't imagine your life without me in it,*" she mimicked.

"He's awkward," I said. "That doesn't mean he's wrong."

Danka's eyes flooded with tears, and I got up to go. I pulled a grass stem from her hair and slid it into my pocket.

"GUESS WHAT?" I say to Daniel when Danka's little black Audi has vanished over the hill. "The Epicurean's going to close."

That is, it will close in a couple of days at which time I might buy out any remaining stock at a fraction of its retail value and in the meantime there will be no more apples in the basket and no more fresh croissants.

"No more licorice either," I add with a grin, but I feel like a black hole in space. I haven't told him how hungry I've been. Late last night on the porch swing I ate a whole, raw zucchinni along with a jar of pickled, pearl onions, and still, when I slept, I dreamt about food. I've never felt like this before, well, maybe one time, but that was years ago and for the life of me I can't remember what Dr. Kirschner said. It was my very first time in her office; a routine exam – pap smear, pelvic, breast palpation. It was winter, I recall, I had a bit of a cough, so she looked in my ears, eyes, and throat before placing the stethoscope over my lungs. How cold the instrument felt, but her fingertips were warm, the nails enameled. She wore a wedding ring, then. On the ceiling was a poster of William Hurt.

"Take a hard breath," she instructed, instead of a deep breath. I smiled. For a moment I just sat there not breathing at all. Then I drew in a breath with an edge like a knife, and held it.

"Very good," said Doctor Kirshner. "Hang on. Hang on. Now, relax," she said, "and tell me how you've been feeling."

"So hungry I could eat this examining gown," I said.

"They are nice, aren't they?" said the Doctor, fondly stroking the cloth of the gown. It was cotton, not the usual paper, with little clusters of strawberries on it.

"I mean it," I said, and I must have said it fiercely, because she left for a minute and came back with a package of oyster crackers.

"Lie down," she said. "Bend your knees. Put your feet in the stirrups. Have a little something to eat. Drink something, too."

She filled a cup at the faucet. I had to drink lying down. I nearly choked on the lukewarm water, which tasted of wax from the paper cup. Through my hunger I could see William Hurt, who seemed to gaze not at me but at the doctor's bent head. Her hair, at that time, was cut not in spikes but in graduated layers, all an even, dull blonde. From overhead she must have appeared demure, even mousy. William Hurt could not see her eyes – no mascara, no liner, no shadow- or the aggrieved purse of her lips. From my damp perspective she only looked annoyed; tapping her pencil, then tossing both pencil and clipboard onto the counter in order to pull on her plastic gloves. The gloves fit with a snap. She slid the speculum into my body and cranked it with more care than any doctor had ever cranked it before. That's when I knew she would always be my doctor. I didn't care how aggrieved she was. I didn't even much care what she said, after that. She cranked the speculum a final notch, then gave a little hoot when she peered inside.

IN JUST A COUPLE of days, Stevie is walking outside as comfortably as if he'd been doing it forever, and as fast. He doesn't wander in circles as most children do, or get distracted by what's to the right or the left, or turn around and walk back to where he was before. For our afternoon walks, we simply set him on the sidewalk and wait for him to take off. Today, for our picnic, he leads us to the golf course and veers through a hedge onto the green itself, where a footbridge crosses a narrow lagoon. Just over the rim of a sand pit, we can see the squat shape of the clubhouse and that the rear service doors have been left ajar. It is Stevie who, ahead of us, first goes inside, and by the time we've caught up he has found the Coke machine. All the EMPTY lights are on, but in the pantry behind the untended bar we find a box of mint-flavored toothpicks in cellophane wrappers.

"How long are we going to stay here?" I ask Daniel, meaning not the clubhouse and not the golf course but the town, but at that moment Stevie heads out again, into the woods. Soon he leads us up the short rise to the reservoir along the trail that is overgrown. It's a big surprise, when we've rounded the top, to see that there's somebody there.

For a moment I feel I've been trespassed, and I know Daniel feels it too although we don't say a word about it, just spread out our blanket. Daniel takes off his T-shirt and shorts but I stay in my dress for the moment. It's the one Gail made from my wedding gown, about the size of a pillow case, Daniel jokes, and rests his head on my belly. Stevie rests his head on Daniel's belly and together we crane our necks for a look at our company, someone sitting in an inner tube afloat in what appears to be the perfect center of the reservoir. Her toes dangle in the water. Her face is tilted toward the sky.

"Who can it be?" I ask Daniel, but he only rocks his head against my belly, sighs, takes my hand, slides it onto his chest and holds it there. His chest is fuzzy and warm. Stevie, also naked except for his sneakers, plays among the flat rocks at the edge of the water.

"Let's eat," I finally say.

"Not until we swim. Otherwise we won't go in at all," says Daniel. He sits up as he speaks, stretches, rises, makes his way past Stevie into the water, steps carefully–slowly–in, then dives underneath and does not come up.

And does not come up.

And still does not come up.

Stevie tosses a rock in the water, while at the center of the reservoir the person in the inner tube has spun slowly around and now lies with her head to the north, her toes to the south.

She's pregnant, I see now, in a bright yellow swimsuit. Her bathing cap is spectacular; white with giant yellow anemones.

Still Daniel has not come up.

I know the terrain; there's the glass studded, rocky bottom, and then a ring, perhaps twenty feet wide, of aquatic plants whose soft leafy tops just barely break the surface of the water, and then, in the center, the deep black water that is the bull's eye that everyone swims for, where the mud underfoot is silty, fine, and cool.

I scan the leaf-pocked surface of the weedy zone for signs of turbulence. None. And no Daniel. Perhaps he cut his foot on a shard of glass, sat down suddenly on a rock on the other side of some bushes, where I'll see him if I walk to the edge of the water.

I take a look.

There's the rock, no Daniel, just a beer bottle browning itself in the sun.

"Oh, no," I say sharply, aloud, recalling suddenly one of the plans we had made – to ride our bicycles to Bloomingham, stop at the God's eye store, buy some sticks of beef jerky and eat them for dinner on the bank of the river underneath the rusting trestle. For dessert we'd buy ice cream sandwiches, take them back to the same spot and sit until sunset. We'll do it tomorrow, I think, and call Stevie to my lap to tell him about it. He has never had an ice cream sandwich before. He wants one now. He begins to cry. I count the fingers of one of his hands, then make a spider that crawls up his arm. He grins, and we invent a game with pebbles and an old, sodden shoe. Perhaps Daniel is surfacing only for brief, quick breaths before diving back under. Perhaps he's floating on his back with just his nose in the air.

Perhaps he's found a breathing straw.

Perhaps his stroke blends invisibly with the stroke of the swimming shadows.

No shadows, however.

The water dances with sparks. When I close my eyes, black spots throb under the lids in a sea of orange, and when I open them again, the pregnant woman on the inner tube has spun full circle, her head to the south, her toes dangling to the north.

"Oh, no," I say again. "Oh, no. Oh, no," and pull Stevie to me and hold him close.

"Where's Daddy?" he asks. No words, just his usual squeal.

"Right here," answers Daniel,

He is lying on our blanket, his wet head at rest on the box of mint toothpicks, the rest of him naked and glistening. His eyes have that stern gaze they get when he knows he should be diplomatic.

"There are a couple of things I have a feeling you might be interested in knowing about," my scientist begins.

"No," I say with fury, "there are no things I have a feeling I might be interested in knowing about."

With this I make my way around the bushes at the water's edge and take a seat on a rock from where I can't see him and he can't see me. I can't remember having ever been angry at Daniel before.

Exasperated, yes.

Frustrated, yes.

Impatient, yes.

Defiant, yes.

But angry?

No.

Never in so married a fashion.

How domestic it feels. I could be sitting in our kitchen, gazing through the window at the blue jay in the pine tree while listening to the clatter of Daniel's fingers on the keys of his computer, every flurry of the keys making me angrier and angrier just because he's who he is, just because he is my husband, just because I love him and am stuck with him forever – just as now his restful silence on the other side of the bushes adds new dimension to this unfamiliar emotion, feeds it and feeds it, until I can't move a muscle, until I can't so much as blink but just stare at the woman in the inner tube who continues to spin, but languidly now as if to linger over each new point of the compass. Round-bellied, she is staring at the sky. Perhaps she is angry at her husband, too. I stare past her at the far, rocky bank of the reservoir until she sits up straight and starts waving at me. She appears to be waving goodbye. The yellow flower on her swim cap bobs like a cheerleader's pom-pom, and at once I know what Daniel wanted to tell me.

THE WATER is silky and warm, and the satin dress billows as I walk gingerly among bottle shards and pop tops to the edge of the ring of water weeds. There I float on my back and am carried along as if on gentle, upraised fingers, the tops of the plants just teasing the small of my back.

And then what I'll ask Emily when I reach her, although she won't remember right away where it was we left off, on that pinnacle of desire we were talking about. Here in the water she won't smell so familiarly of jasmine, but of the wedge of lemon perched on the rim of the drink floating beside her in its own miniature inner tube.

I didn't jump off it, if that's what you mean, she might answer after a moment. *In fact I never came down at all, really. I settled into the desire as it settled into me. It's all right, you just have to get used to it. Don't tamper with it, and never let it get away, and don't overindulge. Just live with your desire, tend it, make a place for it, the way they used to have to carry their fires around. Keep it hot, keep it flaming, but don't get burned. Eventually I went home to Buzzy. Next day I was pregnant.*

I'm pregnant, too, I'll tell her.

She'll lift her drink in a gesture of cheers, tell me she already knows, offer a sip from the curlicue straw. The straw is blue tinted glass and seems to have its own fruity, cool flavor.

I didn't know I was pregnant until Daniel told me, I'll tell her. *I mean, until he was going to tell me. I mean, until after he was going to tell me but he didn't. He didn't tell me it was you out here, either. I didn't let him. I didn't know that I was pregnant until I saw that it was you. I mean, I didn't know that I knew it. I thought it was licorice. Dr. Kirshner said–*

The ring of water weeds has ended; the very center of the reservoir is deep and black, as inviting as a mirror. With the palms of both hands I touch the silt at the bottom, somersault, open my eyes, look up through dark water at the heavy round shape of the inner tube as I glide underneath it, holding on for as long as I can just to anticipate the sound of Emily's voice.

But having broken through the surface of the water I find I've come up short; blinking water from my eyes I see not Emily in her bathing cap but my son and husband on their blanket in the distance, playing with stones and the ancient shoe.

How small they appear, how isolated, waiting patiently for me.

And when I've turned toward the inner tube, Emily isn't on it. In her place is Arnie Junior, clicking his tongue, his massive beak open and raised toward the sky. At the base of his throat, a single red feather curls away from the others, quivering in the air. His black belly gleams. Around the pupils of his eyes are two bright, narrow rings of the purest yellow.

When he cocks his head, I can see that his beak is as thin-walled, as translucent, as a shell. He's not looking at me, but I know that he knows I am here.

"Hello, Arnie Junior," I say.

Arnie Junior bows.

Just next to the inner tube floats the drink in a tall glass, placidly bobbing. There's no curlicue straw, but a stirrer in the shape of a palm tree. I lift the glass, take a sip. It's beer and lemonade, a cooling-off drink, only this one is warm, the beer nearly flat, the lemonade cooked to a syrup. Arnie Junior's head swivels. The tongue-clicking intensifies, reaches a high pitch, purrs, then slows, lapses, stops altogether. Arnie Junior yawns, but the yawn makes no sound. I balance the drink in place on its miniature inner tube, and give it a gentle push. It drifts past like a boat. I'm hungry and cold. Daniel has stood on the blanket and has started dressing Stevie; first the red T-shirt, then the gym shorts, then the hat.

"How long are you going to stay here?" I ask Arnie Junior, meaning not the town and not the reservoir but the inner tube itself. Two-footed, he hops along on the circumference.

Twice he goes round.

Three times.

Four.

Then he stops, reaching with his beak for the strap of my dress. He takes a seed pearl in his beak, and bites. The two halves of the strap slip off of my shoulder.

Then he bites the other side.

Daniel, on shore, is dressing himself; first the shorts, then the sneakers, then the shirt. I imagine the smell of his skin underneath it, musky and warm, and his nipples, taut from the breeze, just now beginning to soften. Dressed, he and Stevie step just to the edge of the water. I know he is squinting, and he knows I am squinting at him. We both know we are formulating another plan. Arnie Junior sharpens his beak, scraping it this way and that on the rim of the floating glass. With the point of the beak he reaches into the glass to withdraw a wedge of lemon. When I swim back to shore, Daniel will dry me with the corners of the blanket, then dress me in its folds, wrapping them over my new, round belly.

I'll step into my thongs, take Stevie by one hand, Daniel by the other.

Under his arm, Daniel will carry the toothpick box.

Such is our plan.

How simple it is. How enticing. We both know that the other is smiling, having come up with it.

Abby Frucht grew up in Huntington, New York, graduated from Washington University in St. Louis, Missouri, and now lives in Oberlin, Ohio, with her husband, a biologist, and their two sons. Frucht's collection of short stories, *Fruit of the Month*, won the Iowa Short Fiction Award in 1987. Her first novel *Snap* was published in 1988. Ms. Frucht has been the recipient of fellowships from the Ohio Arts Council and the National Endowment for the Arts.

The type for this book is Caledonia,
set by The Typeworks, Vancouver, B.C.
Text and cover design by Tree Swenson.